THE GETAWAY BLUES

Books by William Murray

THE
GETAWAY
BLUES

William Murray

BANTAM BOOKS

NEW YORK • TORONTO • LONDON • SYDNEY • AUCKLAND

THE GETAWAY BLUES
A Bantam Book / September 1990

Library of Congress Cataloging-in-Publication Data

Murray, William, 1926–
    The getaway blues / William Murray.
       p.   cm.
    ISBN 0-553-07029-0
    I. Title.
    PS3563.U8G4   1990
    813'.54—dc20   90-33635
                                                    CIP

Published simultaneously in the United States and Canada

Bantam Books are published by Bantam Books, a division of Bantam Doubleday Dell Publishing Group, Inc.
Its trademark, consisting of the words "Bantam Books" and the portrayal of a rooster, is Registered in U.S.
Patent and Trademark Office and in other countries. Marca Registrada. Bantam Books, 666 Fifth Avenue,
New York, New York 10103.

PRINTED IN THE UNITED STATES OF AMERICA

O   0 9 8 7 6 5 4 3 2 1

This one is for Al and Trudy Sokol,
who outclass most of the field.

"Horse sense is what a horse has that keeps him from betting on people."

—W. C. FIELDS

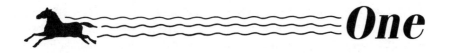 **One**

CHARACTERS

Lucius J. Bedlington had been planning his own death for months. I had heard about it from Charlie Pickard, who trained horses for him and whom Lucius liked to have around, mainly because Charlie could tell good stories and could keep his eccentric owner amused. Also, Charlie wasn't the sort of man who could be cowed or impressed by money and Lucius liked him for that. The owner would come around Charlie's shedrow once or twice a week, after the morning workouts, and sit in Charlie's tack room to drink tepid coffee from a Styrofoam cup and listen to him talk. No one had better tales to tell than Charlie, once you got him started on his reminiscences and observations from having been around racehorses all of his life, and I guess it must have taken Bedlington's mind off his own troubles, whatever they were. It's hard to feel too sorry for a man with as much money as he had, but something must have been bothering him a lot if he was actively conniving at his own demise. At least, that's the way it struck me, when Charlie first told me about it at Santa Anita early one morning.

We were standing at the rail at Clockers' Corner, watching the horses go by in the early-morning mist of what promised to be a clear, cool late-January day, when Charlie shook his head and sort of clucked to himself. "Crazy old coot," he mumbled. "He ain't got but about forty million in the bank and he don't know what to do with himself."

"Who's that, Charlie?" I asked, knowing there'd be a good story behind it. Charlie usually favored an oblique approach to a narrative, but once he got inside he'd illuminate it with the appropriate details. I had a feeling this time would be no exception.

"Lucius J. Bedlington," he said. "Man wants to kill himself. Sits up there all day long in that big ugly house of his trying to figure out the best way to do it. Even asked me if I knew some good horse medication he could get hold of to put himself down. 'No pain,' he says, he can't stand pain. Loony as a hoot owl in heat."

"He's serious?"

"You bet. Old Lucius, he ain't the kind of man that shoots his mouth off just to hear himself talk, though he sure can talk a stream," Charlie said. "When he says he's gonna do it, he'll do it. He's just figuring out how he's gonna do it. He don't want no pain and he don't want no mess neither. 'A quick, clean, and gracious exit' is what this old boy says to me the other day. Oh, he'll do it, all right. You can bet on it."

Before I could pursue the topic any further, Charlie picked out a horse beginning to work from the three-quarter pole, across the infield from us, and raised a pair of scarred binoculars to his eyes. "This is one of Bedlington's right here," he said. "I'm working him six."

"What horse?"

"He's a maiden," Charlie said. "Name of Rudolph."

"The red-nosed reindeer?"

"Don't be funny. Bedlington calls all his horses after them two English guys that wrote a whole bunch of operas."

"Gilbert and Sullivan?" I asked. "I guess I knew that. He had that nice filly, Elsie Maynard, a few years ago. And wasn't Ko-Ko his horse?"

"Sure. He could run some," Charlie said, his gaze fixed on the animal now nearing the turn for home. "I must have had about twenty horses from Lucius, off and on, over the years, and they all get funny names like that."

"I guess he must be an enthusiast," I observed. "You ever been to a G and S, Charlie?"

"Me? Opera?"

"Well, they're more like musicals than opera," I said. "They're funny, too."

"Not so's I can tell," Charlie said. "About eight or nine years ago, when I first started training for Lucius, he took me to some performance, a whole bunch of people dressed like Japs running around and singing in some kind of funny English accent—"

"The Mikado," I cut in.

"The what?"

"The name of the opera you went to," I said. "It's called *The Mikado.*"

"Whatever. I didn't get one word of it. And I'm tone deaf, least that's what Lucius says to me, so I didn't get nothin' out of it." He lowered the glasses as Rudolph swept past us and clicked the stopwatch he held in his left hand. "One fourteen flat, about right. I'll blow him out on Monday and run him Wednesday."

"Open maidens?"

"Thirty-two thousand. He ain't much," Charlie said, stuffing the binoculars back into the side pocket of his lumberman's jacket. "No, that man is more than a little crazy."

"Why does he want to kill himself? Has he told you?"

Charlie grinned in spite of himself. "He's bored, he says. Can you believe that? He says he's bored and that nothing going on today grabs him. How do you like that?"

"He sounds like a genuine eccentric."

"A what?"

"An oddball."

"You got it, Shifty. That's what that man is, all right. Can you imagine? He hardly ever comes to the races anymore and he used to be a regular. Took a real interest in his horses. He's got one running today, but he ain't likely to show up. Want some coffee?"

"Sure, it'll take the chill off."

As we headed toward the refreshment counter, I took a look at my program for the day's card and found Bedlington's entry. He was a four-year-old maiden of no discernible ability named Dummkopf. "And what the hell kind of a name is that?" Charlie asked, as we sipped our coffees and watched the pale sun begin to burn away the mist, while all around us horses and riders flashed past, on their way to and from the main track. Above us loomed the empty grandstand, while the sounds of the horses, the muffled beat of their hooves on the soft brown dirt of the oval, seemed to punctuate our talk and the chatter of the other watchers around us. I liked these early mornings at the racetrack, during which you could enjoy the spectacle that racing provides divorced from the grind of having to bet on the animals in an actual race. I came as often as I could, maybe two or three times a week when I wasn't working, also because I enjoyed the company of the horsemen, especially the older ones like Charlie Pickard, who had been around and had stories to tell. "So I ask you, what kind of a name is that?"

"It must be from one of the operas," I explained. "Maybe *The Grand Duke*. That's the last one the boys wrote."

"Don't Dummkopf mean dumbbell in German?" the trainer asked.

"I think so, Charlie."

"That's what I mean. It's insulting to the horse."

"Not the way he runs."

"He ain't fast, but he might win later on, when I stretch him out. And he might be all right on the turf, if I can ever break his maiden on the dirt. Anyway, Shifty," he cautioned me, "you don't want to go knockin' no horse till it's dead. You never know in this game. I learned that from Whittingham, who's the best damn trainer I know. I once had me a little old gelding that couldn't win for twelve-five on the dirt, but I stuck him on the grass and he won three stakes for me up north. And maybe this colt will do the same. He's got the big feet you need on this turf course. I might run him on it anyway and not wait till he breaks his maiden. Hell, in this game you never know. If I did know, I'd be as rich as old Lucius."

I liked Charlie Pickard a lot. I'd seen him around the track for years before I got to know him in the backside kitchen one morning, only a few months before. He'd been around quite a while, first in Chicago, then out in California since the late sixties. He was short and on the chunky side, with a round, pink face and a prominent, bulbous nose. His hair was gray and thin on top, but I might not have recognized him without his cap, a brown Irish one that he kept clamped to his skull night and day; I was sure he slept in it. "Keeps the chill off," he once told me. "Gettin' up at dawn, like I do, you get chills. I hate colds," he explained, "so I wear it." I told him I figured it had attached itself to him by then and he probably couldn't take it off if he'd wanted to. He didn't disagree with me.

Charlie was a good horseman, too. He had a string of twenty or twenty-five horses every meet and won his share of races, even though he rarely made the trainer standings and sometimes the wins came few and far between. He didn't know how to butter up owners or con them and he didn't have the flashy style to get himself expensive animals. And he wouldn't train for anybody he didn't like personally, which left him with three or four small owners and a stable of claimers. The only money man he knew was Bedlington, but they'd never had an important horse together. Mostly, Charlie bought his animals at the periodic local sales and he never paid more than twenty-five or thirty thousand for a yearling, which meant essentially that he only acquired mediocre stock. He was a survivor, not a winner, but it didn't seem to bother him much. He enjoyed his life, liked what he did for a living, and he could spread cheer around him like a carnival barker promising forbidden delights. I had been seeking him out lately, enjoying his company and lapping up his improbable accounts of life inside the traveling circus that is the world of the Thoroughbred.

"So I guess, if you're right about Bedlington," I said to him as we strolled back toward the rail, "you're going to be out your wealthiest owner. When do you think he's planning to do it?"

"Soon," Charlie answered, "pretty soon."

"I'd like to meet him. He must be a real character."

"He's one of the ones," Charlie said. "Come by before my horse's race. He probably won't show up, but if he does, I'll introduce you to him."

I was planning on going to the races that afternoon anyway and I didn't feel like driving back to my apartment in West Hollywood, so I decided to hang around after the workouts. Charlie and I had breakfast together at a place a couple of blocks from the track, after which the trainer went home to catch up on his sleep before having to come back in time for the fourth race, the one in which Dummkopf was entered. I bought the L.A. Times, drove back to the Santa Anita parking lot and settled down in my seat to read until half an hour before post time for the first race, at noon.

It hadn't been a good meet so far. I love Santa Anita as a place to go racing, but I've always found it a tough place to pick winners. Maybe it's because the meet opens every year the day after Christmas, just before all the horses officially become one year older, on New Year's Day. Three-year-olds, who have been competing only against their own kind, suddenly turn four and are thrown into competition with older animals. Easy winners at one level in their own category, they abruptly find themselves unable to take the heat against the same sort of horses with more experience. A three-year-old is like a twenty-one-year-old human athlete, suddenly out of the amateur ranks or up from the minor leagues, being asked to perform against seasoned pros six or seven years older. Some make it, some don't, and it's not easy to predict who will and who won't. Also, horses come out from New York and the other eastern circuits about whom you know very little. The Daily Racing Form, the horseplayers' Koran, provides useful statistics, but there's no substitute in handicapping for having actually seen a horse run in a race. The Santa Anita meet buries a lot of bettors early every year and I have been among them. This season was proving to be no different and now, a month into the meet, I found myself down about a thousand dollars, which was a lot more than I could afford at that time of my life.

It had been a slow fall and winter for me. I had picked up a two-week gig in Las Vegas, once again substituting for my old pal Vince Michaels at the Golden Nugget, and I had gone out on a couple of cruises down the Baja coast; but all that these jobs had succeeded in doing was keeping me alive. Currently I was working three nights a week at the Magic Castle, in downtown Hollywood, but the pay was survival money. My agent, Happy Hal Mancuso, the Torquemada of show business, had been trying to land me jobs in various TV series and he had gotten me on the *Tonight* show, with Johnny Carson, but not much had come of any of these ventures. Being a close-up magician is not a remunerative profession, a fact Hal had never failed to remind me of nearly every time we met. "Why don't you get up a real act, like Siegfried and Roy or Doug Henning?" he'd ask me. "You know, make elephants disappear, change naked women into leopards, saw broads in half, shit like that. You could do it, Shifty. And I could finally make some money off you, you bum."

I'd explain to Hal that I was a magician, not a celebrity. "That stuff is show biz, Hal," I'd tell him. "It's all done with mirrors and construction. That's not what I'm about."

"What you're about is poverty," Hal would say, "destitution. You're a terminal loser. I don't know why I waste my time on you."

I knew why. It was because I was one of the few clients he had any respect for. Most of his people were lounge comics or TV actors or bimbos. I remembered Hal sitting in the close-up room at the Magic Castle one night, a few weeks after we met, watching my act. He sat there for three hours, through three complete shows, during which I didn't repeat a single effect. "You're a genius, kid," he'd said to me afterward, "a fucking genius. I've never seen anything like it." And so he had agreed to take me on, knowing from the start that he wasn't going to get rich off me, but it galled him just the same. And then, when he found out that I was also a confirmed devotee of the bangtails, he'd had his excuse to start knocking me. But, oddly enough, I think that if I had taken his advice and stopped being a real prestidigitator, he'd have lost all respect for me. As if Horowitz had decided to turn himself into Liberace. Anyway, I had to live my life on my own terms, Hal knew that, which was why, despite his best instincts as an agent, he went on representing me. And I'd have taken a job in a TV series or a movie, especially one that enabled me to practice my craft, but it had never quite worked out for me. Not yet.

I had been in these tight financial spots before, so it wasn't as if I wasn't used to the feeling. If something didn't turn up for me soon in my profession, I'd have to get some sort of job to survive. I wasn't proud. I'd take almost any kind of job, if I had to, as long as the work didn't endanger my hands. They were the only asset I had and I had to guard them as carefully as if they were made of glass. Once I had broken a little finger when trying to clean my windows and had had to go to work in the children's book section of a department store for some weeks. I didn't mind it, but I had been terrified I'd never be able to make my best moves again. It had taken many hours of practice to bring myself most of the way back and I wanted never to repeat that experience.

If only I had been able to pick some winners, I thought as I sat there in my car that morning. But not even my old friend Jay Fox, the best professional handicapper I know, had been able to straighten my action out this meet. The horses we came up with kept running second and third or winning at odds too low to play. I have an aversion to risking money on any animal at odds of less than two to one, a rule that in the long run has saved me a lot of grief, but it wasn't helping me now. Unless I could come up with a couple of big winning days very soon, I'd be back behind the counter of some magic store or working for a valet parking service somewhere, the kind of jobs I had taken frequently at other stages of my spotty career. I didn't mind too much, but, after nearly twenty years as a practicing magician, considered to be one of the best around and maybe *the* best with cards, I found myself occasionally getting a little winded in the face of my shrunken bank account.

This is all by way of explaining how I happened so unexpectedly to find myself involved with Lucius J. Bedlington. I had pretty much forgotten about him, especially as I had managed to pick a modest daily double and was nursing a small profit of about a hundred dollars by the fourth race. I hadn't been planning to bet this contest at all, but in glancing over my program I was reminded of my earlier conversation with Charlie Pickard. So, about twenty minutes before post time, I strolled out into the paddock to have a look at his animal.

As I waited on the grass for the horses to file into the walking ring from the saddling stalls, I realized that I wasn't alone at the spot where Charlie's untalented maiden would be led. I was standing a few feet away from a slender, very elegant-looking old man dressed in a perfectly tailored double-breasted dark blue suit and leaning on the silver knob of a cane. He had a small mustache and a full head of curly white hair, combed straight back. A polka-dotted handkerchief stuck out of his breast pocket and a red carnation perched in the buttonhole of his lapel. He was also wearing a foulard around his neck, which made him appear to be a figure out of a Thorne Smith novel.

"Excuse me," I said, "are you Mr. Bedlington? I'm a friend of Charlie's."

He turned to look at me, as if I had unexpectedly crawled out from under a manhole cover. His eyes, a pale blue set off by his pink cheeks, seemed to be staring at me from a considerable height, even though he was no more than an inch or so taller than I. "Indeed?" he said, in a light, metallic voice with what sounded at first like a faintly English accent. "I hope he hasn't betrayed your friendship by persuading you to wager on this beast."

"No, but I thought I'd come down to look at him anyway." I held out my hand. "I like his name. Mine's Anderson, Lou Anderson. My friends call me Shifty."

"How odd." He allowed me to shake his hand, but withdrew it quickly, as if afraid I might contaminate him. "Are you a toiler in these dismal vineyards?"

"No, just a player. I'm a magician."

"Then perhaps you can put a spell on this animal and make him run."

I smiled. "Afraid not. I'm only good with small objects, like cups, balls, and playing cards. Horses are out of my league."

The old gentleman sighed. "Then I'm afraid you're useless here," he said. "We need real magic."

"Try 'the resident Djinn at seventy Simmery Axe,' " I suggested.

Bedlington looked surprised. "Charlie spilled the beans, did he?"

"He said you were a Gilbert and Sullivan fan," I explained. "I know that song, anyway."

"One of my favorites," Bedlington declared. "John Wellington Wells, the family sorcerer."

Our conversation was interrupted by the arrival of Charlie with the horses. Eddie, Charlie's ancient groom, led Dummkopf up to us, as the trainer did a small double take at Bedlington's presence. "I didn't think you were coming out here anymore, Mr. Bedlington," he said. "I see you two have met."

"I've been rotting at home for two weeks, Charles," the owner declared. "My driver has abandoned me and, as the state of California will not permit me to operate my own vehicle, I am condemned to rely on the kindness of strangers. Actually, I summoned a taxi. It was driven by an appalling Israeli with a seemingly endless fund of uninteresting stories about his dreary family. After we watch Dummkopf run his customary losing race, I shall retire to the Turf Club and summon another conveyance to whisk me out of here."

Charlie grinned and looked at me. "He always talks like this," he said. "Did you understand him?"

"I caught the general drift," I answered. "Why won't they let you drive, Mr. Bedlington?"

"He used to average ten traffic tickets a month," Charlie explained. "He thinks any street is a speedway and I've never known him even to slow down for a stop sign."

"A slight exaggeration, Charles," Bedlington said. "You have a fanciful imagination."

"Whatever you do," the trainer advised me, "never let him get behind the wheel of any car you're in."

"Most amusing, Charles," Bedlington said, gazing disapprovingly now at his horse, an undistinguished-looking gray colt. "He looks half-asleep."

"He'll run a little better today," the trainer said, "but he don't have any speed. I figure he'll maybe come in third or fourth. Next time I'll stretch him out and we ought to win with him."

"Ever the optimist," the owner said.

Tim Lang, the journeyman jock Charlie had engaged to ride Dummkopf, walked smilingly up to us. He looked, in Bedlington's black-and-rose polka-dotted silks, like a small spring bouquet. He nodded to us, then listened absentmindedly as Charlie told him not to let Dummkopf fall too far out of it before making his late run. Lang had ridden the horse before and knew the animal had no speed. His gaze roved past Charlie's lowered head toward the fine-looking knees of a tall blonde in a white miniskirt, who was standing a few feet behind us with another group of owners. When the paddock judge called out riders up, Tim grinned at the blonde and went on staring at her, even as the horses filed out through the gap toward the track.

"I don't know what it is about these riders," Charlie said. "They all go for these big tall broads."

"Women, Charles, not broads," Bedlington said. "How long have we known each other?"

"Ten or twelve years, I don't know."

"And I still can't manage to educate you." He looked at me. "Mr. Anderson, horse trainers are beyond redemption, wouldn't you say?"

"I guess so. But we can't do without them."

"That remains a matter of conjecture." And he walked briskly away from us toward the Turf Club.

"Quite a character," I observed.

Charlie shook his head. "You don't know, Shifty. This guy is a real oddball."

"It's hard to believe he's planning to kill himself."

"That's because you don't know him. But he's a perfectionist. He's going to do it right."

"Maybe if you could get him a couple of winners, he'd change his mind."

"I got a nice three-year-old filly who may turn out to be something, but she ain't gonna run for another month or two," the trainer said. "The way Bedlington talks, he ain't gonna be around that long."

"What's her name?"

"The filly? Mad Margaret."

"From *Ruddigore*. That's another Gilbert and Sullivan."

"How come you're so up on them guys?"

"I used to like them, till I discovered Verdi."

"What? Who?"

"Old Joe Green, the Eyetalian composer." I laughed. "Skip it, Charlie. You wouldn't like it."

"I like Lawrence Welk, does that count?"

"No. Play an accordion, go to jail. I'll see you, Charlie," I told him, as we reached the escalator leading to the grandstand. "I can tell by the necktie and jacket you've put on that you're going to watch the race with Bedlington."

Charlie looked glum. "Yeah," he said, "he wants me to. He ain't a bad guy, Shifty, but his friends . . ."

"The rich are different from most people, Charlie. They're more boring."

"Yeah. And dumb. How'd they get the money in the first place?"

I went back to my seat in the grandstand to watch the race. Dummkopf broke poorly, made a small move on the turn for home, then flattened out and came lumbering in fifth, beaten ten or eleven lengths. I knew Charlie would be disappointed and annoyed by his race, so I made no effort to find him later. I placed one more bet of my own, on a horse in the seventh Jay had pointed out to me, but the animal ran out of the money. Nevertheless, I went home with a profit of about eighty dollars for the afternoon, feeling better about myself and my future prospects than I had in a couple of weeks. Even a small winning day can make the sun shine on a bettor. The track is a world of new beginnings, which is one of the reasons I'm addicted to it. I forgot all about Lucius J. Bedlington, also because I figured Charlie must have exaggerated.

I was dozing in front of my television set that night, when my phone rang. It was Charlie Pickard. "Shifty? What are you doing?" he asked.

"I was watching TV and I fell asleep. What time is it?"

"Nine-thirty."

"It's late for you, isn't it, Charlie?"

"Yeah. I just got back. I had to drive Bedlington home and he made me stay for dinner. He wanted to talk, I guess."

"About killing himself?"

"No. This and that. He's lonely. Lives all alone in that crazy house of his. No wonder he's nuts. Just him and this old butler he's got, some deaf old guy who's about two thousand years old who's been with the family ever since the Civil War, I guess."

"It must have been a fun evening."

"Actually, it was okay. I mean, this guy is no dummy, Shifty," Charlie said. "He's got a thousand stories to tell and they're pretty interesting. But that's what I'm calling you about."

"His stories?"

"No, no. Didn't you tell me this morning you're broke and need a job?"

"Unless things turn around for me very soon, yes," I answered. "But I don't want to get up at five A.M. and hot-walk for you, Charlie. I need a real job."

"Forget it, I wouldn't let you near any horse of mine. You're a player, you're too dangerous. No, I'm talking about Bedlington."

"What about him?"

"He needs a driver. You work only a few hours a day, maybe not every day. It's a little money. I suggested you and he jumped at it."

"He hasn't seen my car, Charlie," I said. "I'm still driving the Datsun 310, the first one the Japanese ever built, which now looks like it was stoned by the Palestinians. No rich man is going to sit in that car, much less allow himself to be driven around in it."

"No, Shifty, he's got the car," Charlie explained. "But he needs somebody to drive it. He's got errands, appointments, only during the day, he says. At night you can still work at the Magic Castle."

"What kind of car does he have?"

"I don't know, does it matter? He used to have a chauffeur who drove a Rolls, but now he has some crazy Eyetalian job. Look, he'll pay you a hundred a day, any day you drive him anywhere, even if it's only an hour or two. Is that bad? You need the money, don't you? And he only lives a few miles from Santa Anita. You can even get to the races most of the time."

"Sounds possible. Why me?"

"He likes you. I guess you impressed him, because you knew about them operas he likes so much."

I hesitated a moment, but only because I had never worked as a driver before and I wanted to sort out how I felt about it. For some reason, perhaps having to do with my opinion of myself, the prospect depressed me a little. "I don't have to wear a uniform, do I?"

"He didn't say nothin' about it," Charlie answered. "Anyway, why don't you go talk to him? He wants to see you tomorrow morning, at about ten. You can always say no."

"I guess."

"And anyway, it ain't gonna last more than a month or two at most."

"Why not?"

" 'Cause he's gonna do it, Shifty, I'm not kidding you. When this guy says he's gonna kill himself, you better believe him. I've known him a long time. He's a straight arrow. He always delivers on what he promises. He's nuts, but his word is better than any contract. I wish all my owners was like him."

"Well, thanks, Charlie. Do I need to call him?"

"No, just be there around ten tomorrow." And he gave me Bedlington's address, on a street I'd never heard of in the foothills of Altadena.

"Is it hard to find?"

Charlie laughed. "You kidding? Just get within two miles of it. You can't miss it."

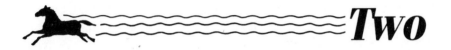 *Two*

UNDERTAKINGS

Charlie was right. No sooner had I reached the end of the long, narrow avenue winding its way up into the foothills of the San Gabriels than I spotted Bedlington's house. It was a huge Victorian monstrosity, with twin towers and odd angles, perched on a knoll at the end of a one-block street branching off the main road. The property was surrounded by a high brick wall topped by shards of broken glass and the gate was made of spiked iron palings, behind which a gravel path curved up a steep slope to the main entrance, hidden under a porte cochere. The grounds had obviously been well tended, but had recently been allowed to go to seed. A strip of front lawn had been mowed, but the flower beds, including clumps of large rosebushes, had not been trimmed or weeded for some time and had deteriorated into a jungle of choked vegetation. Here and there the brilliantly hued heads of various blossoms poked up through the mass of green, but the overall effect was one of neglect and decay.

All this I saw as I stood beside my car at the front gate, waiting for someone to answer the bell I had found embedded, and all but hidden by ivy, in the wall to my left. After several minutes, just as I was about to ring again, the gate creaked open and I quickly got back into my car and drove up toward the mansion. I parked at the main entrance and walked up a short flight of steps to the front door, which swung open just as I reached it.

A very old man in a wrinkled black suit ushered me inside. He was completely bald, with only a wispy fringe of white hair, and he was stooped over, so that he had to peer up at me as if from under a ledge. "Mr. Anderthon?" he said, whistling through what I took to be a set of badly-fitting false teeth. "Thith way, pleathe."

He tottered ahead of me, leaning on various pieces of furniture and the wall to keep himself from toppling over, and led me into a large living room toward the rear. "Make yourthelf comfortable, thir. Coffee on the tray. Down in a few minith." And he staggered out, shutting the door behind him.

I'm no expert on art, but I knew at once that I was in the presence of beauty. One wall was decorated with three exquisitely detailed framed drawings of ballet dancers, one leaning over to adjust a slipper, the other two exercising at the bar. They looked like Degas to me, but I assumed they were reproductions. The curtains over the large windows were drawn, so that the light in the room was muted, soft, as if to blur reality, to shut out the hard light of day. The furnishings were antique and an enormous wood-burning fireplace provided on its mantelpiece a resting place for a number of handsomely framed photographs of Lucius J. Bedlington in the company of various beautiful women. Next to it, alone on a wall of its own, hung a large, dark oil portrait of an austere-looking man in a mid-nineteenth-century business suit. A glass-fronted cabinet housed a number of silver trophies, most of them won by Bedlington at various international horse shows. One whole wall was composed of bookshelves containing mostly classics and, I soon discovered, first editions of Dickens, Trollope, Peacock, and other English literary giants. I had the feeling the books had been read and were not merely on display.

Intimidated by my quick tour of the room, I retreated to a rose-colored settee in front of the coffee table and poured myself some coffee. The pot, I noted, was sterling silver and the cups were made of porcelain. I sipped uneasily and waited. Charlie had obviously not exaggerated about Bedlington, but nothing he had told me had quite prepared me for this room.

It was another ten minutes before Bedlington appeared, suddenly strolling casually in as if he had misplaced something. "Ah, Mr. Anderson," he exclaimed as I rose to greet him, "how nice of you to come."

As we shook hands, sat down, sipped coffee, and chatted about the failure of Dummkopf to run well in his race the day before, I was trying to figure out how old he was. I guessed in his middle or late sixties. He was wearing black Gucci loafers, black slacks, a white silk shirt, an ascot, and an expensive-looking, old-fashioned paisley smoking jacket. There was something faintly dashing about him, the romantic, engaging air of the professional rake, even though his conversational tone was languid, world-weary. He made no effort to bring the conversation around to my purpose in being there and I began to wonder if I had misunderstood Charlie, or whether perhaps Bedlington had forgotten.

"About this possible job—" I began.

"Ah, yes," he interrupted me, "of course. I expect Charles explained it all to you."

"Well, he said you needed a driver."

"Yes, not every day. I don't go out much anymore," he said. "I'm entombed here. The state of California, in its entrenched mediocrity, refuses to allow me to drive myself. And there are some things I have to attend to during the next few weeks. Charles did explain that the job was temporary?"

"Yes, he did."

"Good. A month or two, at most. I'll pay you a hundred dollars a day, whether you work an hour or two or more. Fair enough?"

"Sure is. I guess Charlie told you I'm a little hard up right now."

"Are you really as skillful as he says you are?"

"I think I am, yes. But it's not a great way to make a lot of money."

"Why should you be the exception, dear boy? We live in the Age of Trash."

"That's what my agent says."

"We pay vast amounts of money to corporate executives, lawyers, bankers, and other such thieves, lavish vast rewards on illiterate teenage idols, producers of horror movies, television mediocrities, and cretinous evangelists, while underpaying scholars, teachers, and artists. Who are you to complain?"

"I'm not complaining. I like my life."

"Do you? Well, you're young."

"And speaking of artists, those drawings are spectacular. They look like Degas."

"They *are* Degas, dear boy. You don't imagine I'd have copies, do you?"

"I didn't know. And the painting? Someone in your family?"

"Heavens, no. That's *Whistler's Father*."

"I didn't know he had one."

"It's been in the family since we acquired it from Whistler himself. It's never been shown anywhere."

"Too bad. It's a great picture."

"Isn't it? Well, one day soon it will be on display somewhere appropriate."

"You're giving it to a museum?"

"I'm arranging to dispose of all these treasures in some sensible fashion. I simply haven't finalized all the arrangements."

"I gather you're not expecting to be around much longer."

"Is that a question or a statement, dear boy?"

"I guess it's a statement."

"Ah, Charles Pickard of the blabbermouth. Yes, that's the idea. But I don't think we need to discuss it."

"No. Sorry."

"Don't be. I'm having the time of my life, if you must know. Now, is the arrangement satisfactory?"

"Sure. When do I start?"

"This afternoon, at two. I have a call to make, in Pasadena. Do you know how to shift gears?"

"Yes. What kind of car is it?"

"An Alfa-Romeo. I think you'll enjoy it."

"I'm sure I will."

"And now I'll ring for Scopes. He'll see you out."

"The butler?"

"I'm afraid he's everything these days."

"I can find my own way out. He seems to have a hard time getting about."

"Yes, poor man. He's been enfeebled by an excess of health food. He became a vegetarian twenty years ago. Would you believe he's only two years older than I am?"

"No."

"He's eighty-one."

"You're seventy-nine?"

"About to be, dear boy. Time to make a quick, graceful exit, wouldn't you say?"

"Why? Lots of people lead active lives well into their nineties these days."

"My compliments to them all." He stood up and pulled a long cord hanging from a corner of the wall. "I'll see you at two, then." And he ushered me out into the hallway.

Scopes appeared out of a side door near the entrance and lurched for the front door. "Good day, thir," he said, opening it and bowing. His teeth clattered to the floor. I pretended not to notice and hastily exited into blinding sunshine.

When I came back at two o'clock, the car was parked out front and Bedlington, dressed in white slacks and a navy blue cashmere sports jacket, appeared at the door himself to greet me. "Shall we go?" he asked. "I'm pleased to see that you're prompt."

"That's quite a car," I said, staring at the Alfa. It was a long, green convertible with a rumble seat and four headlights. "I've never seen one like it."

"There were only six built that particular year, I think it was 1931," Bedlington said. "It has an overdrive and can still cruise comfortably at ninety. I used to drive it back and forth to San Francisco, when I was married to Helen Verdun."

"The silent-movie star?"

"An impossible bitch, with the sybaritic tastes of a Roman empress. We lasted four years, until she ran off with a studio mogul."

"I think I once read something about it, but that was a long time ago."

"The Paleolithic era of my courtships," Bedlington explained. "Helen was an early failure. There have been others."

"How many others?"

"Too many to count, dear boy."

By this time we were inside the car, with the top down, and Bedlington proceeded to instruct me into the mysteries of his ancient but spectacular roadster. It had five forward speeds, two horns, and three controls for the headlights. "These over here are for fog," he said. "You don't have to bother with them. Or with these, really, since they're mainly for mountain driving. Just worry about this button here. But we'll be back before dark. Shall we go, dear boy?"

He sat up in the front seat beside me, where I soon realized he would become a menace. He pointed out various sights and told me where to turn only at the very last minute, so I would be forced to brake and often jump lanes in order to get over to the correct side of the road in time. Nor was it an easy car to maneuver, having been built long before the era of power steering and disc brakes, and I had my hands full. I also noted that the speedometer was not working, but when I pointed this fact out to Bedlington, he laughed. "No matter," he said. "You can't go too fast in town, dear boy. But do take care. This car does have a tendency to take off on its own sometimes and it never fails to attract the attention of the bulls. I'm fairly well known around here and they'd love to catch me behind the wheel again."

"What would they do? Put you in prison?"

"At the very least," he answered. "There's a municipal judge in this town who longs to impose the death penalty on me."

"Have you killed someone in this car?"

"No, but I've come close. Jaywalkers, mostly. They're drawn to it like moths to a searchlight. But I've never had a major accident. I'm an excellent driver."

"Then why did they take your license away?"

"I'm weak on rules, dear boy."

During the twenty minutes or so it took us to reach our destination, a cream-colored, neo-classical, two-story building a few blocks below the Arroyo Seco Freeway, in South Pasadena, Bedlington kept up a running discourse on the idiocies of speed limits and traffic regulations, all of which, he maintained, had been imposed on society because of the incompetence of most drivers, the majority of whom should never have been licensed to operate a vehicle in the first place.

"Are you saying that only the rich in their fast cars ought to be allowed to drive?" I asked, at one point.

"No, dear boy, only the competent, of whom there are damn few in the world, in any category."

"How are people supposed to get around?"

"On public transport, which we have systematically destroyed here in order to build freeways," he continued. "There used to be an excellent trolley service, the famous Red Cars, all over the Los Angeles basin, you know. It was eliminated in a conspiracy of the oil companies with the automobile manufacturers, back in the late thirties and forties. The result is that we are saddled with millions of incompetent drivers, traffic jams, and smog. One of the many detestable aspects of modern life."

I parked in the circular driveway in front of our destination and prepared to sit it out, but Bedlington urged me to come in with him. "You might enjoy this," he said.

"Where are we?"

He waved casually toward a small sign I had failed to notice beside the front entrance. "Eternal Peace," it said. "Funerary Arrangements."

"A funeral home?"

"I'm afraid so," he confessed, "but the owner's a remarkable fellow. It took me quite a while to find the right person."

The colonnaded building, set behind a lawn and well-tended flower beds, was surrounded on three sides by tall cypresses that shaded it and kept it in a state of perpetual gloom. In the dimly lit reception room, whose walls were decorated by large prints of ruined Greek temples, a sallow-looking young man rose from behind his desk as we entered. "Ah, Mr. Bedlington," he said, in a wispy tenor oozing servility, "please go right in. Mr. Thanassis is expecting you."

"Good afternoon, Pericles," Bedlington said, as we walked into a small inner sanctum even more gloomily illuminated than the reception area. "I want you to meet my friend, Mr. Shifty Lou Anderson. He is not, as you might suppose, a pickpocket or a confidence man, but a practicing minor sorcerer."

This odd introduction didn't seem to faze Pericles Thanassis, who, I quickly gathered, was the boss of Eternal Peace. He was a small, stooped man in his fifties with a large, bald head and a round, pale face like that of the Man in the Moon in some children's tale. Dressed in severe black, with a white stiff shirt collar that seemed to cradle his chin, he came bobbing and weaving out from behind his desk to place his hand in mine, where it lay briefly like a wounded bird. "Delighted, sir," he exclaimed, in a husky, dark voice. "Necromancy?"

"I'm afraid not," I said. "Close-up. You know, cards, coins, bits of this and that."

"I haven't seen him work yet," Bedlington declared, "but I'm told he's very good. He's helping me out these last few weeks."

"Yes, I understand," the little man said, retreating behind his desk again while continuing to bob his head up and down like an agitated bird. "I'm so happy to see you, Mr. Bedlington. I have almost everything ready."

"Indeed?"

"Yes, sir. I have the velvet samples here for you to pick out."

He fished around in a drawer and pulled out a leather case, which he deposited on his desk and snapped open for Bedlington to inspect. "If these won't do, I have a new shipment due in any day," he said, picking out a strip of cloth for his client to look at. "Here's a beautiful cloth, sir. We used it last year to line the casket of a very prominent evangelist. The gold embroidery is hand-sewn."

Bedlington fingered the material, but did not seem impressed. "Not quite what I had in mind," he said. "I wanted an off-white, elegant but simple. Repose, quiet good taste, you know what I mean."

"Oh, perfectly." He produced another sample. "Perhaps this one?"

"Yes, that's better. A bit glossy for my taste."

"Some very prominent people repose on this fabric, sir. It blends well with most complexions."

"It isn't perfect, but never mind."

"A lovely cloth, sir. Resists the humidity wonderfully."

"I can die with it," Bedlington said.

"Oh . . . ah . . . yes," Thanassis said, flustered. He snapped the case shut and put it back in the drawer.

"And the casket itself?"

"Coming along beautifully. Today we're finishing up the trim, then we'll install the silver knobs you sent us from Venice. Fine workmanship."

"The best. And the Egyptian lamps?"

"They're being rewired on a timer. The Carrara marbles will be delivered next week, I'm told." He seemed about to soar out of his chair with delight.

"And the fountain?"

"In the center, at the foot of the bier, as you requested."

"Excellent."

"About the music—"

"No music."

"No music, sir?" Thanassis seemed genuinely distressed.

"Not one wretched note, Thanassis," Bedlington said. "I thought I made that clear."

"I'm sorry," the little man said. "I had thought—-with your love of Gilbert and Sullivan—"

"And Cole Porter," Bedlington said. "Hardly appropriate."

"Many people have music now," the little man insisted. "Usually something inspirational. Hymns from the Hollywood Bowl or a medley of Liberace's favorite études—"

"What an appalling idea. Pericles, if a man can't live in peace, at least he can lie in it."

"Yes, of course."

"When can I see everything?"

"I'll call you in a few days, without fail," Thanassis answered. "All but the final minor details. We'll finish the casket today or tomorrow. The upholsterer will be in tomorrow morning for the lining."

"That's it, then. Have we covered everything?"

"Yes, sir, I think so."

"Good." Bedlington nodded to me and we rose to go.

"By the way, sir, your illness . . . you'll excuse my asking . . . there's no hope?"

"None at all," Bedlington said cheerfully.

"And may I ask . . . when—when you'll . . . I mean, how soon—"

"A few weeks."

Thanassis shook his head sadly, as he escorted us out into the lobby. "So soon, so soon. It just doesn't seem possible," he mumbled.

"Nice of you to be concerned, Pericles."

Thanassis clutched his hand and stopped him before we could get out the front door. "If only they were all like you," he said. "The trouble is that, in my profession, the arrangements are never made by the client himself. And the relatives, sir—you must know what they're like! No care paid to the essential details. No thought given to the future comfort of the loved one. No effort spared to rush through the ceremony as economically as possible. No pains taken to maintain decorum. No elegance, no dignity. Above all, no taste. Things aren't what they used to be. You take the Etruscans or the Egyptians, sir—*there* were people who knew how to pass away. They simply exchanged one palace for another. A man like me was a person of consequence in the community."

"My dear Pericles, we die as sordidly as we live," Bedlington said, beaming with pleasure. "Death should be treated with the same gallantry once devoted to the conquest of a beautiful woman. She ought to be elaborately courted, showered with gifts, and welcomed when she calls. Today we treat death as a prostitute and haggle over the fee."

"Oh, yes!" Thanassis exclaimed, his eyes alight with messianic fervor.

"We die as ingloriously as flies under the swatter," Bedlington continued. "Believe me, Pericles, surrounded as I am by the stench of the living, I long only for the hygienic solitude of death." He patted Thanassis on the shoulder and we swept grandly out the front door toward the car. "We'll be in touch," he called back, as he settled himself beside me and I started the engine.

He said nothing more until we turned into the street leading up to his house, but contented himself with humming a tune I couldn't identify from one of his favorite operettas. "What do you think of all this?" he asked me, as I turned toward the gate.

"What do you mean? Everything?"

"I suppose that's what I mean."

"Does it matter what I think?"

"Not really. I'm just curious."

"I think you're either playing an elaborate little game or you're as nutty as a fruitcake."

He laughed. "You're honest," he said. "I like that."

As I drove the car through the gate, he said, "Get out, I'll take it from here."

We switched seats and he suddenly slammed the gears into action, roaring up the driveway and coming to a screeching stop under the porte cochere. "I'll walk next time," I said, extricating myself.

"I miss driving this machine," he explained. "It's a magnificent automobile. They don't make them like this anymore." He reached into his wallet, extracted a single crisp one-hundred-dollar bill and handed it to me. "Thank you," he said. "Call tomorrow at nine. Scopes will tell you if I need you. Is the arrangement satisfactory?"

"Fine," I said. "Thanks."

He walked briskly up the steps into his house without a backward glance.

I made the last three races at Santa Anita that afternoon and found Jay Fox enthroned in his box. He had been having a good day and was feeling expansive, with several of his retinue on hand. Arnie Wolfenden, a recent émigré from New York, was slumped in one of the rear seats, his eyes burrowing into the *Form* from about an inch away, while Fido, Angles Beltrami, and Whodoyalike were listening to Jay's good-humored analysis of the rest of the card. He broke it off when he saw me. "Too bad, Shifty," he said. "We're on our way to a monster day here. Where have you been?"

"I have a part-time job," I explained, "driving a very rich man around on errands."

"How rich is he?" Angles asked. "Could we interest him in our action?"

"I don't think so," I said. "He has weightier matters on his mind." I told Jay who he was. "Charlie Pickard trains for him."

"Oh, yeah, I know who he is," Jay said. "An elegant old guy who looks like he's right out of the twenties."

"You got it. Anyway, it's easy, maybe a couple of hours a day, not every day, and he hands me a hundred dollars. I get to drive this incredible car."

I started to describe it to him, but the bugler sounded the call to the post for the seventh and Whodoyalike bounded to his feet. "Who do ya like?" he asked the box at large.

Arnie looked up from his *Form*. "The four horse in here is the only speed," he said. "He'd be worth a bet, if he weren't even money."

"Better a winner at even money than a loser at a hundred to one," Fido chirped. "I gave him out on the service, my best bet of the day. I'm going to hammer this one." And he rushed away toward the betting windows, followed by Whodoyalike.

"Them two bums can't resist even money," Angles said. "A couple of jerks."

"Why do I despise that man?" Arnie asked, wiping his nose with a blue handkerchief the size of a face towel. He stood up. "But I suppose Fido's right. I'm putting him on top only in Exactas to the four and seven. Jay?"

The Fox shook his head. "I'm passing," he said. "The value isn't there, because the favorites figure to run one-two."

Arnie, who looked standing up like a small army tent with the face of a ruined academic protruding from the top, eased himself out of the box and shuffled away down the aisle. "Look at him," Angles said. "If he don't stop eating, he's gonna croak out here one day."

"Arnie's dream is to die with a winning ticket in one hand and a loaf of French bread in the other," Jay observed. "He's happy. Don't worry about him."

"Who's worried?" Angles snapped. "Why should I worry? Anyway, the speed don't win here. The five horse can lay up close and pick him up at the sixteenth pole. I'm bettin' only to place." He followed Arnie out.

"So you're having a good day," I said.

Jay grinned. "I'm ahead eight hundred and if this favorite wins, I have five in the Pick Six," he said. "It should pay four or five hundred and I've got it twice. Too bad you weren't here."

"My timing is off in everything these days," I answered. "Except magic."

"Tell me some more about this guy," Jay said. "He sounds like a real character."

"He is." I quickly filled Jay in on everything, including Bedlington's passion for the works of Gilbert and Sullivan. "In fact, he's got so many things going for him, including this car, his horses, and an incredible art collection, that I still can't convince myself he means it about doing himself in."

"Sounds pretty bizarre," Jay agreed, picking up his binoculars to focus on the horses, who were now being loaded into the starting gate below us.

I had left my own glasses in the glove compartment of my car, but the race was of no interest to me, so I sat back to enjoy it merely as a distant spectacle, for once. It went off about as Jay had predicted it would, with the two favorites carving out leisurely fractions on the front end and the rest of the undistinguished field bunched up behind them. I allowed my gaze to wander over the infield to the dark brown, arid-looking slopes of Old Baldy against the cool, blue sky and was relaxing with my eyes half-closed, when I heard Jay mutter, "What the hell's going on?"

I looked back toward the horses, now on the turn for home. The two favorites were still running one-two, without having had to expend themselves, but the longest shot in the race, a seven-year-old gelding with a total of two lifetime wins in a career of thirty-eight starts, had begun to close ground on the rail and was mounting a threat. "He'll die," Jay said. "The fractions are too slow."

The horse in question was Balls of Fire and he was being ridden hard by a jockey named Lonny Richards, whom we all knew well and distrusted profoundly. He was a forty-five-year-old journeyman rider, who had once been a top jock around the California tracks. He should still have been in his prime, but his career had declined. He had always had great natural ability and had once ridden good horses from rich stables, had even finished second twice in the Kentucky Derby and had won a Belmont, but lately good mounts had become few and far between. Over the years he had acquired a reputation for leaving horses in the gate at the start of races, especially when he was up on favorites in nondescript contests for small purses, and the professional hard knockers at the track had learned to lay off him unless the price was right. "The only time to bet that bum," our late pal Sour Sam had once said, "is when he's an overlay in an Exacta race. Then he'll ride like a demon for you." Mostly, it was safer not to risk any money on him at all and over the years owners and trainers of cheap horses had learned not to engage his services. He had recently been relegated to one or two mounts a day and he no longer rode important horses for anyone. He also reportedly had a drinking problem and liked to chase young girls. Sam used to call him the Undertaker, because he had buried so many bettors, and the name had stuck to him, also because he had a narrow face with a long nose and was not known for his good humor.

His horse today, however, was not dying, as Jay had predicted he would. At the head of the stretch, the two leaders swung a bit wide and Richards cracked his mount with a right-handed whip. Balls of Fire shot through the narrow gap, scraping paint along the inside rail, and engaged the leaders. The three animals came straining toward the finish line together, but in the last few yards Balls of Fire, with Richards slashing and driving on the inside, stuck his head in front at the wire. The photo-finish sign blinked on, but we knew who had won. "Incredible," Jay said. "That sonofabitch can still ride when he wants to. I'm glad I passed."

Balls of Fire paid $88.20 for every two-dollar ticket, an event that did not enliven our box. Fido, in fact, returned to it screaming. "Did you see that? Did you see that?" he shouted, his face crimson with fury, as he hurried toward us. "That Richards, I could kill him!"

"I should have looked at the price," Angles said. "Richards at forty to one, I should have had something on him."

"They let him through on the rail," Fido said. "They opened it up for him. If he doesn't go through, he can't win."

"They were waiting for him," Angles said. "You think this game is honest?"

"They were riding all out," Jay said. "Nobody quit in the race, Fido."

But Fido wasn't listening. "How can they do this to me?" he asked, clearly not expecting an answer. "How can they get away with this stuff?" And he rushed away from us, perhaps to look for a more sympathetic hearing elsewhere. Angles followed him out. "Fuckin' Shakespearean actors, that's what they are," he said, leaving. "They could win Academy Awards with their acting talent."

Arnie sighed. "The paranoia factor at racetracks is not to be discounted," he said, rising majestically to ease himself out of our box. "I've had enough for one day. See you tomorrow, gentlemen."

I made no bets of my own that afternoon, but I hung around to chat with Jay through the last two races. He had blown his Pick Six, but was still going to go away with a nice profit on the afternoon, so he was at peace with himself and his milieu. Our conversation, as it often did, strayed over a variety of topics, with Jay making occasional pointed observations on the vagaries of human existence. He was my best friend at the racetrack, where we had met eleven or twelve years ago, and I enjoyed listening to him talk. Unlike most horse degenerates, he had other interests besides the ponies and was well informed on doings outside the locked-in world of racing. So we chatted casually through the last two contests on the card, neither of which Jay thought was worth even a token wager, and we headed out toward the parking lot together. "Coming out tomorrow?" he asked.

"That depends on Lucius J. Bedlington," I said. "I can use the money."

"You'll turn it around," he assured me. "By the way, watch yourself with this guy. The whole thing sounds weird to me."

"It *is* weird," I agreed, and waved goodbye to head for my car.

Ahead of me, as I turned up an aisle between rows of automobiles, I saw a young woman in a tight miniskirt clipping along on high heels. She had dark blond hair and a large black handbag draped over one shoulder, but the reason I noticed her was that she had the finest pair of legs I had seen in months. I'm definitely a leg man, so I paused long enough to watch her for a few seconds. When she turned and disappeared suddenly between two cars, I headed back toward the Datsun.

A few minutes later, as I headed out of the lot, I saw her again. She was at the wheel of a battered white Mustang convertible, with the top down, and had parked next to an entrance to the backside stable area. I couldn't see her face, because she was looking away from me, but I was sure it was she. The hair looked the same, a pageboy cut, and the big black shoulder bag rested in her lap. I had to slow down and then stop in the heavy outgoing traffic, so I was there to note whom she was waiting for. Lonny Richards came walking out from between the barns and hurried toward her. She raised the black bag and shook it at him, as if it contained a treasure, and he smiled. When he slid into the seat beside her, she leaned over to kiss him and dropped the bag in his lap. I was hoping to see what she looked like, but the line of cars in front of me had begun to move again and some irate loser directly behind me was leaning into his horn. I put the Datsun in gear and drove off. Richards had obviously made a killing on his win, but it was that frail with the splendid legs I envied him, not the loot.

Three

DOING
NUMBERS

I saw Bedlington nearly every day for the next couple of weeks, usually for two or three hours, while I drove him around town on various errands. Most of them had to do with his funeral arrangements or with matters relating to the future disposition of his estate. One night we attended a performance of *Ruddigore,* one of the less known of the Gilbert and Sullivan operettas, put on at the Ambassador Auditorium in Pasadena. In the second act, an entire picture gallery of ancestors came to life, a plot twist that amused me. The piece turned out to be one of Bedlington's favorites and we left that night with him humming the various tunes. "An enchanting conceit, dear boy," he confided to me, as we settled ourselves in the Alfa for the drive home. "How splendid it would be, if I could simply disappear into a portrait and come to life from time to time to chastise my descendants, 'at the dead of the night's high noon,' eh?"

One afternoon we drove up into a canyon above Altadena to a secluded plot of land hidden from sight by a row of fat cypresses and nestling in the curve of a dirt path winding past a rocky outcropping. I parked the car and we got out to walk the last fifty yards or so to a gate set in a high concrete wall. Behind it, in isolated splendor on a circular patch of lawn, rose what looked like a miniature Greek temple, complete with Corinthian columns and a triangular portico. "You see?" Bedlington said, pointing to the structure.

"What is it?" I asked, looking around. The building was in the open, but shielded from view on all sides by the high wall and stands of trees, mostly cypresses and pines.

"My final resting place, dear boy," he said. "I thought you might appreciate it."

"Seems an odd spot for it."

"Really? Where should it be?"

"In a cemetery, I suppose."

"Precisely the reason I had it erected here," he explained, "where I can be entirely at peace and not hemmed in by the rabble." He unlocked the gate and led me inside. "You see?" And he pointed to an inscription engraved over the entrance. It read:

Is life a thorn?
  Then count it not a whit!
  Man is well done with it . . .

"Gilbert?" I asked.

"Of course. *The Yeomen of the Guard.* Apropos, don't you think?"

"I suppose so, if that's the way you feel."

"Want to go in?"

I shook my head. "No, thanks."

"No need to," he commented cheerfully. "It's not finished yet, anyway. Thanassis is slow. But it will be splendid, eventually. I presume you'll come when I'm safely ensconced within."

"I may."

Oblivious to my uneasiness, he led the way out toward the gate. "I couldn't allow myself to be entombed in a public cemetery, dear boy," he said. "Have you noticed the odd thing about cemeteries?"

"What about them?"

"How they all seem to contain only nature's noblemen? Loving fathers and husbands, heroic sons, angelic daughters, great statesmen, victorious generals, public benefactors, humanitarians. I wonder where all the crooks, liars, and cowards are buried? Do you suppose they simply vanished into thin air one day?"

I laughed. "It's a mystery."

"Indeed it is, dear boy. I'm going to be happier here, on my own private plot, than somewhere surrounded by such excessive public virtue."

By this time I had decided that Bedlington was not merely an eccentric, but certifiably loony. As far as I could tell, he had every reason to want to go on living, including the money, apparently, to indulge his every fantasy. It made me more than a little impatient with him, especially when I considered the number of miserable people in the world who would have happily traded places with him. I took the matter up with him on our drive back from his private mausoleum.

"I know about the poor, dear boy," he said. "They will always be with us."

"True, but you're in a position to help."

"How? Charity? I give generously every year. It has not made the slightest dent in human affairs. I'm afraid I agree with Shaw, who once declared that the world is populated in the main by people who ought not to be alive."

"I imagine Hitler felt the same way."

"And Stalin and all the people like him since the beginning of history. Dear boy, humanity is a hopeless cause."

"If I felt that way, I'd—" I suddenly realized that I couldn't finish the sentence.

Bedlington smiled. "Exactly, dear boy. You do see my point," he said. "No, no, I've made the right decision."

After that discussion, I decided not to debate the point anymore with my self-destructive plutocrat. Besides, I was having too interesting a life of my own to be put off by his snobbism and rampant pessimism. I had begun to work on what I hoped would be some dazzling new effects for my act and I was breaking them in at the Magic Castle, the Victorian mansion in the Hollywood foothills that has become a Mecca for magicians from all over the world. If I could perfect them, I thought perhaps Hal might be able to get me back on the *Tonight* show or on some other late-night television talkathon to dazzle the rubes. To change the subject, I told Bedlington about them.

"Sounds mildly entertaining," he said. "Perhaps I'll pop in on you one night."

"I'll pick you up."

"Why not, dear boy? If you could make real magic, of course, I might change my attitude, you know."

"I wouldn't want you to do that. You're having too much fun as it is."

He laughed. "Very perceptive of you, my lad."

Three nights later he did come, but without giving me any warning. He just appeared beside me at the bar around ten o'clock, between my two shows, and ordered himself a glass of port. "I thought it was unfair to call you at the last minute," he informed me.

"You took a taxi?"

"Of course."

"Then I'll drive you home. No charge."

"Don't be absurd, Shifty," he said. "A bargain is a bargain. Besides, on the drive down here, I was very nearly asphyxiated by the fumes from the taxi driver's cigar, which was evidently composed of dried goat turds from his native Armenia."

"You won't like my car."

"I'll tolerate it, dear boy."

For Bedlington's benefit, I worked in one of my new effects, this one with my specialty, a deck of cards. I began my act in the close-up room by asking a middle-aged woman named Betty, who was sitting in the front row, to draw a card from the pack I extended toward her. "I'll lay you ten to one, Betty, that I can find your card," I told her, after she had made her selection. "And I'll do it without looking." I shuffled the deck behind my back, then took three cards and held them out to her. "Find your card," I told her. She pointed to the bottom one, but I turned over the top one. It was her choice, the jack of spades. "Oh, but you wanted the bottom one," I said. I turned that one over, too, and it was also the jack of spades. Then I flipped over the middle one, again the jack. I turned over every card in the pack and came up with nothing but jacks.

"Hell, that's easy," said the burly man sitting next to her. "The pack is all the same card."

"Really?" I said, looking surprised. "You must be this lady's husband. Am I right, sir?"

"You betcha," the man said. "And I know a phony trick when I see one."

"Is that so?" I answered, suddenly riffling the deck and turning the cards over on the tabletop in front of him. It looked like a normal pack. "Almost," I said. "Only there's no jack of spades at all."

"You got that other deck in your pocket," the man said.

"Do I? Let's check this one first," I said. I picked up the cards, shuffled them, then spread them out again. This time they were all blank.

"Oops, sorry," I commented, giving them one more go and turning them over for the last time. "Ah, you're right, sir!" I exclaimed, smiling. "There are the jacks!" The whole deck was again composed of the jack of spades. My small audience of about twenty people applauded, except for poor Betty's sour spouse.

"Sensational, Shifty," Bedlington said later, as we headed out toward my car.

"I adapted it from another magician I know and I got lucky," I explained. "That woman's husband turned out to be a great shill. I couldn't have planted a better one myself."

"What normally occurs?"

"The same pattern of action, but I have to generate the doubt on my own. This guy saved me the trouble."

"I don't think he was very happy about it."

"Well, people don't like to be shown up."

"The love affair of humanity with itself is the great romance of history," Bedlington declared, as we rumbled out of the parking lot toward the freeway. "By the way, what *is* this vehicle?"

"It's a Datsun 310."

"Where did you have it customized? In Tijuana?"

"It's paid for and it gets me around," I said.

"I was always indifferent to practical considerations, dear boy."

"That's because you were born with money, right?" I said. "You've never had to work for a living."

Bedlington sighed. "No, that's true," he said. "Why do I feel I haven't missed much?"

When I left him that night, he turned back to me before going inside. "Oh, that horse of mine you saw a couple of weeks ago . . ."

"Dummkopf?"

"Yes. He's entered day after tomorrow. Charles thinks he'll run pretty well."

"Are we going?"

"Why not? I have to fill these remaining days somehow."

When I got home that night, I found a message on my answering machine from a man named Derek Flanders. He sounded old and distinguished and introduced himself as a close friend of Bedlington's. Would I please call him at my earliest convenience?

I thought no more about it, but I remembered to call him back before going out for breakfast the next day, around ten o'clock. "Coutts, Riley, and Flanders," a brisk female voice chirped in my ear.

"What are you?" I asked.

"I'm sorry?"

"A law firm?"

"Yes, we are. Whom did you wish to speak to?"

"Mr. Flanders." I gave her my name and credentials.

In a matter of seconds, Flanders himself came on the phone. He had a dark, gruff, friendly manner. "Mr. Anderson, thanks for calling," he said. "I'm an old friend of Lucius's. I'm also his lawyer. I'd like very much to talk to you."

"What about, Mr. Flanders?"

"Well, Lucius has told me about you and I thought maybe we could have a chat."

"Sure, I guess so."

"Not on the phone," he continued. "Can I persuade you to drop in to see me?" And he gave me the address of his firm, which was a block or so off Lake, in Pasadena.

"Does Mr. Bedlington know about this?"

"Of course not. He probably wouldn't want you to talk to me. I won't tell him we've met."

"You can, if you want to."

"Fine. Can you come in this afternoon, around three?"

Bedlington hadn't called and I had no plans of my own. I went first to Santa Anita and made a couple of small losing bets, then left after the fifth race to meet Flanders. His firm, evidently a prestigious one, occupied an old two-story mansion on a side street, in what had once been an elegant residential area. Most of the old houses on the block, shaded by large oaks and ancient pines, had been converted into offices, but at least they hadn't been torn down. I parked on the street and walked up to the front door. "Mr. Anderson?" a smiling young woman said, as I entered. She was sitting behind an antique desk and I guessed she was the same person who had spoken to me that morning. "Mr. Flanders is expecting you." And she rose out of her chair to escort me to his office. She was attractive, but not making much of her looks. She was dressed in a dark gray business suit, sensible low-heeled shoes, wore no makeup, and her brown hair had been pulled back into a bun; she looked dismayingly efficient. Her no-nonsense delivery was clearly part of a studied act and I decided that I was dealing with a conservative law firm probably specializing in corporate accounts. "Here you are," she said, in that cool, studied voice of hers, while opening the door for me. "Mr. Anderson," she called into the room.

Derek Flanders came out from behind his desk to meet me. He was a small, trim-looking man with an angular, intelligent face built around a long, sharp nose. He was bald, with only a thin fringe of white hair, and slightly stooped. I guessed that he was in his seventies, but he seemed much older than his client. He wore a conservatively cut dark blue suit with a vest and a striped old-school tie, and the nails on his delicate-looking little hands were perfectly manicured. "Mr. Anderson, thank you for coming," he said, shaking my hand firmly and ushering me into a comfortable padded seat facing his desk.

The phone rang. "Excuse me a minute," he said, picking it up. "Freeman? I can't talk to him now. Tell him I'll get back to him as soon as I can . . . Yes . . . And hold all my other calls, please."

I looked around. The room was dark, heavy with law books that rose floor to ceiling against one wall, while the two large windows behind Flanders's desk admitted only the light shaded by the large trees outside. Old English hunting prints and several ancient maps adorned the other wall. It was a room designed to impress, not one to party in.

"I know about your connection with Lucius, of course," Flanders said. "I hope you don't mind if I ask you a bit about it."

"No, I don't mind. I would, if I were you." I told him exactly how I happened to have become involved with Bedlington. "He pays me generously for the little I do for him."

"Oh, Lucius has plenty of money," the lawyer said. "Inherited most of it, but he made a good deal on his own. He was a shrewd investor."

"I gather you've known each other for a long time."

Flanders chuckled. "Since the gaslight era," he said. "We met in college, at Harvard, then roomed together our last two years there. Over five decades now. That's quite a while. I've handled his legal affairs for the past thirty-two years. What do you think of him?"

"I like him," I said. "I think he's nuts, but I like him. I also think he has everything to live for, so I have a hard time taking this scheme of his too seriously. But I guess he means it."

"Oh, absolutely," the lawyer agreed. "Under that airy, lighthearted exterior, Mr. Anderson, is a whim of iron."

"I wondered if he had some terminal disease and wasn't telling anyone about it."

"I've checked his doctors and I've seen all of his medical records," Flanders assured me. "He's so healthy he could outlive us all."

"Then I guess I feel sorry for him."

"Don't let him know you feel that way about him, or he'll drop you immediately," Flanders said. "The last thing Lucius wants is pity. He's far too vain." The lawyer paused and sat back in his leather swivel chair, his eyes now focused on the tranquil view from his windows. "I wonder . . ." he murmured, then seemed to come to a decision and turned back to me. "Mr. Anderson, I'd like you to do me a favor."

"Sure, if I can."

"The next time Lucius arranges to have you come by his house to pick him up, would you please call me?"

"Why?"

"Because I'm trying to get him to see me. He'll talk to me on the phone, but I haven't been able to meet with him for several weeks."

"Why not?"

The lawyer sighed. "Because I keep trying to talk sense to him and he says I'm boring him. He hangs up on me. I want him to see a psychiatrist. I'm trying to save his life, damn it. I've got to get him to listen to me. The way things are, I can only write him letters, most of which he answers with acerbic little notes. Sometimes he has that decrepit butler of his call me. You've met Scopes?"

"Oh, yes."

"I can hardly understand what he says and I have to get him to repeat everything at least twice on the phone. It's exasperating. Of course, that's exactly why Lucius does it."

"To exasperate you?"

"Oh, yes. I've always been a straight man for his jokes. But this time, Mr. Anderson, it's not funny. It's a matter of life and death."

"How would my notifying you help?"

"I'd arrange to show up as you arrive," he said. "That way he'll have to see me."

"He'll know I tipped you off."

"I'll tell him I've been having the house watched and that I followed you in, which is exactly what I'll do," he explained.

"Well, I guess so," I said. "It's for a good cause."

"You do like him?"

"Yes, I do. Do you think this'll help?"

Flanders shrugged and rapped his small hands on the arms of his chair. "Who knows? It's worth a try," he said. "And by the way, there will be something in it for you. I'll have Miss Clark draw you a check."

"No, thanks. Not necessary. I can't do that."

"Ah," Flanders said, smiling, "a man of integrity. I like that."

"I have my price," I said, "but this doesn't really fit in anywhere. I'd feel funny about it. Anyway, I hope it works."

"It's a long shot," the lawyer admitted, standing up to ease me out of his office. "Thanks, Mr. Anderson, I appreciate it. And if it works, I'll remember you, I promise."

On my way out, I stopped by Miss Clark's desk. She was on the phone, chirping mechanically into it, a smile frozen on her pale features. The caller at the other end was evidently not being accommodating, but she persisted, locked into her uncomfortable public persona. After hanging up, she looked up at me, the professional smile still in place. "Do you like horse racing?" I asked her.

"I—I've never been to one," she confessed, surprised. "Is there some way I can help you?"

"Sure. You could come to Santa Anita with me this Saturday and help me pick winners."

"I—I don't know a thing about it," she stammered, a bit rattled. "I'm afraid I—how could I help you?"

"I don't know. Just by being there, I guess. It's fun. Really."

"Oh." She looked puzzled, as if the word was unknown to her. "Well . . . I don't know—"

"Do you have a first name?"

"Me? It's—it's Amber."

"Mine's Lou. I'm also known as Shifty, because I do card tricks. Want to see one?"

She glanced quickly back toward the interior of the building. "I couldn't possibly," she said. "You really must excuse me—" The phone rang and she reached for it.

"I'll call you later, Amber," I told her. "You'll love Santa Anita."

I let myself out and walked toward my car. I wasn't at all sure why I had asked Amber Clark for a date. There was just something about her that interested me. I guess I was curious about what might lie beneath that frozen exterior. I'm known in my circle for the occasional impulsive gesture.

I had to call her early the next morning, however, and back out of my invitation, because Saturday turned out to be the day Dummkopf was entered and I had to squire Bedlington to the races. She couldn't come on Sunday, because that was the day she always went on nature hikes with her group, she said, but I did convince her to let me take her out to dinner on Tuesday night. She lived in West L.A., not too far from my place in West Hollywood. "I don't eat meat," she informed me. "Is that all right?"

"Fine. We'll go Chinese," I said. "That way you can gorge on bamboo shoots and snow peas, while I stuff myself on shrimp and beef."

"Oh, Chinese? MSG is an evil chemical."

"We'll get them not to use any," I assured her. "I know a place where the owner's a friend of mine and the food is great. Okay?"

She sounded doubtful, but gave in. "And I don't smoke," she added.

"That's fine, neither do I. See you then." And I hung up quickly before she could tell me anything else about herself. I was wondering by then if she would also turn out to be some sort of religious fanatic, but something about her made me want to pursue her. She had become a small challenge and challenges can sometimes be exciting.

Dummkopf had been entered in the ninth, the last race on the card, so I picked up my millionaire owner right after the seventh on Saturday and we arrived at the paddock just as the horses were being led into the walking ring. The day had turned dark and windy, with a hint of rain in the air, and Charlie was standing on the grass in an old gray topcoat that came nearly to his ankles. "Ever the fashion plate," Bedlington observed, as we came up to him. "Hello, Charles, are we in for another minor failure?"

Charlie grinned and shook his head. "Maybe not, Mr. Bedlington," he said. "This horse is gonna like the grass. He just might fool us."

As I watched the entries file into the ring, I gazed idly about me and spotted the blonde with the terrific legs again. She was standing off to one side, all by herself, the large black shoulder bag dangling off her hip. Despite the chill in the air, she was dressed in another tight miniskirt that hugged her buttocks and revealed her splendid legs, long and brown, lightly muscled, with trim ankles and shapely knees. I had to force myself to look above them to her face, which, I was relieved to note for my peace of mind, was undistinguished. She was conventionally pretty, with streaked, straight blond hair framing an oval face of the sort that grace beer commercials or cavort in the background of sleazy movies made for teenagers. I tried not to look at those legs again and made myself concentrate on the horses.

Tim Lang came out of the jockeys' room and joined us, as we watched the animals being walked around us. He shook hands with us and Charlie leaned over to talk to him. "Listen, Tim, I have a feeling this horse is gonna like the grass," he said. "He ain't got no speed, which you know, so just ease him on over close to the rail on the first turn. At a mile and one-eighth you got all the time in the world. He should start pickin' 'em up at the quarter. Try not to get him boxed and I think he'll give you a good run at the finish."

Lang didn't seem to be listening to any of this. His eyes were on the blonde in the miniskirt. "That lucky shit," he mumbled.

"Who?" I asked.

"Richards," he said. "How does he rate something like that?"

"Who is she?"

"Some actress he picked up. She could move me up a couple of lengths."

"Tim, did you hear me?" Charlie asked. "This sucker's gonna run some today."

"Sure, Charlie, I heard you." But his gaze never strayed from the girl, even after the paddock judge called out riders up and the mounted horses made one last turn around the ring. The blonde was standing by herself, gazing smilingly up at Lonny Richards, who was riding the animal in the one hole and leading the post parade.

I checked my program. The horse's name was Elongate, a lanky sort who had already run well at the distance on the turf and was being made a lukewarm favorite by the bettors, at odds of five to two. As I watched the horses move toward the gap leading to the track, I saw Richards lean over his mount to pat him lightly on the neck with his left hand. The blonde gave a little chirp of delight and grabbed the strap of her shoulder bag with one hand, as if afraid it might be snatched away from her. No sooner had the entries filed out of the paddock than she began to move swiftly toward the grandstand, trotting along on her spiky high heels.

I glanced at Charlie but he had seen nothing of this little drama. His gaze had been on Dummkopf, who had looked his usual placid self, about as alert as an old cow being led to pasture.

"I shall be at my usual station, Charles," Bedlington said, heading for the Turf Club stairway.

"You better get ready to come down to the winner's circle, Mr. Bedlington," Charlie said. "I got a feeling he's gonna run real good."

"*Well*, Charles, not good," Bedlington corrected him. "Your misuse of the English language is one of the many crosses I have to bear."

"I ain't got time to talk English," Charlie said. "I got horses to train and I got jockeys and vets and agents and stable help to talk to. How do you expect 'em to understand me if I was to talk well English?"

"Good English, Charles. You're incorrigible." He waved to us. "I shall not descend to confront the rabble after the race, Charles, regardless of the outcome. Shifty, I'll see you at valet parking ten minutes after the finish." And he left us, walking briskly through the flow of spectators, like Charlton Heston parting the Red Sea.

"Charlie," I said, as we rode the escalator toward the grandstand boxes, "I think Richards is going to stiff the favorite."

"What makes you think so?"

"I got a hunch."

"Hunches and tips is how bettors go broke, Shifty," he said. "You can bet my horse across the board. He's thirty to one and I think he's gonna get some part of this."

"I think so, too."

I went straight to the windows and bet twenty dollars across the board on Dummkopf, then went outside to watch the race from a corner of an aisle near a box I knew Richards frequented on days when he had no mounts. I was hoping for another glimpse of the blonde, but I didn't see her. I raised my glasses to watch the race just as the starter sprang the horses loose and they came bobbing toward us down the stretch for the first time.

I could tell right away that Dummkopf liked the surface. He was striding purposefully, head bowed under Lang's tight hold, as he swung over toward the rail and tucked in, only two wide, around the clubhouse turn. As the animals swept past and headed for the backstretch, I tried to find Elongate.

It wasn't hard; he was battling three wide on the lead with a couple of speedballs, who were setting sizzling fractions. Elongate's best style, according to my analysis of his form, would have been to take back a couple of lengths behind the speed, then move at them on the turn for home. By using himself up early, he was being deprived of any chance to win. When the timer on the tote board flashed a minute and nine seconds flat for the first six furlongs, I knew that my hunch had been correct. The Undertaker was up to his old tricks again. He must have bet on other horses in the race, probably in exotic combination wagers involving various long shots. Stiffing the favorite and causing him to finish out of the money is one of the commonest forms of cheating in a horse race, especially one in which a bettor stands to make a large sum of money by speculating on the long shots. I recalled the ecstatic expression on the blonde's face in the paddock and I assumed that Richards must have clued her in on his action. The pat on the horse's neck could have been a signal. Maybe she was betting for him as well.

I looked back toward the pack for Dummkopf. He was running next to last along the rail, with about twenty lengths to make up, a seemingly hopeless task. But now, as the tiring leaders turned for home, several of the trailers, including Bedlington's plodder, began to close ground. Dummkopf, I realized, was closing fastest of all, but to get clear Lang had to take him five wide around the last turn. An eighth of a mile from the finish line, at the head of the lane, three other closers had picked up the leaders and were charging for home. Dummkopf had several lengths still to make up, but once in the clear he put his head down, dug in again and came on like a stakes horse. Fifty yards from the wire he had picked up two of the leaders and was battling head to head with the third choice in the race, a seasoned gelding named Triple Play. The latter, ridden by Bill Scarpe, long one of the dominant jockeys in the country, had saved much ground by staying close to the rail and moving up between horses to make his run. Now he found enough left to fight off Dummkopf and gradually pulled away from him to win by a neck.

Triple Play paid $12.60 to win for every two-dollar ticket, while a five-dollar Exacta, a combination bet requiring two horses to finish first and second in exact order, was worth eleven hundred and forty-two dollars even. Dummkopf paid $24.80 to place and twelve dollars to show; I was three hundred and eight dollars richer and my losing streak had definitely come to an end. I headed for a pari-mutuel window, my winning ticket in my hand.

Angles Beltrami was standing in the line next to mine and he spotted me. "Hey, Shifty," he said, smiling cynically, "you caught that action, too, huh?"

"I bet the second horse across the board," I confessed.

"That pig? Nah, that's not what I meant," Angles said. "I got the winner and I got him good, for like a grand."

"That's good, Angles. That's good handicapping."

"Handicapping, my ass," he snapped. "The favorite shoulda won by five, only I figured the angle."

"What was it?"

"Richards and Scarpe, man, they been pullin' this shit for years," he said. "One of them stiffs the favorite, the other one wins with a long shot. Fuckin' crooks."

"Triple Play was only five to one."

"Yeah, but this was an Exacta race, Shifty. What's the matter with you?" His face darkened with anger. "A couple of fuckin' bandits, that's what they are!"

"What are you so sore about?" I asked. "You're cashing, aren't you?"

"I been stiffed by them little bastards so often this don't begin to make up for it," he said. "I figured the angle this time, but you pay to get an education with them pricks. I hope they both fall off someday and break their fuckin' necks."

This seemed an uncharitable view of events to me, but I let it pass. Angles lived in a world in which conspiracy reigned supreme and all human actions were suspect, but who was I to contradict him this time? I pocketed my winnings and headed out toward the Turf Club exit.

The blonde was standing in a corner of the betting area, a few feet beyond the end of one of the bars. She was angry and talking in a loud voice, but hard and fast, to a vaguely familiar-looking man of about fifty whom I'd seen around the track for years. He seemed to be trying to placate her, but without success. Her eyes were full of tears and her cheeks were flushed. Suddenly, the man grabbed her by both arms and shook her, his head leaning in toward her, as if telling her something she had better pay attention to. Whatever it was, it stopped her in her tracks. The color drained from her face and she shook his hands off, scurrying past me on those wonderful legs toward the unreserved grandstand section. I paused to watch her go, then looked over at the man. He, too, had been watching her departure, but his face looked thoughtful, even concerned. I thought he might be genuinely worried about her.

I was going to be late picking up Bedlington, so I started to walk very fast, only to come up against Jay Fox emerging from the men's room. "Hey, Shifty, where have you been?" he asked. "Did you like this last boat race?"

"I loved it," I said. "I bet on Charlie Pickard's horse."

"That bum? How could you do that?"

"I haven't got time to explain, Jay. I have to meet Bedlington. But listen—" I said, suddenly pausing in midflight to cock a thumb back toward the man the blonde had been talking to. "See that guy, over at the corner of the bar?"

"Which one?"

"He's by himself. Long, wavy brown hair, in the blue wind-breaker."

"What about him?"

"Who is he?"

"Him? That's Jack Leone, Richards's agent. Don't ask me how he survives."

"I think I know."

"Yeah, I do, too."

"Only this time I don't think they caught the Exacta," I said. "I'd bet they didn't use Charlie's horse."

"Well, he was the only maiden in the field," Jay said. "You can't use 'em all. I wouldn't have used him either."

"You might have, Jay, if I'd had a chance to tell you what Pickard said to me before the race."

"No, I don't think so," he said. "You know me, Shifty. I'm a one-way bettor."

"Yes, your way."

"That's how I survive out here," he explained. "I don't listen to tips, I pay no attention to information and I'm indifferent to what anyone thinks. The numbers have to add up, that's all that matters."

"No mystery and no romance. I'll see you, Jay." And I bolted for my rendezvous with Bedlington.

When I emerged, a little breathless, from the Turf Club exit, I found him waiting for me. He was sitting placidly in the open passenger seat of the Alfa, parked off to one side beyond the flow of cars being returned to their owners by the valet-parking attendants. "I'm sorry, Mr. Bedlington," I said, as I climbed in behind the wheel. "I had a nice ticket to cash on your horse and then I got waylaid by an old friend of mine."

"Lucius, Shifty," he said. "I think we know each other well enough by now."

"Okay." I started up the engine and put the car into gear. "Charlie was right," I said, as we eased into the outgoing traffic. "That colt of yours is a different animal on the grass."

"Did he really run that well?" he asked, indifferently.

"Didn't you see the race?"

"No. I bumped into a very old acquaintance of mine at the bar and we were doing a bit of reminiscing." He chuckled. "Poor Henry was astonished to learn I had a horse in the race and didn't even watch him run."

"I can believe it."

"Dear boy, I've seen too many of them run over the years."

"Why bother to come, then?"

"Good question. It moves me about a bit, you see. I spend a lot of time alone and I get bored. Actually, I'm bored most of the time."

"I've never been bored at a horse race."

He looked at me sadly. "Where did this animal finish?"

"You don't know? Second. And he almost won."

"Oh, yes, I remember. I'm happy for Charles."

"That's all?"

"Ah, Shifty, 'in the evening of my day, with the sun of life declining, I recall without repining all the heat of bygone noon,' " he recited.

"G and S again. Which one?"

"A minor adaptation of *The Yeomen of the Guard,* dear boy."

He remained silent after that and I concentrated on driving his difficult machine. I glanced at him as we roared up the road toward his house. He was sitting straight up in his seat, his hands resting lightly on his knees and staring straight ahead. I realized that I had never before met anyone associated with a racehorse who didn't care whether the animal won or lost. That was the moment I became convinced he was serious about killing himself.

 # *Four*

SMOG

I didn't hear from Bedlington again until late Monday night, when I got home from a disgusting horror movie about dead people living in the sewers of New York to find a message from him on my answering machine. He wanted me to come by the next morning, at about eleven, to take Scopes shopping. "I've drained the wine cellar, dear boy," his voice informed me, "in the forlorn hope that my last bottle of Romanée-Conti would coincide with my departure from the scene. Unfortunately, I've outlived my expectations, due to the intolerable delays occasioned by my pet raven's inability to conclude all the essential arrangements. I may not be able to see you, as I am in seclusion at the moment, so a grisly grim good night to you. 'Oh, to be wafted away'—" He was obviously off into Gilbert and Sullivan again, but my answering machine cut him off in full cry.

Tuesday was also the day of my date with Amber Clark, which I reminded her of when I telephoned Flanders shortly after nine o'clock.

She seemed doubtful about wanting to go through with it, so I was glad to have caught her before she had definitely changed her mind. I was curious enough about her by this time to insist on seeing her, even if it would mean a disastrous evening in her company. I'd been alone for several months by then and hadn't found anyone recently I wanted to spend much time with. I also had a feeling that she would at least be too odd to be merely boring. So I agreed to all of her conditions and promised to bolt the eatery I had selected at the merest hint of chemicals in her egg-flower soup. "Well, all right," she finally conceded, "I suppose so." She wouldn't let me pick her up either, but insisted that we meet at the restaurant. "Just because I'm a woman," she said, "it doesn't mean I can't go to an appointment by myself."

"That isn't exactly what I thought," I objected. "I just thought—"

"You're a man," she said sweetly, "I know what you just thought." She concluded by telling me she would give Flanders, who hadn't come in yet, the message. "I'm so sorry, but I have another call," she added, and cut me off. Not only odd, I decided, but ruthless. I began to look forward to my date.

Scopes was waiting for me outside the mansion gate when I showed up there promptly at eleven. He was dressed in his wrinkled black suit, with a battered black bowler on his bald pate and badly fitting dark glasses on the end of his nose. He looked unreal in the California sunlight, as decayed and pallid as the walking corpses I had seen in the horror movie the night before. "Good morning, thir," he said, as I got out to help him into the car. "Tho kind of you."

"No problem, my pleasure," I said, as I lowered him into his seat and strapped him in. "Where to?"

He handed me a slip of paper with the address of a liquor store in Beverly Hills, then slumped down into his seat and almost immediately dozed off. He didn't come to again until after I had parked and shaken him by the shoulder. "Here tho thoon?" he mumbled. "Dothed off. Alwayth happenth." His eyes closed and he slumped down again, but I opened the door and hauled him out. "Thank you, thir," he said, and began to totter off in the wrong direction across the parking lot. I grabbed him again and guided him to the entrance of the shop. "Tho kind," he said. "Long time thinth I've been here. Thank you."

The store turned out to be a luxurious emporium specializing in imported wines. We spent nearly an hour in it, during which Scopes managed to drop his teeth on the floor twice and knock over a pyramidal display of Italian Barolos being offered at a discount. He broke two bottles, but no one minded because of the size of his order. He only picked out two cases, a total of twenty-four French clarets, but the cheapest one in the lot cost over a hundred dollars. We were smilingly escorted back to my car not only by the young clerk carrying the wine, but by the manager, whose servile grin faded from his face when he saw the Datsun. He excused himself to rush back inside, undoubtedly to confirm the solvency of the check Scopes had scrawled for the order.

I pulled up at the mansion gate a little after one, with Scopes snoring loudly beside me, his derby tilted rakishly to one side, his mouth open and his plate resting precariously on his lower lip. As we waited for the gate to open, a dark blue BMW sedan pulled up behind us and then followed us into the grounds. I parked under the porte cochere, with the BMW in my wake. By the time I had woken Scopes up and pried him out of the car, Derek Flanders was standing on the front steps, waiting for us.

Scopes finally noticed him, but evidently failed to recognize him right away. "Thir?" he asked, peering intently at him. "May I—"

"Scopes, it's me," Flanders said. "I have to see Mr. Bedlington."

"Oh, Mr. Flanderth," Scopes exclaimed. "He . . . he'th indithpothed—" The word was too much for him; it expelled his teeth into the driveway, as if a small animal had sprung from his lips. He leaned over to grope for them and I had to rush to his side and grab him by the arm to keep him from falling on his face. We sank together to the gravel to retrieve his mouth.

"What, may I ask, does this scene represent?" I heard Bedlington say. "I mean, apart from its lugubrious comedic aspects."

He was standing above us in the open doorway and elegant as always in loafers, navy blue slacks, and his smoking jacket. Flanders started up the steps toward him. "Lucius, I have to talk to you," he said. "I've been sitting in my damn car waiting all morning for a chance to get in here."

"What about?"

"You know damn well what about."

"Not today, Derek. I'm not in the mood."

"I absolutely insist," Flanders said. "I will not leave until we talk."

"Write me a letter."

"You don't answer them."

"Telephone me."

"You put Scopes on to talk to me."

"He knows everything I care to tell you, Derek."

"Not good enough, Lucius. I'm not leaving until you see me. I just want to talk. I promise not to quarrel with you."

"What is there left to say, Derek? We've told each other all we know, haven't we?"

"Lucius, we've been talking to each other for over sixty years," Flanders said. "The least you can do is give me another half hour."

Bedlington was clearly annoyed, but evidently realized he was not going to be able to put his old friend off. "Well, damn it, come in then," he said. "Shifty, can you give Scopes a hand?"

"Sure."

"Then please join us. I want to make sure this man leaves the premises."

Flanders turned to me and held out his hand. "I'm Derek Flanders," he said, "Mr. Bedlington's attorney. You're Mr. Anderson?"

"Right."

"How did you know that?" Bedlington snapped.

"You told me you had a driver, remember?" Flanders answered. "One of the few times I've been able to get you on the phone recently."

"My memory's going, along with everything else," Bedlington said. "Fortunately, I'll be on my way before I degenerate into a zombie." He turned on his heel and walked briskly back into the house, followed by the lawyer, who paused just long enough to nod his thanks to me.

It took about half an hour to put the two cases of wine away. With Scopes tottering precariously down the narrow stairs ahead of me, I carried them into the cellar, about a third of which had been used to store Bedlington's now depleted collection of vintage bottles. All of the bins, about two hundred in number, were empty and I guessed he had stopped buying at about the time he had decided to ease himself out of life. Scopes insisted that each of our day's purchases be placed in the exactly appropriate slot, which managed to spread them out across an entire wall. "We can't bunch them, right?" I asked. "What happens, Scopes? Do they contaminate each other if they huddle together for warmth or something?"

"Beg your pardon, thir?" the butler answered, his pale, wrinkled countenance a mask of incomprehension. "Huddle, thir? I'm thorry, but—"

"It's okay," I said. "Just making a little joke. Forget it."

"Ah, a joke, I thee." He smiled hideously. "Very amuthing, thir." The effort caused him to look like a minor gargoyle and I decided never to risk trying to make him laugh again; I thought it might kill him.

I offered to help him up the stairs, but he insisted he would be able to manage on his own and I left him there, beginning to haul himself up by the railing one torturous step at a time.

". . . or rather I've been fool enough to unburden myself to you," I heard Bedlington say, as I appeared in the entrance to his funereal living room. "There's hardly—ah, Shifty, come in, dear boy." He peered at me through the gloom. "Want a drink?"

"No, thanks."

"Come in, come in, sit down."

"Lucius," Flanders objected, "this is really private business—"

"Nonsense," Bedlington said, cutting him off with the wave of a hand. "Shifty knows all about it. Or enough about it, anyway."

"There are some matters I can only discuss in private—"

"Precisely why I've asked him to join us, Derek. I'm not going to allow you to bore me with mundane trivialities. Whatever you wish to say to me that my conjuror here cannot listen to, you can entrust to the lethargic incompetence of the U.S. Postal Service. Sit down, Shifty, this will only take a few minutes."

I joined them around the coffee table and a brief, uncomfortable silence ensued. The lawyer was scowling, a development that evidently pleased Bedlington. "As I was saying," the millionaire finally resumed, "there's hardly anything you don't know about me, Derek, and that irritates me. It's really humiliating. I feel as naked in your eyes as a newborn babe and it offends my sense of modesty." Apparently carried away by his own eloquence, he rose out of his chair and began to move about the room as he talked, his old friend's gaze fixed dourly on him. "We men are, after all, the modest sex," he continued. "Women, on the other hand, live in a perpetually fluctuating state of nudity. But I—"

"Oh, come off it, Lucius," Flanders objected. "I've heard all this before."

"Then why the hell don't you leave me alone?" Bedlington answered. "All you have to do is humor me for another week or so."

The lawyer sighed. "How are you going about this nutty scheme?"

"None of your business, Derek. All you need to know is that it will be final and not too messy. No one is going to be able to get to me in time, pump me out, and plug me into any machines, that I can assure you." He paused in his calculated pacing and smiled at his old friend. "You do think I'm crazy, don't you? You'd commit me, if you could, wouldn't you?"

"No. I mean, crazy, yes. But commit you? No."

"Only a lunatic would decide to do as he pleases with his own life. My God, Derek, you took philosophy courses in college. How in hell did you pass them?"

"Simple. I cheated."

Bedlington suddenly struck a dramatic pose by the fireplace, his right arm extended like a dancer's. " 'Oh, to be wafted away from this black

Aceldama of sorrow,' " he declaimed, " 'where the dust of an earthy today is the earth of a dusty tomorrow!' "

"Okay, okay. *Patience*, Act One, Bunthorne," Flanders said wearily, as if they had played this game many times before.

"Very good, Derek, you haven't lost your touch," Bedlington said. "I haven't slipped a quote past you in years." He smiled at me. "That's how we became friends, Shifty. A shared passion for the work of the immortal partnership."

"This is absurd, Lucius," Flanders declared. "You can't make a joke out of death."

"Why not? It's actually one of life's funnier ones."

"My God, you're rich, you're in good health," the lawyer insisted. "You haven't any reason—"

"I'm bored," Bedlington said, interrupting him. "I don't find the human comedy amusing anymore." He walked over to the nearest window and pulled the drawn curtains. The hazy light of a smoggy southern California day flooded into the room. "There used to be a beautiful garden out there, Derek, remember? Full of flowers in the spring, bright with turning leaves in the fall. I can't get anybody to work in it anymore, except for the illegal aliens, whom we exploit and underpay, and I'm not going to do that. Of the last two gardeners I hired, one turned out to be a thief and the other a drug addict. And the smog is so bad it's killing half the plants anyway. I can't even bear to look at it now." He pulled the curtains shut again.

"Lucius, it's your head that's full of smog. You're just depressed—"

"No, I'm exhausted, Derek, I've finally come to the realization that I've lived a ridiculous life," he said, resuming his pacing and seeming to talk as much for his own benefit as ours. "And what's left for me? Not even women interest me anymore. Boredom has deprived me of my vices and my vices were all that was left. I'm out of date. Scopes and I totter through each day together here like a couple of characters out of an old silent flick—no sound, no fury, just lingering ennui. If it weren't for my various little errands, forcing myself to go out with the help of my agile prestidigitator here, I wouldn't go out at all."

"If you took an interest—" the lawyer began.

Bedlington cut him off with an impatient gesture. "The outside world appalls me," he continued. "It's become a commercial enterprise dominated by venal scoundrels and elbowing louts. If we could only export our ignorance, greed, insensitivity, and bad manners, we'd solve our economic problems overnight. And what, Derek, does the future promise? We're going to pollute ourselves into extinction or blow ourselves up.

Eventually, I suppose, we'll all perish by the billions, packed in next to each other on this rotting planet like anchovies in a tin can, as comfortably at home as on a freeway at rush hour, breathing in great healing lungfuls of exhaust fumes and dying the same slovenly way we've lived, standing on each other's feet. I don't think I want to hang around for that glorious day. Perhaps, instead, you'd like to join me. We could make a clean exit together, after a quiet supper, a good bottle of wine, and a few cheerful reminiscences. How about it?"

"No, thanks," the lawyer said. "You know, Lucius, it's a good thing I'm fond of you, because—"

"You shouldn't be."

"Why not?"

"I've always taken advantage of you."

"How?"

"Women, for one thing."

"You were richer and better-looking than I was."

"Well, a couple of years after you and Grace got married—"

"I'm not sure I want to hear this."

"We had an affair. It began when you were in New York for four months, on the Pritchard case. And it lasted until Christmas, when I broke it off."

"You're lying."

"She wrote me a number of letters, the first one from London, when you went over there that summer. I still have them. Want to read them?"

"No."

There was an uncomfortable pause. "Well?" Bedlington said.

Visibly disturbed, but doing his best to control himself, Flanders stared at his old friend. "I guess I knew about it," he said at last, "but it was so long ago and she's been gone for so many years, you could have spared me this—this dismal confession."

"Why? Because I've shattered your illusions? It wasn't just me. That woman put horns on you for years and you knew it. You simply pretended not to notice because, I suppose, you needed her money and her social position." He sank happily into the chair facing the lawyer and grinned at him. "So now your sorrow at my untimely end will be happily tempered by an occasional twinge of genuine satisfaction," he added. "Fine. I don't want my casket bathed in tears. It might stain the mahogany."

"I know exactly why you're doing this," Flanders said calmly, "and I'm not going to play along with you. I know very well that behind that cynical posing you're really a generous—"

"Generous? Of course I've been generous," Bedlington said. "It's one of the social duties of the rich to be generous, a duty we all perform admirably because it deprives us of nothing we really need and gratifies our vanity. My dear Derek, it's all deductible."

"You're telling me?"

"Hey, try this one," Bedlington said, leaning in toward his friend. "'Whene'er I spoke sarcastic joke replete with manner spiteful, this lawyer mild politely smiled and voted me delightful!'"

"King Gama, *Princess Ida,* Act Three, slightly adapted," Flanders shot back. "Now listen to me, Lucius—"

"Derek, you're an ass!" Bedlington said, bouncing up out of his chair again to resume his restless tour of the room. "I bare my soul to you, I reveal the depths of my infamy, and you sit there chattering about what a lovable, charming fellow I am. The truth is, I've treated my friends shabbily and my women abominably." He smiled wanly. "I doubt if any of my ex-wives, and a fine brood of withered chickens they must be by now, cherish any tender memories of me. I didn't really love them; I loved only the spectacle of myself in love with them. And when they began to bore me, I got rid of them with no more regret than I devote each day to putting the trash out. That's my dreadful secret, Derek. I've never really cared for anyone or anything." He stopped pacing and leaned up against the mantelpiece. "'And . . . so . . . farewell,'" he added, in a soft, drawn-out monotone.

"*Pirates,* Act Two, Frederic to Mabel," the lawyer said, heaving himself up out of his seat. "I'll go, Lucius. But I want one small favor from you."

"That depends."

"I want you to see a friend of mine," he said, as they walked out into the hall. I followed them.

"Who is it?"

"He's a specialist."

"A psychiatrist?"

"Franz Heidrich. He's a great one, Lucius."

"You want me to trade my coffin in on a couch?"

"Not exactly the way I'd put it, Lucius."

"No, of course not. Look, Derek, the thing is, I haven't enjoyed myself so much in years. You have no idea how entertaining it is to make your own funeral arrangements." He took Flanders by the arm and walked him firmly toward the door. "Now don't disappoint me, Derek. I'm counting on you for the ceremony. You and Scopes and maybe Shifty here will be the only authentic mourners." He glanced back at me. "You *are* planning to attend?"

"I wouldn't miss it for anything," I assured him.

"See, Derek? Any other last requests?"

The lawyer didn't answer. At the end of the hall, however, he turned back. "Where . . . I mean . . . here?"

"Surely you don't think I'd make an exit in some squalid motel room surrounded by traveling salesmen and joiners in funny hats?" Bedlington said. "I'll see to it that no one is seriously inconvenienced. I'll notify the police and make all the arrangements for the disposal of my estate. I suppose that my doctor, that expensive quack, will be present at the autopsy, which, I understand, I can't legally avoid. A horrid business, but at least I won't have to witness it myself."

The lawyer looked past him to me. "Good-bye, Mr. Anderson. I hope *you* can think of some way to put a stop to this madness."

"Not a chance, Derek," Bedlington said cheerfully. "Good-bye."

"Well, I'll go now," Flanders said, still standing in the doorway.

" 'Yes, but you *don't* go!' " Bedlington recited.

Flanders grimaced. "*Pirates,* Act Two, the Major-General." And he walked out the front door, which Bedlington promptly closed behind him.

"I guess I'll go, too," I said, "unless you need me for something else."

"Not a thing, dear boy. Thank you for sitting in. I'd have never gotten rid of him." He peered into the dark hallway. "Who's that?"

I turned around in time to see Scopes totter out from the landing above the cellar steps. It had apparently taken him all this time to negotiate them; he leaned against the wall, gasping for air.

"Ah, Scopes," Bedlington said. "Nasty steps, those. Catch your breath, old boy, then we'll have a pot of tea. Shifty?"

"No, thanks, Lucius. I'm on my way."

"Where to? The track?"

"It's Tuesday, Lucius," I reminded him. "I only go when it's open."

When I drove out of the grounds a few minutes later, I had the odd feeling I had just emerged from a dream; the line between it and the reality of my relatively uncomplicated daily life seemed as hazy as the foul air that blurred the slopes of the surrounding hills.

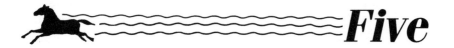 *Five*

CONVERGING

"Who are you?" she asked. "I mean, really?"

"I told you," I answered. "I do card tricks."

"You're not telling me anything."

"No? Watch." I took the pack of cards I always carry with me out of my pocket and showed her a few moves. Not too many, because you never know about people and magic and I didn't want to risk boring her. First I shuffled, showing off a riffle or two, then I demonstrated how I could deal from the bottom, the middle, or the second from the top. Not complicated stuff, just basic legerdemain. I think the shifts, including a couple of the variations worked out by a famous master of the card table named S. W. Erdnase, at least surprised her. I concluded my little demonstration with a cull that brought three aces together from various parts of the deck, then I shuffled again and spread the cards out before her in perfect order by suit and number.

"Well," she said, "quite impressive. What else can you do?"

"I could keep you here with cards alone for a couple of hours and never repeat a move," I said. "And after that, I could show you some effects with coins, sponges, balls, cups, little bits of this and that."

"You mean tricks."

"In close-up magic we mostly don't like to use that word," I explained. "They're not really tricks, you see. They're moves."

"I can see that it takes skill," she said. "Do you have to practice?"

"Several hours a day," I told her. "And I'm always working on something new. You have to in my profession."

"You do this for a living?"

"Yes, I'm a magician," I said. "My kind of magic doesn't pay a hell of a lot, but I'm only interested in close-up. I show up in L.A. at the Magic Castle, especially when I'm trying out the new moves. Then I work clubs, private parties, dining rooms, conventions, cruise ships, just about any place that'll pay me. I've done a little TV, too, and I'd like to do more, because the money's so good, but it's hard to come by. My agent—"

"What good is it?"

"I beg your pardon?"

She took a sip of her hot tea and looked intently at me over the rim of her cup. "I mean, what does it accomplish?"

"Accomplish?"

"In the world as a whole."

"Nothing, absolutely nothing," I had to confess. "It gives me pleasure and it amuses the people who like it, that's all. Anyway, it's the only thing I do really well, besides handicap horses and that's much too chancy to count on for a living."

"It's sad," she said, sipping thoughtfully.

"Why? I'm happy. And I make a few other people happy. What's sad about that?" She didn't answer, so I tried to reassure her. "Look, Amber, I'm not a neglected, starving artist, if that's what's bothering you," I continued. "I love what I do, I love my life. I wouldn't want to do anything else."

"That's what is sad," she said, with a little sigh, like a schoolteacher confronted once again by a promising but incorrigibly lazy student.

Our conversation was interrupted by the arrival of our order, which consisted of several succulent-looking dishes, all but one of them vegetarian. Mr. Xu's, the restaurant I had selected for my first date with Amber Clark that night, was a small, square, brightly lit room with booths along the sides and a handful of tables packed in close together in the center. The whitewashed walls were decorated by a few undistinguished

Chinese prints, and a single, large bamboo screen stood next to the entrance. The establishment was skimpy on charm, but the food was reasonably priced and its Szechuan dishes were my particular favorites. I had figured Amber Clark for a woman who would care less about amenities than substance and I had expected a favorable reaction to the spicy, garlic-laden eggplants, string beans, black mushrooms, and snow peas now reposing so temptingly before her. But she merely leaned over them and sniffed warily. "Did you speak to them about the MSG?" she asked.

"Twice, didn't you hear me?"

"I just want to be sure. It's a deadly chemical."

I spotted our Chinese host, Mr. Xu himself, standing, arms folded, by the kitchen door and I beckoned him over. He was a small, wrinkled ancient dressed in a plain black suit and his black hair lay slicked down against his skull. As a young man, during the Second World War, he had played slimy Japanese villains in Hollywood war movies and had retained ever since the hairstyle imposed on him by the studios. "Yes, Mista Sifty," he said, bowing and smiling as he came toward us. "How you ah, Mista Sifty?"

"I'm fine, Mr. Xu, thank you," I assured him, and then outlined our concern to him. "Miss Clark here is allergic to MSG."

"Ms.," Amber said.

"Miz?" Mr. Xu echoed her. "Is no Miz heah." He leaned over and sniffed the steam rising from our plates.

"MSG, Mr. Xu," I explained.

"Is no Miz," he said. "Is good food. You eat." And with another, this time frigid, smile and a little bow, he returned to his post by the kitchen.

"That wasn't exactly reassuring," Amber commented.

"Well, some things you have to take on faith," I said, helping myself to the feast before me. "Think of all the people in the world who are starving to death. We're not going to waste any of this, are we? It would be a crime against humanity."

Caught between two conflicting commitments to the welfare of mankind, Amber compromised by eating about a third of what was on her plate. I could tell that the way she picked suspiciously at her food distressed Mr. Xu, who passed by our table during his periodic tours of the room to make sure everyone was being properly served and eating well. Each time I kept him away from us by giving him a shrug, a deprecating smile, or a little wave, as if to assure him we were all right and not to worry about us. Mr. Xu was one of those restaurateurs who took his clients' welfare personally and was genuinely distressed by any failure of his product to please.

Amber Clark, I had decided by that time, was probably going to be more of a challenge than I cared to undertake. I had arrived at the restaurant five minutes late, having been delayed by a phone call from my agent regarding a possible club date in Gardena, and found her already seated. "You're late," she said, as I joined her. After I'd apologized and explained the cause of my tardiness, she merely nodded and observed, "I consider it rude to be habitually late. I just want to make that clear."

Not a promising beginning to a relationship, but it was offset at first by her appearance. She still wore very little makeup, but she had unbound her hair so that it fell loosely about her shoulders, framing her pale face and focusing attention on her large, oval-shaped, bright-blue eyes. She also had a beautiful mouth, with straight, perfectly even, very white teeth; but she was so difficult to amuse that I didn't become aware of this feature until I was finally able, over our mandarin oranges, to force a wan smile out of her by assuring her that they had undoubtedly been preserved in organic chemicals. "Straight from the vat to us," I said, "without any polluting natural ingredients to offset the taste."

Even beauty, however, has its limitations. After an hour and a half, I was worn out from trying to entertain her. She seemed to be interested in nothing that wasn't directly concerned with the welfare of the environment and the survival of every living organism in it, from the beleaguered marmosets in the shrinking Amazonian rain forest to the oil-fouled otters of Alaska. It was exhausting, not because I didn't approve of most of her causes, but because I feel that our own survival on the planet depends in part on our being able to enjoy what's left of it. I tried to explain this to her. "You have to lighten up a little, Amber," I said, "otherwise the bastards will get you down. And anyway there are still great things to do and see, if you know where to look."

"And where would that be?" she asked.

"Oh, the oceans, the rivers, the forests, the mountains, lots of places," I answered vaguely. "There's open spaces everywhere, places we haven't screwed up yet."

"Most of them are polluted," she said, "even at the poles. And then there's the ozone layer. We're destroying that, too, and soon we'll be dying of radiation. You've heard of the so-called greenhouse effect?"

I admitted glumly that I had.

"Well, it's further advanced than even most scientists will admit." And she proceeded to launch into a fact-riddled lecture on the environmental catastrophe about to overwhelm us. During the course of it I managed to signal to the waiter for our bill and was in the process of paying it when I heard Amber's voice drone to a halt. "Friends of yours?" she asked.

I looked up. Jay Fox and Arnie Wolfenden were standing in the entrance, waiting for a table. Jay was grinning at me and waved, while Arnie seemed to be sniffing the aromas around him like an overweight ocelot scenting a kill. "Excuse me, Amber," I said, getting up. "A couple of pals of mine from the track and one of them owes me money. I'll be right back." Any excuse, I thought, to get away from the rain of horrifying statistics she had been drowning us in.

"Hey, Shifty," Jay said, as I came up to him, "nice-looking girl. Who is she?"

"That is not a girl," I said. "That is Ralph Nader in drag." I filled him in quickly on the progress of our date. "I just had to get away from her for a minute. What are you guys up to?"

"Arnie knew about this place," Jay explained. "We're here to do some important eating. You? What now?"

"I'm going to take Ralph home," I said, "and then I'm going to go out and buy a *Form* and pick some winners."

"She looks good enough to eat," Jay said, looking back toward my table as Amber got up and headed for the rest rooms. "And it's nice to see her move, if you know what I mean."

"You wouldn't enjoy it, Jay," I assured him. "She has more numbers on her tongue than you have in your charts. I'm limp from numbers."

"My experience with women has convinced me that they are as spontaneous as the Talmud," Arnie observed. "I abandoned the pursuit some years ago, in deference to my peace of mind. Food, wine, and winners, not necessarily in that order, are all that concern me now."

"Speaking of winners, take a look at Jim Jam in the fourth tomorrow," Jay advised me. "This horse is working so good I hear even the clockers are betting on him."

"Then he won't pay anything."

"There's a Dummy-God horse in the race," Jay said. "He won't win, but every time out he looks like he can't miss and the dummies will make him odds-on again, I guarantee it. We should get five to two on Jim Jam."

"Thanks, Jay, I'll take a close look."

Mr. Xu came over to lead Jay and Arnie to an empty table and I returned to my own to finish paying the check. Before Amber came back from the ladies' room, Mr. Xu came over to make certain I hadn't been disappointed. "You not eat much," he said. "Food no good?"

"The food was great, Mr. Xu," I assured him. "The lady was a little picky. She's afraid of chemicals and other preservatives. She thinks the world is poisoning itself out of existence."

"Wheah you meet this lady?" he asked.

"In a law office, Mr. Xu. This is our first date. I don't think it's a success."

"Ah, no?"

"No. I doubt we'll be seeing very much of each other in future."

Mr. Xu nibbled thoughtfully for a moment on this estimate of our chances, then nodded as if he had made up his mind. "You betta off," he said and retreated again, with a tiny farewell nod, toward the kitchen.

I couldn't have been more mistaken about how the rest of my evening with Amber Clark would turn out. No sooner had we emerged from Mr. Xu's into the street than she turned to me and asked, "Are you a dancer?"

"No, I'm a magician. I thought I—"

"No, no, that isn't what I mean," she said. "Do you like to dance?"

"Sure, but what kind of dancing? I don't think I'd be much good at ethnic do-si-dos to summon the goddesses of the harvest," I said, "or bouncing to beating drums in order to placate the evil spirits."

"What are you talking about?"

"And there is no dance, except at the windows, for the Dummy God."

"The what?"

"The deity who watches over the dummies who bet on obvious favorites," I explained. "I guess I'm not making myself clear."

"You are the strangest man I've ever met," she observed, staring at me out of those dismayingly blue eyes, as innocent of humor as those of a Chinese politician. "What do you mean?"

"My incorrigible penchant for treating life lightly," I said. "Do you mean actual dancing, as in disco?"

"Oh, not that stuff!" she objected. "No, I mean the real thing. I know a couple of places."

"Foxtrots, tangos, waltzing to Welk?" I asked, as we headed toward my car, which was parked halfway up the block on Santa Monica Boulevard.

"How depressing," she said. "Do you mind if I call you Lou?"

"Call me anything you like."

"Good. Shifty sounds evasive."

"And you're nothing if not direct. Are you sure you want to do this?" I asked, as I opened the door for her.

"Thank you." She sank quickly into her seat. "Oh, yes. We need the exercise and dancing is the most healthful way of maintaining muscle tone and arterial circulation."

"Well, I knew it wasn't just for the hell of it."

"Let's go to Sundown. Turn left on Melrose and go east to Fairfax, then right to Venice, and I'll show you from there."

"Right. Want to drive?" I asked, before letting myself in.

"No, I don't trust this car," she said. "How long has it been since you've had your catalytic converter checked? You're probably polluting."

"I'll bet I am," I agreed, starting up the engine. "You know what I'd really like to do right now? I'd like to go out and harpoon a whale somewhere."

"I don't think that's funny at all," she said. "Look out, you'd better get over in the left lane!"

She turned out to be an expert sideseat driver and we made it to Sundown in less than twenty minutes. I knew about the place, but had never been there. A large, square, metal-sided building located in an outback between Venice and Culver City, it had once been a warehouse, then a drive-through market, and had since been converted into a rock palace featuring live bands, a different one every night. Something called Space Shuttle was in session that evening and Amber knew all about the group. "They're great," she said, as I bought our tickets and we headed inside. "They've got a great beat and they write a lot of their own songs." She took my hand. "Come on, Lou, we'll get a table."

It was only about nine o'clock and the band wasn't scheduled to go on for another half hour, but that didn't deter Amber. She led me through the cavernous building, still less than half full of revelers, and across a spacious dance floor to a table on a balcony above the scene. From there we had easy access to the dancing area, but we were far enough away from the action to talk to each other. Three of the musicians, long-haired young thugs dressed in gunmetal-gray space suits, were setting up their equipment, while a bearded fat man dressed in torn jeans and a black T-shirt was hooking up a snarl of wires to microphones and instruments. Some recorded soul music was being piped in through speakers over the floor, but no one was out there. The young crowd now beginning to come into the place was mostly milling about the two bar areas on either side of the room and obviously waiting for the live music to begin. I looked around for a waiter, but couldn't spot one. "I'll get us something to drink," I said. "What do you want?"

"Mineral water," she said, "any kind. I don't drink."

"Oh, I guess I knew that. Bad for you, right?"

"Alcohol destroys brain cells and damages the liver," she said. "It's also a cancer-causing agent."

"And how about soft drinks? Don't tell me!" I held up my hands. "Poisonous chemicals?"

"Of course, didn't you know? They're full of carcinogenic substances."

"Sorry, I keep forgetting. I'll be right back," I said, heading for the nearest of the two bars below us.

The crowd was lined up three-deep at the counter and it took me about fifteen minutes to get served. When I returned with our order, Amber had left. Then I spotted her out on the floor, moving all by herself to an old Neil Diamond song. I set our drinks down and watched, mesmerized. She was a spectacular dancer, with all kinds of elaborate little moves of feet and hands and shoulders and hips moving in perfect sync with the music. I didn't even consider joining her, partly because I was completely intimidated by her skill and partly because what she was doing out there was a lot of fun to watch. I wasn't alone either. A couple of dozen other people were looking at her, but she was so absorbed in herself and the music that she paid no attention to anyone else. When the piece ended, she simply walked away, while several of the watchers, myself included, applauded. "I'm sorry," she said, as she rejoined me, "but I couldn't resist the beat. And you were gone for so long."

"I had no idea you could dance like that," I said. "You never mentioned it."

"You never asked."

"I guess I just assumed you were a career secretary or something," I confessed.

"Like most men, you make easy assumptions," she said. "But that's all right, I understand about men."

"Do you? Remarkable. I don't even understand myself, much less an entire category of people. So what about your dancing?"

"I've been studying ever since I was eight, but I'm not interested in classical ballet or in prostituting my talent for purely commercial gain," she declared. "Dancing is simply a release for me. It's something I've always wanted to do, but without corrupting it."

"So your job with the law firm—"

"It's just a job," she said. "I have secretarial skills and I'm very well paid. The firm represents only conservative investment and insurance companies and a few individual clients, none of them associated with polluters or manufacturers of toxic products."

"You checked that out."

"Of course. I work mostly for Mr. Flanders. Mr. Coutts is retired and Mr. Riley is very old and only comes in twice a week. Mr. Flanders is really the operating partner," she explained. "He's very nice and strictly business. And there isn't very much to do, really. It's a quiet office."

"It's not a career for you, I gather."

"Oh, no. My real concern is the environment," she said. "This is just a way of paying my living expenses." She suddenly stopped herself, as if embarrassed, and looked away from me.

"What's wrong?"

"Oh, you might as well know," she said glumly. "I'm rich."

"Wonderful! How rich?"

"I have a trust fund that pays me over six thousand a month."

"So why are you working at a job that doesn't interest you?"

"Because it's family money," she said fiercely.

"So?"

"My father is the Clark of Clark-Halliday. You've heard of it?"

"It's a big conglomerate or something? I'm not up to date on matters of high finance."

"Yes. They own twenty-two companies, eight of which make toxic products and two of which are paper manufacturers, destroying the forests. I haven't spoken to my father in four years. I see my mother, whenever she comes down to visit, but not often. She's so weak and she won't stand up to him. They live in Carmel, but my father's away a lot, busily corrupting and laying waste wherever he goes."

"Well, he hasn't cut you off from the money."

"He'd like to, but he can't," she said. "The trusts were set up for me and my two brothers when we were born and we began drawing income from them when we became twenty-one."

"What do your brothers do?"

"They work for the company. I don't talk to them either."

"So you refuse to live off this tainted money. What do you do with it?" She started to explain, but I cut her off. "Don't tell me, let me guess. You contribute it to worthy causes. You're using it to help atone for your father's misdeeds."

"You make it sound trivial and stupid."

"No, Amber, I didn't mean that," I said. "I respect the way you feel and I guess I subscribe myself to a lot of the things you've been saying all evening. It's just that you can't go through your whole life without having any fun. There has to be a time to cultivate your own garden."

"Voltaire said that, in *Candide*."

"I only steal my ideas from the best."

"Well, it's not enough. But I have my dancing."

As if on cue, Space Shuttle suddenly blasted into action, sending shock waves of amplified sound over the crowd now milling about the room. We couldn't have gone on talking, even if we had wanted to. Amber bounced to her feet, her face alive with excitement, took my hand and led me down into the pit.

We stayed out on the floor for an hour and a half, till the end of the first set. I needn't have worried either about feeling inadequate as a partner for Amber. She danced like a soul possessed and her inventive skill inspired me into moves I didn't know I had. Space Shuttle was deafening and raucous, but the group had a terrific beat, with varying but solid tempos that supported anything we wanted to try. And out there in front of me, like an inspiring muse, I had Amber, all shoulders and hips and long legs, as sexy and wild in this physical aspect of her life as she had been dogmatically humorless and dull in the rational part of it earlier that evening. Her face, too, was radiant with pleasure, her eyes shining, white teeth gleaming as she moved. My God, there was life and fun in her after all! We danced on and on, totally caught up in the music and oblivious to everything but the joy we had in it and in each other.

When the band took its first break, she grabbed my hand and led me off the floor. "You're good," she said. "You can really dance."

"Not like tonight, Amber," I told her. "You're an inspiration."

"It's such a release," she said. "I couldn't live without dancing."

She excused herself to go to the ladies' room and I began to push my way back toward the bar to pick up another round of drinks. Space Shuttle must have been a hot item, because the big room was packed with revelers by now, a huge crowd for a Tuesday night. It was about ten minutes before I could get close enough to order and, as I was inching forward, Lonny Richards suddenly pushed past me. He was holding three bottles of beer in one hand and using his free one to open up a small path for himself back into the main room. He didn't notice me and I watched him cross the dance floor toward a corner table to the left of the bandstand. I couldn't see whom he was with, but as soon as I had picked up my own drinks, I made a detour in that direction before heading back to my own table. The light in Sundown was muted, a soft orange glow that dropped shadows into the corners, so that I couldn't tell at first who else was in Richards's party of six or seven people. But I did spot the leggy blonde I'd seen with him at the track. She was sitting between the jockey and a soft-looking, gray-haired man I soon recognized as Maury Levine, better known to me as the Mooch, because of his skill at never carrying his own weight at check time and for copping freebies. I also spotted Jack Leone, who was busily engaged in making up to a bimbo with flaming red hair and enough paint on her to decorate a billboard. It looked like a happy party and I guessed they were celebrating some sort of betting coup, the only occasion at which anyone would have tolerated the presence of the Mooch. I don't know why it interested me, but I've always felt that it pays off at the races to keep an eye on what the riders are up to and whom they're associating with, even though I think that most of them are honest. "Little Shakespearean bandits" is what Arnie Wolfenden called them, but then he had a more cynical view of human affairs than me. And as far as the Undertaker was concerned, I couldn't disagree with him.

Amber and I stayed through the second set, which ended well after midnight. I came off the floor drenched in sweat, feeling as if I had worked off every ounce of extra weight. I'd had a terrific time, however, and I'd have stuck it out till the end, at two o'clock, but she suddenly looked up at me very seriously and said, "If we stay, we won't be able to have a meaningful physical convergence."

"What did you say?"

"Must I be coarse about it?" she answered.

"You mean you want to have sex with me?"

"Do you object?"

"Certainly not."

"I'll have to go right home afterwards," she added, as we walked out into the parking lot. "Will you mind?"

"I'll try not to."

I dropped her off near Mr. Xu's so she could pick up her car, told her where I lived, and then raced home to tidy up before she arrived. I had definitely not expected to be entertaining her at my apartment on our first date, so I hadn't bothered either to make my bed or clean up the breakfast dishes in my kitchenette. I was afraid that she'd consider my place a toxic waste dump and leave before our so-called convergence, an event I have to confess I was now looking forward to. If she made love with the same commitment and wild but disciplined grace she had displayed on the dance floor, I was in for an adventurous night.

I did the best I could during the ten minutes I had alone before my doorbell rang and even managed to put clean sheets on the bed. I left only one light on and found an FM station playing soft rock, then went down to let her in. She probably wouldn't approve of my place, I thought, but it suited me and maybe she wouldn't notice the ramshackle conditions I lived in.

She smiled briefly when I opened the door for her, then walked briskly in, pretty much ignoring her immediate surroundings. My apartment was on the ground floor at the rear of an undistinguished-looking two-story complex built around a small swimming pool flanked by an old oak tree and a couple of dilapidated palms. We threaded our way through a tangle of rickety aluminum beach chairs, past an open barbecue, then up a short flight of steps to my front door. "Who lives here besides you?" Amber asked, as I fumbled in the darkness for my key.

"Mostly losers," I confessed, "the people who pursued the American dream but didn't quite catch up with it. But it's cheap and the old man who manages the building is a friend of mine." I opened the door and let her in.

She stepped inside and looked around. "I like it, Lou," she said. "It's you."

She was right, it was. Everything that mattered most to me was reflected in this room. Apart from the basic furnishings, which included a queen-sized bed, an armchair, an old chest of drawers, and my kitchen equipment, every other object testified to my enthusiasms. A stack of old *Racing Forms* soared up from the floor in one corner, blowups of horses in action galloped across one wall, while over my stereo posters of Houdini and Giuseppe Verdi, my two favorite magicians, loomed benevolently. Next to my bed, on a long table under several other portraits of celebrated conjurors, lay the peculiar, tiny tools of my trade—packs of cards, cups, balls, sponge-rubber animals, bits of string, coins, and a row of the basic books on prestidigitation. Above the bed, two sets of old racing silks had been nailed over the headboard, looking in the soft light like brightly colored flags. "What are those?" Amber asked, pointing at them.

"Racing silks," I told her. "In case we have a photo finish."

"Are you ever serious about anything, Lou?"

"Not if I can help it. Sorry."

"I'll just be a minute," she said, heading for my bathroom. "You can get undressed, if you want."

"I thought we might help each other do that together."

"I don't think we have time for leisurely courtship and foreplay," she said. "I need at least eight hours' sleep."

While she was in the bathroom, I began to wonder if we were going to be able to go through with the convergence, mainly because I've never been able to regard the sex act merely as therapy or a form of aerobics. So I was still fully dressed, sitting nervously on the edge of my bed, when Amber reappeared, five minutes later. She was naked and the sight of her took my breath away. "You're still dressed," she said. "Please take your clothes off."

Whatever reservations I may have had about Amber's clinical approach to the carnal romp were wiped out by the sight of her. She had a beautifully proportioned body, with long, well-shaped legs, small but firm breasts, a flat stomach, and a waist I could almost get both hands around. Desire for her soared up from below, clouding my reason in a pink haze of lust, and I pulled her into my bed like a carnivorous plant hauling in a succulent butterfly. "Listen, I don't mind being ravished," she said, pushing me briefly off her as I struggled simultaneously with my clothes, "but I do expect you to take your shoes off."

I managed to get everything off and we tumbled over each other like a couple of uninhibited spider monkeys. Amber was amazing. She was a ruthless taker in bed, completely indifferent to the comfort and welfare of her partner, but she took such pleasure in the act that it aroused me to the same sort of improvisational frenzy that had characterized my dancing with her. I came the first time long before she did, but she persisted with me until she had satisfied herself and also brought me to a climax a second time. And all, I realized with astonishment, in less than half an hour. "You're very satisfactory," she answered, as she immediately began to dress. "Thank you for a fulfilling evening."

Slightly dazed, I sat up and reached for my clothes, which lay scattered about the floor. "I'll see you out."

"Don't be silly. I'm quite capable of getting home on my own," she said. "You must stop thinking of women as helpless victims, Lou."

"Oh, I've never made that mistake, Amber. But I thought—"

"I know what you thought," she said, closing the bathroom door behind her. "You're a man."

I gathered she didn't mean that as a compliment, but I didn't care. I smiled and relaxed, propped up against my pillows. When she reemerged five minutes later, she looked as pristine and unsullied as when I had first seen her. "Good night, Lou," she said on her way out.

"Amber?"

She paused at the door. "Yes?"

"I don't suppose you'd consider another fulfilling convergence with me?"

"I don't see why not, Lou," she said, "but in future we'll go to my house."

"I'm sorry about the mess," I explained. "I didn't imagine we'd be making love on our first date—"

"You're so sentimental."

"I guess I am. Anyway, I promise to improve my attitude—"

"It isn't what you think. It has nothing to do with you."

"If it's enough sleep, you could stay over."

"No, no," she said. "You're in a danger zone."

"A what?"

"You're living in a danger zone."

"I know it's not the Bel Air Hotel, but it's safe enough," I said. "We haven't had a major crime in this building since I've been here and only one dope problem, an aging starlet who—"

"Haven't you read Paul Brodeur's *Currents of Death*?"

"No. What is it, a mystery?"

"Honestly, Lou, you're hopeless," she said. "No, it's about electro-magnetic pollution. You have a power relay terminal in front of your building."

"What's a relay terminal?"

"All those power cables, the overhead lines going up the street, where they come together, those are relay terminals," she explained. "Your building is being zapped every day by megavolts of electric pollution. I'll bet you have a very high incidence of miscarriages on this block."

"Well, not in this building," I said. "We're short on mothers. In addition to the aging starlet, we have a couple of lesbian soap-opera regulars, a forty-year-old stripper and her gay live-in boyfriend, a retired schoolteacher, and a divorced insurance adjuster who hates men."

"Well, it's not only women—" she began.

But I cut her off. "It's okay, Amber, we'll go to your place."

She looked at me intently and shook her head. "You're being victimized by reckless industrial practices and you don't even care," she said. "I don't know if we *should* see each other again."

"You know, you and this guy Lucius Bedlington have a lot in common," I said. "He also thinks the world is a shitheap."

"But he's doing nothing about it," she snapped. "I despise that man. He's so equivocal about everything."

"You've met him?"

"Once, when I first came to work there, about a year ago," she said. "He came in to see Mr. Flanders and they had an argument, I don't know what about. But I talk to him on the phone and he's always making fun of me. I can't stand him. He thinks I'm some sort of dumb little floozie he can charm with his sexist little remarks. Ugh." And she shuddered, clasping herself in her arms. "He's awful."

"He's an old man and he's given up, that's all."

"He hates everything."

"No, he doesn't. And anyway, the only person he's harming is himself."

"That is no excuse."

"Oh, you're hard, Amber," I said. "Look, we'll just go to the races and then go dancing and then maybe a little more converging—"

She stepped out into the hall and shut the door in my face.

 *Six*

REUNION

"I detest this sort of thing," Bedlington said. "Why do people persist in suddenly emerging from history, redolent of past failures? What can we possibly have to say to each other after all this time? I knew Isabel as she was, not as the ruin she must be . . ."

"Which ex-wife is this?" I asked, as we drove up the Sunset Strip toward Beverly Hills.

"The third one, I think."

"You don't know?"

"When you get as old as I am, my lad, it's hard enough to remember your own name, much less those of your discarded partners," he said. "I couldn't believe it when she called me out of the blue yesterday. Of course I didn't want to see her, but she insisted. If I hadn't agreed, she'd have descended on me like a pestilence of gnats. Imagine, she wanted to come to the house!"

"Well, it would have been easier—"

"I'd never get rid of her," he said. "She hardly ever stops talking long enough to listen to anything anyone else is saying. No, this is much the best arrangement. And with you along, I'll be able to get away from her."

He was going to introduce me to her as his personal live-in therapist and I was to remind him, if the lunch lasted past two-thirty, that he had a doctor's appointment in Beverly Hills at three. It was my job to get him out of there. "What the hell does she mean by crawling out of my past like this?" he complained. "God knows what she looks like after all this time! Jesus, I haven't seen her in twenty years at least! And the two most dismal decades in human history have trampled over her since then. I can't imagine what she wants."

"Money?"

"No, no, I checked that out with Derek," he answered, a little ruefully. "I made my usual generous settlement on her and I did hear, a long time ago, that she had remarried. I gather she's been living abroad. Oh, hell, who knows, dear boy? We'll get through this somehow and after next week it won't matter."

"Is that the scenario?" I asked.

"Oh, yes, it won't be long now," he said cheerfully. " 'And I, war-worn, poor captured fugitive, my life most gladly give—I might have had to live another noon.' "

"*Yeomen* again?"

"Of course, dear boy. You're becoming as adept at the game as Derek."

I hadn't heard from Bedlington for three days and I had begun to wonder about him. I had finally called the house, but Scopes had informed me that the master was in his room and did not wish to be disturbed. At least, I think that's what he said. So then I had called Amber, as I'd been doing all week in a fruitless effort to make another date with her, and asked her to inform Flanders. I was pretty sure by then that my part-time employer's manic fits of cheerfulness were probably succeeded by equally extreme bouts of depression and I felt I owed it to the lawyer to keep him informed. I wasn't about to stand in the way of Bedlington's planned departure from the scene, but I wasn't going to make it easy for him either.

We pulled up in front of the Beverly Hills Hotel at about one, making quite a splash in the green Alfa and successfully upstaging the Jaguars, Rollses, and Mercedeses all around us. "Wow, what a set of wheels!" the young parking attendant said, grinning broadly, as he opened the door for Lucius. "What is that?"

"It's called don't touch," Bedlington snapped. "My associate here will park it."

"I'm afraid that's against the rules, sir," the boy said. "If you'll show me—"

Bedlington handed him a twenty-dollar bill. "Rules were made to be bent," he said. "Consider this a small insult."

"Insult? Yes, *sir,*" the boy said, quickly pocketing his bribe. He pointed down the driveway toward the boulevard. "You can put it into the first space you can find, on the right. How long will you be?"

"Long enough to eat lunch," Bedlington said, then looked at me. "I'll wait for you right here. And remember, you are not to leave my side."

When I came back from parking the Alfa, we walked into the great pink palazzo together, then through the lobby and the bar to an outdoor patio packed with show-biz types indulging themselves in power lunches. A tall, slender woman in her early fifties rose up from a corner table to our left and waved. "Lukie!" she called out in a loud alto. "We're over here, darling!"

Her chief characteristic seemed to be an astonishing animal vitality, enhanced by a wild-looking mane of dyed red hair and large green eyes outlined by heavy mascara and a curving sweep of plucked eyebrows. She was dressed in an elegantly tailored white suit, cut low in front to reveal a surprisingly large, lightly freckled bosom. Gold chains encircled her neck, gold hoops dangled from her earlobes, and bulbous-looking stones sparkled on her fingers. Standing beside her was a small male doll attired in a pin-striped suit that seemed to have been pressed on him. He was in his forties, with delicate features, slick black hair combed straight back, and eyes hidden behind dark sunglasses. They seemed to have stepped out of an old Italian movie about the idle rich at play in an exotic foreign locale. "Darling Lukie," the woman said, as we came up to them, "how wonderful to see you again!" She threw her arms about Bedlington and kissed him on both cheeks.

"Hello, Isabel," he said, disengaging himself. "This is my friend Lou Anderson. He's also my physical therapist."

"Well, of course," she said, without even glancing at me. "At our age we all need to be massaged regularly." Still beaming, she held Bedlington out at arm's length. "Let's have a look at you! Why, you sweet thing, you've aged adorably. You know, you're even better-looking than when I met you."

"That's very kind of you," Bedlington said.

"And what about me? How do I look?"

Bedlington smiled coldly. "You seem to be tottering toward the abyss with the grace of a capering carnivore."

She threw her head back and roared with laughter. "Oh, God, how you put things!" she said. "You bet your ass, baby! I intend to go down with all flags flying! Every year I go to Switzerland and have everything lifted!" She cupped her hands under her breasts. "And what do you think of these? The miracles of surgery, my dear. It's perfectly terrific what they can do these days! All wops, you know, love big tits!"

"Ah . . . yes," Bedlington said uneasily. "By the way, you haven't introduced us."

"Oh, this is Filippo," she said, presenting him as if he were a house pet. "Isn't he cute? I'm the Countess Fracasso now. Isn't that a howl? Filippo, darling, this is Lukie." She blinked at me. "And your name?"

"Anderson, Lou Anderson."

"Ah, yes, of course," she said, "the masseur. How democratic of you, Lukie."

Bowing and smiling, Filippo stepped forward to shake hands. "Is fabulous to knowing you, man."

"Anderson is *not* my masseur," Bedlington said. "He's—"

"Actually, I'm a magician," I cut in.

"How marvelous!" she said, beaming. "I'm sure he must work wonders for you, Lukie! Wherever did you find him?"

"Pleasure," Filippo said, pumping my hand up and down once. "Is totally rad, man."

"What is he saying?" Bedlington asked, as we sat down.

"That he's enchanted to meet you," she explained. "It's the American century, darling. We've corrupted the whole fucking world!"

"Charmingly put, Isabel," Bedlington said. "But please don't call me Lukie. You know I don't like it."

"Yes, you always were a little stuffy. Do you still live in that mausoleum of a house with that appalling butler? What was his name?"

"Scopes."

"Oh, my God, yes, Scopes. I thought he'd be dead by now."

"Not quite."

"I never understood how you could stand it there. And all those unbearable Gilbert and Sullivan recordings, do you still play them all the time? And the horses, do you still have horses? God, it's been ages, you know!"

"I know."

"Filippo, darling, see if you can snag one of these incompetents and get us some drinks," she said. "Champagne? We have to celebrate our reunion, after all these years."

She was so hyper I was convinced she was on something. So was Bedlington, who asked her about it at one point, as we were waiting for our order to arrive. "Oh, a little sniff of this and that now and then," she answered. "It's so good for one's sinuses and Filippo has only the best."

"That can be addictive, Isabel," Bedlington said.

"Don't be ridiculous, darling, I've been doing it for years!"

She chattered endlessly on through the entire lunch, even as she picked sparingly at her prosciutto and melon and then a green salad. She must have been afraid to stop, as if a moment's pause could prove fatal to her self-image, cause it to shatter and crumble her into dust. The words washed over us as inconsequentially but annoyingly as the sound of a television sitcom coming through the wall of an adjacent room. Filippo appeared to be dozing behind his shades.

Bedlington glanced at his watch. "Isabel—"

But she rattled on: ". . . and two days ago I was still in Rome, that gorgeous whore of a city! How I hate airplanes! Plastic food, I was sick the whole time! And last week, you'll never guess, I bumped into Pookie at the Excelsior one night. You remember Pookie, don't you? That English exquisite we adopted in Monte Carlo the day you lost your yacht playing roulette at the Sporting Club? Well, there was Pookie again, camping out along the Via Veneto, and we had such reminiscences! Remember the night in Cannes, when I painted my tits blue and your fig leaf fell off at the Prince's costume ball?"

"No, I do *not* remember," Bedlington said.

"Darling, you didn't used to be quite so stuffy. But I suppose times have changed."

"Yes, they have."

"Well, I don't regret any of the wonderful times we had together," she continued. "Remember Mimsy's house party, when you did your back flip over the Princess Mignarotti's table and landed on the salmon?"

"No, and that's enough, Isabel," Bedlington said, turning hastily toward Filippo. "What are you doing in Los Angeles, Count? Business?"

"Ah, *sì,*" the little Italian answered, nodding. "We come here for the film, no? Is big *serata.*"

"You're an actor?"

"Darling, he makes them," Isabel said. "Great trashy epics of sex and violence, people being slashed to ribbons, monsters from outer space, vampires tearing at people's jugulars, teenage werewolves, that sort of thing. You haven't heard of Fracasso Productions? Very big, darling. We're in town for the gala opening of *Inferno.*"

"Dante's *Inferno?*"

"Don't be absurd, pet! It's all about satanic cults, the devil showing up in Bloomingdale's or somewhere, people being sodomized and dismembered in lingerie, babies being sacrificed in the toy department, oh, it's all too deliciously sordid! That Swedish sexpot plays the high priestess, Davida what's-her-name—"

"Is very big bust, man," Filippo said.

"The film is a failure?" Bedlington asked.

"No, no, no," Filippo objected, waving his hands about his head, then cupping them in front of him so that we'd be sure to grasp the main point about her talent. "Davida is very big bust. The movie is making much money, is very high *concetto,* how you say?"

"Concept?" I guessed. "Very commercial?"

"Ah, *sì,* we make a fortune, *mio caro.*"

"Isn't he adorable?" Isabel said. "Aren't we darling together?"

"Very high concept," Bedlington said.

"I knew you'd like each other. I've always had a wonderful instinct for people."

"That's one way of putting it."

"Isabel tell me you very *simpatico,*" Filippo said. "You dig?"

"No, not anymore. I don't get out in the garden at all now."

Isabel shrieked with laughter. "Oh, God, how divine! Lukie, you're too precious for words!"

Filippo abruptly stood up. "Is screening at Paramount *alle tre,*" he said. "I go now." He shook our hands briefly and nodded. "Is nice to meet you, man." He gave Isabel a peck on the cheek. *"Ciao."* And he scurried away between the tables like a lizard in flight.

"The little shit," Isabel said, smiling. "But he's amazingly hung, you know. Odd about these little men, how they love big women and have these huge—"

"Isabel, we have to leave, too," Bedlington said hastily. "Let me get the check . . ." And he signaled for the waiter.

"Oh, no, darling, it's already been taken care of," she said. "After all, I invited you, didn't I?"

"Yes, you did," Bedlington agreed. "And you also said you wanted to talk to me about something."

"Yes, well?"

"Well, what?"

"Didn't you get my letter?"

"What letter?"

"Oh, God, don't tell me I forgot to mail it! I must have. I always forget to mail letters. It used to make those dreary tax people furious. So annoying—"

"Isabel, what was in the letter?"

She paused, but only for a moment, then smiled brilliantly at him. "It's Melinda," she said. "I want you to take care of her for a couple of weeks. Filippo and I have to leave tomorrow and—"

"What are you talking about?"

"Melinda's never been here before and she's led rather a sheltered life," she continued. "Convent schools, private camps, all that sort of thing. I couldn't keep her with me all the time, after I met Filippo. We travel so much and I couldn't send her to her father in Houston, because he'd have kept her and I'd never have gotten her back and then, when she was old enough to make up her own mind, he keeled over on his rig one day, so—"

"Isabel, for God's sake, who is this person?"

"Well, my daughter, of course. Who did you think I was talking about?" she said. "Honestly, Lucius, you *have* slowed down, haven't you? I have this clinic in Lausanne, they feed you monkey hormones or something, you could—"

"Absolutely not," Bedlington said. "I haven't the slightest intention of playing host to anyone, Isabel. Besides, I'm leaving—"

"Where are you going?"

"On a very long trip."

"It can't be that long. You can go anywhere these days in a matter of hours."

"Well, not where I'm going."

"Surely you're not about to be shot off into space, are you, like some sort of astronut?"

"Well, actually, something like that."

"How tiresome of you, Lucius. But it can't take that long. When are you going?"

"Next week sometime."

"You can see her before then," she insisted. "You don't need to put her up or anything like that, if you don't want to—"

"Out of the question."

"—but you can at least see her and make sure she's all right, meets some nice people, give her some pointers."

"What for?"

"Because she doesn't know anyone and she's never been in California before, except for a couple of quick trips," she said. "What's the matter with you, Lucius? You used to be the most generous man, whatever your other many faults."

"No."

She seemed stunned. "You refuse?"

"Ah, I think the message is beginning to seep through." Bedlington turned to me. "What time is it?"

"Quarter of three."

He stood up. "Let's go."

"Oh, sit down," the Countess said, reaching into her purse and producing a large sealed envelope. "Here." She dropped it on the table.

"What is it?"

"The proofs."

"Proofs? Of what?"

"That Melinda's my daughter."

"That is a matter of supreme insignificance to me, Isabel. Why should I care about that?"

"Because, for all I know, she may be yours as well."

"What?"

"You heard me, darling."

"You always were fond of nasty jokes."

"It's true. And frankly I don't give a damn whether you believe me or not."

Bedlington gazed at her coldly. "Isabel, what are you up to?"

"Up to?"

"You need money, is that it?"

"Money?" She threw her head back and laughed. "Don't be ridiculous, Lukie. My previous two husbands were in the oil business during the OPEC boom. Melinda was born in Switzerland, four months after our divorce and seven months after our separation in London. I was pretty sick of you by then, sweetheart, and I saw no reason to tell you."

"You didn't?"

"No. We'd both been playing around and you never wanted children. So I gave her one of the billionaires for a father and brought her up myself. She's American, of course, but she's spent much of her life abroad."

"We didn't have much to do with each other those last few months, as I recall," Bedlington said. "What makes you think I could be her father?"

"Well, we did hop into bed a couple of times, I remember, after Dodie's party and on the Prince's yacht one night," she said, clearly relishing Bedlington's discomfiture. "And she does look like you."

"Damn you, Isabel!"

"Anyway, she hasn't a clue about any of this," the Countess said, "and you don't have to tell her anything about it, if you don't want to."

Bedlington picked up the envelope, tore it open and began sorting through its contents. "What is all this stuff?"

"Birth certificate, childhood snapshots, school papers, medical and dental records, and so on," the Countess said, ticking them off on her fingers. "You'll find the blood analysis interesting. I checked our old records and it matches yours. You're both A-positives."

"That does not prove that I'm her father," Bedlington said.

"No, but it means that you could be," she said, obviously enjoying herself hugely.

"What about the other men you went to bed with?"

"Really, darling, should we be discussing this in front of your masseur?"

"That's okay, I'll go," I said, starting to rise.

"Sit down!" Bedlington snapped. "And he's not my masseur! Isabel—"

"I didn't ask them for blood tests, Lucius," she said. "They were passing little flings to help take my mind off how rotten you were being to me. And this was long before AIDS."

Bedlington sank back into his chair. He looked suddenly older and no longer so spry. "You waited all this time to come and tell me this?"

The Countess shrugged. "What difference does it make?" she said. "Melinda knows nothing about you except that we were once married and you can forget all about it. I just thought you'd be curious. I would like you to see her. I mean, you could just meet her once, couldn't you?"

Bedlington thought it over for a moment. "Where is she now?" he asked.

"In New York, it's the only place she knows fairly well," the Countess said, "and she wanted to see some plays. We had to come straight through, because of Filippo's movie business. She's on a TWA flight from New York, coming in Sunday night. I forget the number, but you can check it. I imagine she'll call you, if you don't call her."

Bedlington rose out of his chair again. "Where's she staying?"

"Here for a couple of nights, then she may look around for an apartment."

"You mean she's going to live here? Don't tell me she's an actress, God help us!"

"She tried that and also a little modeling, but it bored her," the Countess said. "She's very bright and very ambitious. No, she's an editor.

Filippo taught her. And she wants to become a director." She smiled. "They have film schools here, I'm told."

"Very good ones," I said.

"Money's no problem, she has plenty of money." The Countess leaned over the table and extended her hand toward Lucius. "Good-bye, Lukie," she said. "It's been marvelous. If you do decide to see her, drop us a line in Rome and tell us all about it. You'll find Fracasso Productions listed in the phone book here and they'll forward your letter. Or you can call. I know Melinda looks forward to meeting you and she's very outgoing, not shy at all."

"I wonder who she got that from," he said, taking her hand and dropping it as if it were contaminated.

"Well, of course, darling, who else? By the way, her last name's Kennedy, don't forget. And if you do write, keep it light and amusing. You weren't always such a downer. No kiss?"

"I'd as soon kiss the head of Medusa," Bedlington said, turning abruptly on his heel and walking away from her.

I glanced back at the Countess as I followed him out. She was laughing.

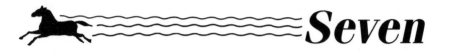 *Seven*

ENCOUNTERS

To my surprise, I didn't hear from Bedlington again until the following Wednesday, by which time he could have been dead. Then he called early in the morning to inform me that he had a horse running that day and wanted me to take him to the track. I knew about the animal, because its name had cropped up among the entries listed in my *Racing Form*. It was Mad Margaret, the unraced three-year-old filly Charlie had told me about in mid-January, and I'd been waiting for her. "I hear she's been working a hole in the wind," I told Lucius. "Maybe I can get rich on her."

"I wouldn't know anything about that, dear boy," he said. "I wouldn't even go, if it weren't for Melinda."

"Oh, so you've met her."

"Indeed I have, dear boy. She called me from the airport."

"What's she like? Is she yours?"

"Mine? You mean, my daughter?"

"Yes."

"I would say definitely not."

"Oh, I thought—"

"Never mind what you thought. It was just one of Isabel's nasty jokes."

"Does she know you could be her father?"

"Shifty, my lad, it's early in the day, Scopes hasn't brought me my tea yet and I'm still a little foggy. What are you implying?"

"I'm not implying anything, Lucius," I said. "I just wondered if you'd discussed it with her."

"Of course not," he snapped. "There's nothing to discuss. Pick me up at noon. We'll go in your car."

"Does she look like you?"

"Shifty, you are overstepping bounds."

"What bounds?"

"Of decency. This is none of your business."

"Right. I'm just curious. I've been calling you, but got no answer—"

"Calling me? What for?"

"I thought—oh, hell, just checking in."

"Well, don't," he said. "I've been very busy, dear boy. Lots to do now and so little time. I'll see you at noon." And he hung up.

I dozed off again for about an hour, then got up, made coffee, and sat down in my kitchenette with the *Racing Form* spread out on the table before me. A pale, wintry sun bathed the little room in light as I sipped and studied the entries. I had made some notes in the margins the night before on certain animals that seemed to me to have a good chance of winning and this was a nice way of checking my estimates, even if my little scrawls would have seemed merely amateurish to a pro. I thought of Jay Fox across town, in his pad at the beach, now well on the way to covering his own *Form* with his multicolored, inked-in notations— numbers, dots, stars, checks, asterisks, loops, lines, and other symbols— the great comforting jumble of statistics, out of which winners would presumably emerge like flowers sprouting out of a bog. It made me smile. What it took Jay six or seven hours of work to accomplish I had the presumption to attempt in less than one, but then I didn't claim to be in his class as a handicapper. And besides, I distrusted statistics and numbers in general, because they seemed to me to be a denial of magic, as if life itself could be reduced to an illuminated equation on a computer screen. Now, however, as I surveyed my own sketchy grasp at the solution to my day, I decided on impulse to call my old friend. I'd been doing much better recently, partly because the job with Lucius had given me the little financial cushion without which I can't operate as a bettor, but I was planning to step out today on Bedlington's filly and it wouldn't hurt, I reasoned, to get a second opinion. After all, I was about to perform some major surgery on my stash. I went into the bedroom, picked up my phone on its long cord and brought it into the kitchen. I set it on the table, poured myself a second cup of coffee, and dialed. Like an acolyte at the mouth of the Delphic oracle, I was prepared for once to sit back and listen. Jay liked to pontificate.

"Well, Shifty," he said twenty-five minutes later, after having analyzed the card and made his strongest case of the day for a tough old gelding named Go For Broke in the seventh, "I don't know enough about the filly. What race?"

"The sixth. Charlie Pickard told me about her and she's working really well."

"I don't have solid figures on the horse," the handicapper said. "She drew the two hole, which is not the greatest place to be for a green filly, and I only see one gate work. We don't know if she has any speed."

"Charlie says she does."

"Well, you know trainers," Jay countered. "They tell you what you want to hear. If she puts on blinkers, that would be a plus, because then we'd know if she's being asked for speed out of the gate. But she'll have to beat D. L. Gantry's filly on the outside."

"Hustling? She hasn't run a lick in two previous starts."

"Ah, but that's Gantry's style, Shifty. His maidens never fire their first couple of times out," Jay said. "Most of them don't even know what a starting gate looks like. They have to educate themselves. But they all have class and some of them can run. Gantry shows you nothing early and then beats your brains out when you don't expect him to."

"That's because he doesn't know himself," I said. "He's the biggest fraud in racing."

"You think so? I disagree. He knows enough to buy the best-bred yearlings around. So what if he can't train and eventually breaks down all his horses? He wins all the big pots around for two-year-olds and a lot of the three-year-old ones as well."

I couldn't argue with him, because I knew he was right, but I intended to bet on Mad Margaret anyway and told Jay so. "Okay, but I'd watch the board," he warned. "If the Gantry filly takes any real money, I'd cut your action down to a minimum. Then you can make a solid bet on Go For Broke. He'll run no worse than second and should go off at decent odds, maybe three to one, and it's an Exacta race. I'd box him with a couple of the long shots, the one and the eight, and maybe play him straight."

"I'll bet him in the place hole."

"A wimpish wager, Shifty. I'm ashamed of you. I mean, if he's good enough to be a good place bet, then he's good enough to win, isn't he?"

"Jay, I'm just coming out of a real bad streak."

"Suit yourself," the handicapper said. "But that's not a good betting style."

I felt better after talking to Jay, because I'd always found him a good source of information to measure my own action against. He always did his work thoroughly, had strong, well-researched opinions, and knew how to bet in order to maximize his chances. If he happened to be wrong, he'd lose, like anybody else at the races, but if he was right, he'd come away a big winner. He never bemoaned his losses, because, after all, there are a thousand ways at least to lose a horse race that have nothing to do with skill, and you have to be lucky, but he was unforgiving about his mistakes. "If you have an opinion at a racetrack and it's based on the good, solid work you've done, there are still going to be days when you'll lose because your luck isn't running," he once explained. "You have to take your losses and wait for the breaks to come your way, because eventually it all evens out. I once lost ten straight photos at Del Mar, then got hot and won six in a row. But mistakes? Oh, no, the track never forgives a mistake. And that's the only time I get angry at myself, because, even if it's hard *not* to make a mistake out here, it's imperative that you don't make too many."

Moses himself, bringing down the tablets of the Ten Commandments to the awestruck, assembled Israelites, couldn't sound as authoritative as Jay in full rhetorical swing. I always found it reassuring to listen to him, even when I strayed away from his chosen path to explore betting avenues of my own devising. I've always insisted on being my own person at the track, but I'd have been a fool not to pay attention to Jay. In life, someone once said, we are all standing on each other's heads.

About an hour later, after I'd shaved and showered, I called Amber. "Want to go racing?" I asked.

"Don't be ridiculous, Lou. I have a job."

"Take the afternoon off. Bedlington has a nice filly running today."

"You don't seem to understand, do you?"

"I'm very dense. When will you see me?"

"I don't know that I should," she said. "I don't think we're really on the same plane of cosmic awareness."

"Really? Why don't we discuss it over dinner again? You could help me, Amber," I said. "I could become a much better and more concerned individual, if you would."

"I know exactly what you want from me, Lou."

"Amber, converging was your idea. Not that I objected. I enjoyed it very much."

"I can't talk to you now," she said. "Mr. Flanders just walked in."

"Good. I need to speak to him."

She put me on hold for a couple of minutes, then Flanders came on the line. "Yes, Anderson, what is it?"

I brought him up to date on Bedlington's activities. "And this morning he indicated it was a matter of days now," I added. "I thought you'd want to know."

"Very decent of you, Anderson," the lawyer said, "but there isn't much we can do about it, is there?"

"Short of physically preventing him, no."

"Anyway, on a hopeful note, he did seem more cheerful yesterday."

"You spoke to him?" I was surprised. "I thought he wouldn't talk to you."

"He called me up," the lawyer said. "We had some business to discuss and then we chatted about this and that. It was like the old days. I gather he's been seeing this girl."

"Oh, he told you about her?"

"Pretty much what you just told me, Anderson."

"Did he tell you she might be his daughter?"

The lawyer laughed. "No. He obviously doesn't believe it. I think he's quite taken with her. He's been seeing her every day."

"Every day?"

"So I gather. He says she's delightful."

"Really?"

"Oh, yes. He's more than a little smitten, I think."

"Already?"

"Anderson, you haven't known Lucius very long," Flanders said. "Women were always his great passion. His great weakness, if you prefer. This may be all for the best, you know."

"You mean, he's going to fall in love with her? He's seventy-nine years old."

"It's never too late, is it?"

"Then you don't think he's going to go through with his plan," I said. "He's pretty committed to it."

"Who knows, Anderson? We'll just keep our fingers crossed," the lawyer said cheerfully. "And thanks for the call."

* * *

Not only had Melinda Kennedy telephoned Bedlington directly from the airport, but she had driven out to see him the very next morning and had burst into his living room like an explosion of light. "Say, you're cute!" she said, throwing her arms around him and giving him a kiss on both cheeks. "You're everything Dizzy said you'd be!"

"Dizzy?"

"My mother, it's my pet nickname for her. She's so weird."

"Very appropriate. Can I offer you a cup of tea or coffee?"

"I can't drink American coffee," she said, "and tea won't do it for me. You don't have an *espresso*? Too bad. I just had breakfast. I don't need anything." She flung herself into a chair and looked around the room. "Wow, Dizzy was right about this place!"

"She always made fun of it. Accused me of being a stuffed shirt."

"Well, it is a little overdone, isn't it?" she said. "I mean, Lucius, it's like a movie set. *Sunset Boulevard*. God, I love it!" And she bounced to · her feet again to make a tour of the room, peering closely at everything in it and firing off a barrage of questions that tumbled over each other at breakneck speed. She seemed not to hear his answers, but later her comments to him about the room, the house, his whole way of life revealed that she had been thoroughly briefed. She struck him at once as her mother's daughter.

"She's very bright, but the extraordinary thing about her is this manic energy she has," Bedlington told me, as we drove out of his estate toward Santa Anita. "Isabel was like that when she was young. She was interested in everything, wanted to see and do everything, you know. Now she's become hysterical and, I suspect, is always on something, probably cocaine. But Melinda has that very same quality. I was stunned, frankly."

She had prodded him into giving her a tour of the premises, at the end of which she had again proceeded to kiss him and assured him that she was looking forward to seeing a lot of him. "Dizzy says you know everything and you could be such a help," she said. "Me, I'm just an ignorant kid. I need a little guidance."

"How can you be that ignorant?" he asked. "You were educated abroad. I presume they taught you how to read and write and you must at least have studied history and art and geography, haven't you?"

"Oh, yes, but everybody does that."

"Not in this great democracy, my dear. Here we are raising a generation of key-punching ignoramuses who can't spell or speak correctly, who don't read, and who don't even know where Peru is. I presume you had a better education than that."

"Oh, yeah, but I was always being sent away," she said. "I absolutely hated it."

Scopes tottered in with a tea tray and, as Bedlington sipped away, she proceeded to regale him with the story of her life. It was brief and served mainly to confirm what the Countess had told us about her during our lunch in Beverly Hills. She was twenty-two years old, spoke fluent Italian and French, and seemed to know everything about him. She even expressed an interest in Gilbert and Sullivan, although she confessed that her knowledge of the immortal duo derived from having once played Peep-Bo, a small part, in a high-school production in Rome of *The Mikado*. "It was in Italian, of course," she said, "and I thought it was silly, but then I didn't know anything."

"In Italian?" Lucius asked. "What did they call it?"

"Il Mikado," she said. "But now you can teach me all about it. And a lot of other things, too."

"Well, you know, I really haven't much time—"

"That's right, Dizzy said you were going off on a trip somewhere."

"Oh, she told you?"

"I'm so disappointed. I really want to see everything. I've always wanted to come here, you know."

"I can't imagine why."

"Oh, lots of reasons. For my work, partly," she said. "But also because L.A.'s become the cultural capital of the world. At least, for my generation. It's all here."

"What is?"

"The movies, TV, the music, you know—like everything."

"Unfortunately."

"Oh, come on, Lucius, don't be such an old fud," she said. "There must be something you like here. Dizzy said you had horses."

"Ah, well, yes. But it's hardly enough to compensate."

"For what?"

"For the collapse of Western civilization."

"Wow, how you talk!" She laughed, moved around behind him, and gave him a hug. "I love it when you do your Mr. Gloom and Doom number! You're so cute!"

"Cute? I'm a fossil, Melinda. I belong in the La Brea tar pits."

"I suppose that's some sort of museum," she said, coming around to snuggle in beside him. "You'd make a great exhibit. Anyway, I know what's wrong with you."

"Oh, really?"

"Yes. You're not having any fun. You're sort of dead inside."

"I'm working hard at it."

"Boring, Lucius, boring! I mean, you know all this stuff about art and literature and music and history and blah blah blah, but what good is it doing you? You need to get out of this place and get in touch again."

"With what?"

"With life, silly!" She took both his hands in hers and forced him to confront her. "And you could be such a help to me, Lucius. Don't you want to? You see, I've never met anyone like you. I was always being sent away to school and camps and stuff. Dizzy was always running off with some guy. I hardly even knew my dad. He was an oilman back in Texas and all they do is—oh, I don't know—"

"Drill."

"Yes," she said, with a little giggle. "Oh, you're so funny, Lucius. Please . . ." This time her arms went up around his neck and she clung to him for more than a few seconds. "Please, Lucius . . . please help me . . . I'm so alone here . . . Please try . . . I do need you . . . I know I'm just a dumb kid, but I have such a funny feeling about you, as if I've known you all my life . . ."

"Ah, yes . . . well . . ." He managed to untangle himself from her, but she seemed to want to fall into his arms again. Flustered for one of the few times in his life, he stood up and took a few steps toward the hall. "I can't imagine why Scopes hasn't come to pick up the tray . . . I'll just see about some more tea. Would you like anything?" He turned again to look at her and was appalled to find her in tears.

"I'm so sorry," she said, standing up. "I shouldn't have come. Dizzy warned me. I guess I must seem like a child to you." She started to leave. "I'll go now. You've been so sweet. Please forgive me . . ."

Inevitably, she had wound up in his arms again. "My dear," he told her, "of course I'll help you, any way I can. I'm not leaving right away, you know. We'll have a little time together. Anything I can do . . . my dear child . . ."

I caught my first sight of Melinda Kennedy when she appeared in the walking ring that afternoon for Mad Margaret's first race. I was standing next to Charlie, watching the filly being led around in a circle. The horse was a little nervous and spooked by the crowd of watchers at the rail, but Eddie had a good hold on her and she looked wonderful. Her chestnut coat gleamed with health and she seemed to be full of herself, an athlete in form on the brink of competing. The more I looked at her, the better I liked her chances and I told Charlie so. "You never know with these young horses," the trainer said. "If she breaks good and don't get too much dirt in her face, she could do it. She's been working just fine."

"If she breaks *well*, Charles," Bedlington said, "and *doesn't* get much dirt kicked up. You are mutilating the English language, dear lad."

"You ain't paying me to talk English, Mr. Bedlington," Charlie answered. "All I know is, the inside ain't the best place to be for a maiden filly first time out."

"You are incorrigible," Bedlington said.

"Hi! I'm sorry I'm late, Lucius," I heard a breathless female voice say. "The traffic on the freeway was just awful and I got off at the wrong exit. Is this your horse? Oh, she's darling!"

I turned around to find myself looking at an authentic beauty. I had imagined from Bedlington's account of his first meeting with her that she would be very attractive, but not the minor miracle I now confronted. She was not very tall, no more than five-four or five-five, but she seemed to be perfectly proportioned, with lovely legs and arms, a slender waist, and the pale, creamy complexion of a Renaissance princess. A mane of black curls framed high cheekbones, full lips, and a pair of lustrous hazel eyes. And she was elegantly dressed in a tailored dark brown suit that showed off her figure without flaunting it. Even Charlie seemed stunned by her. By the time Bedlington had introduced her to us, the trainer's chin had sagged open in bewildered admiration. "Control yourself, Charles," Bedlington admonished him. "Haven't you ever seen an attractive woman before?"

Melinda laughed, a sound of cheerful bells in a distant meadow. "I've heard so much about you both," she said, taking Bedlington's arm, "and I'm so excited. I've never been to a horse race before."

"I told her it was a highly overrated spectacle," Bedlington said, "but she insisted on coming."

"Oh, he's always so negative about everything," she said. "But we're going to change all that. And I *know* she's going to win."

"I'm glad to hear that," Charlie said, "on account of I could use a sure thing. Ain't ever found one yet."

"My goodness, who is that?" Melinda asked, staring across the ring at a big, dark bay filly that had suddenly reared up and kicked out with both forelegs, nearly hitting her groom and sending the onlookers nearest to her in the paddock scurrying for safety.

"The Gantry filly," Charlie said gloomily. "She's crazy, but I hear she can run."

"She hasn't yet," I said, "but you never know with that guy."

We watched while the groom and Gantry himself, a tall, studious-looking man in dark gray slacks and a lemon yellow cashmere sports jacket, struggled to calm the animal down. It took a couple of minutes, by which time the filly had broken out into a sweat, a lather forming against her neck and inside her haunches. "She's washing out," I said. "She isn't going to run a step."

"Don't count on it, Shifty," Charlie warned me. "She's an Icecapade and they're all a little crazy. But they can run."

"Not the kind I can hammer at the windows, when they look like that."

"They all got speed," Charlie said, "and sometimes the worse they look, the faster they run."

"I think it's just fascinating to hear you two talk," Melinda said. "I don't understand one word, but I love the sound of it."

"Horse people don't talk, Melinda," Bedlington explained, "they sing the siren songs composed by the muses of ruin."

"Honestly, I think it's so sweet," she said. "I'm going to find out what it all means. Shifty will help me, won't you?"

"Are you lucky?" I asked.

"Oh, yes," she said, "always."

"Then you don't need to know anything," I said. "In fact, you're better off *not* knowing."

"I think you're decidedly a very cute person," Melinda said. "Lucius was absolutely right about you."

"What did he say?"

" 'Merely corroborative detail,' " Bedlington declaimed, " 'intended to give artistic verisimilitude to an otherwise bald and unconvincing narrative.' "

"Oh, Lucius," she said, smiling sweetly. "Which one is it?"

"*The Mikado,* my dear."

"How funny!"

The byplay between them had already assumed a pattern of intimacy that surprised me, if only because they had known each other for such a short time, and I found myself unable to believe in it. But she had an aura about her that was authentically bewitching and, whatever her motives, I found myself rooting for her. If anybody was going to be able to dissuade our eccentric plutocrat from doing away with himself, it was obviously going to be this girl. Bedlington seemed mesmerized by her.

"Oh, look at those adorable little men!" Melinda exclaimed, clapping her hands together. "Have you ever seen anything quite so cute?"

She was referring to the jockeys, who had suddenly appeared in the paddock and were heading for their mounts. Tim Lang was among the last to arrive, but came trotting toward us, then stopped in his tracks at the sight of Melinda. His greedy little gunslinger's eyes undressed her from head to foot, but Melinda seemed either unaware of his lust or indifferent to it. "It's *so* nice to meet you," she said, when Bedlington introduced her to him. "You're so sweet to ride our horse. I just know you're going to win."

"Do try, Timothy," Bedlington said. "This is Miss Kennedy's first visit to the races."

The jockey nodded, but never took his eyes off her. Charlie leaned in over his shoulder. "Tim, this filly's got speed and she's worked fine out of the gate," he said, "but she may not like the inside. If she backs up when the dirt hits her, take a hold, don't rush her. If you get clear, she'll run for you."

The rider nodded and smiled at Melinda. "You need the money, right, Mr. Bedlington?"

"Oh, no, he doesn't," Melinda said, shaking her pretty curls, "but we do so want you to win. Please do your best, it would mean so much to us."

Lang seemed dazed by her and could only nod. Even after Charlie gave him a leg up into the saddle for the parade to the post, he continued to stare at her. Then, as the horses moved out through the gap toward the track, he smiled and waved at her. "He's such a sweet boy," Melinda said. "Does he ride all your horses, Lucius?"

"Most of them," Bedlington said. "Charles seems to think he can ride."

"Oh, I just know he can," Melinda said, "and he seems like such a nice young man."

"I don't know about nice," Charlie said.

"Well, bright."

"Bright? He'd get lost in a round room," the trainer said, "but you don't hire a rider for his brains. He's got good hands and he can get you out of the gate. He could be one of the top riders here, like a McCarron or a Pincay, if he'd listen."

"Oh. Why won't he?"

"Like I told you, miss, because he's dumb. Most jockeys are dumb. It's hard to get a lot of brains inside a size-four hatband."

"My goodness, but you sound so cynical, Mr. Pickard," Melinda said. "You sound just like Lucius."

"You're very young, my dear," Bedlington said. "After you've seen a bit more of the world and grappled daily with mankind's lumbering

imbecilities, I suspect you'll be more appreciative of the older generation's negative assessment of the human condition."

"Sounds right to me," Charlie said, "even if I didn't understand half
of what you just said."

Melinda laughed and took Bedlington's arm as we headed toward the
grandstand. I fell in behind them, next to Charlie, who glanced slyly at me
as we trailed after them. "Where'd he meet this chippie?" he asked.

"She's the daughter of one of his ex-wives," I explained. "I met the
mother and she's quite a lot like her. Lots of manic energy."

"She'd wear me out pretty fast."

"Maybe you just don't like women, Charlie."

"It ain't that I don't like them, I just don't understand them."

"Were you ever married?"

"Once, a long time ago," the trainer said. "The three worst years of
my life. She spent most of her time shopping. You know how to paralyze
a woman from the waist down, Shifty?"

"I give up."

"You marry her."

We all sat together for the race in Charlie's box, which was in the
lower grandstand area, about halfway between the sixteenth pole and
the finish line. I had bet fifty dollars to win on the filly, figuring that she
would either run her race and win or finish out of the money, so I kept my
binoculars trained on her all the way to the post. If she had misbehaved or
washed out, I would have rushed back to the betting windows and sold my
ticket, but she seemed to be perfectly calm and well within herself as Lang
brought her to the starting gate. Gantry's filly, on the other hand, was all
lathered up and tossing her head about, fighting the attempt of her rider,
Gary Leavenworth, to control her and get her settled down. She was going
off the favorite, at eight to five, with Mad Margaret the third choice, at
seven to two. A couple of minutes before post time, I lowered my glasses
and sat back in my seat to await the start of the race. "She looks fine," I
said to Charlie, who was sitting quietly beside me, his arms folded across
his chest. "Gantry's filly is a mess."

"Don't pay no attention to that," the trainer said. "She'll run this
time, I guarantee it."

As we sat there, I realized that Melinda had not stopped talking since
leaving the paddock. She had snuggled in next to Lucius in the front row,
her arms entwined in his, while she commented ecstatically on everything
she observed, from the bright emerald green of the infield and the majestic
rocky slopes of the Sierra Madre mountains, against which Santa Anita
nestled like an old art-deco jewel, to the beauty of the horses themselves,

the colors of the silks the jockeys wore, the elegance of the women in the Turf Club boxes, the amusing-looking characters who swarmed about us. She chattered away about everything and nothing, interspersing her observations with questions to which she evidently expected no answers. But instead of being exasperated by her, as any serious horseplayer would have been, Bedlington appeared to be enchanted. He sat quietly in place, beaming, his left hand over one of hers, as the horses began filing into the gate.

When the race started and the animals burst out of their stalls, with the jockeys pumping them out of there to get position before they hit the turn, Melinda leaped to her feet directly in front of me and began to scream. "Oh! Oh! Come on, sweetie! Come on, Maggie, you can do it! Oh! Oh! Come on, come on!" she shouted, jumping up and down. "Hurry up, hurry up! Come on, Maggie! Please! Please! Oh! Oh!"

She had caused me to miss the start of the race and I had to stand up myself in order to see what was going on. Mad Margaret must have broken slowly, because, by the time I picked her out of the pack of eleven horses moving along the backstretch, she was next to last, along the rail about eight lengths out of it. "She got left," Charlie said. "The damn starter took too long to get them out of there and she went to sleep."

By the time they hit the turn, Gantry's filly, Hustling, had opened up two lengths. Mad Margaret had room and had begun to move strongly up on the inside, but was facing a hopeless task. Even if she handled the clods of dirt now showering up into her face, she would either have to run too fast too early to make up the ground lost at the start and she would tire or some other horse would move over in front of her on the turn and shut her off. I kissed my fifty dollars good-bye, but kept my glasses glued to her just to see how she would respond to the hopeless challenge she now faced. There would be a next time, as there always is in racing.

Nothing that had happened in the race made the slightest impression on Melinda, who continued to scream and bounce up and down as if the filly were dueling for the lead. I stepped out into the aisle behind our box to get away from her and so I could make out what was happening. Instead of allowing his mount to relax and settle down, Lang was now pumping hard, asking her to run. "Dumb jock," I heard Charlie say, as Mad Margaret moved up steadily on the inside, running with her head down and seemingly unfazed by the dirt in her face. Luckily, no one came over on her as they hit the turn and she continued to make up ground, so that by the head of the stretch she was third and still closing. "Oh, wow, where is she? Oh, there she is, there she is! She's going to win, she's going to win!" Melinda shrieked.

There was no way she could have won. Gantry's sweaty speedball had opened up four lengths on the field by that time and she continued to run hard down the lane, stretching her lead to six lengths at the sixteenth pole. Mad Margaret was second by then, but the effect of rushing up against a fast pace finally took its toll. She tired in the last few yards and came in fourth, seven lengths behind the winner, but still trying hard as Lang urged her on along the rail. "Oh, that's so sad, so sad," Melinda said, falling back into her seat. "What happened, Lucius? I just *knew* she was going to win! What happened?"

Bedlington put his arm consolingly around her as he began to explain a few facts of racing life to her. Charlie stood up and said good-bye. "I'd better go down and make sure she came out of it okay, Mr. Bedlington," he said. "Nice to have met you, miss."

I followed him out into the aisle. "She ran a hell of a race, Charlie," I said, "all things considered."

"Yeah, only I don't know how much Lang took out of her, that dummy," he said. "All he had to do was wrap up and let her get a taste of it. Instead he goes all out when it's hopeless. You can ruin a green young horse like that. These damn jocks, Shifty, they can kill you, you better believe me."

"I believe you, Charlie," I answered, as the trainer headed down toward the track. He was right about Lang, of course, and by using the horse hard that way he had tipped her quality to every smart horseplayer in the stands. In her next race she'd go off the favorite, maybe at prohibitively low odds. And all just because Lang must have wanted to impress Melinda Kennedy. Oh, well, I thought, nobody ever said this was an easy game. I headed back toward Jay's box, a couple of aisles away, to see if he still felt positively about his hard knocker in the seventh. I'd have to bet about a hundred on it now to salvage my day and I wanted to make no mistakes.

"Hey, Shifty, who is she?" Jay asked, as I joined him. "We saw you in the paddock. That's a Rose Bowl queen."

"Yeah, what's the angle on that?" Beltrami echoed him. "I got a blue-veiner just from looking."

"I'll explain later," I said. "Right now, Jay, I need a little reassurance. I had fifty on Bedlington's filly and she ran a hell of a race. Next time."

"Right," the handicapper agreed, smiling. "Go For Broke will not blow, Shifty."

"I'm glad to see the priorities observed," Arnie said. "The trouble with women is that you can't put saddles on their backs and whip them down the stretch."

"I don't need no saddles," Angles declared. "All I need is half an hour and a nice motel room."

"Angles is strictly a sprinter," Jay said. "Quick out of the gate and quick to finish."

"In the cheap claiming ranks," Arnie observed, "where the losers flourish."

"Ah, what do you know, Wolfenden?" Angles said, turning on him. "You ain't been laid in twenty years, I bet. I bet you ain't even had a hard-on since then."

"I keep calm, Angles," Arnie said. "Excitement of any kind scrambles the brain cells and this is a place that rewards tranquil contemplation."

"Ah, what do you know? Nothing, that's what you know," Angles said. "You don't figure the angles, you don't weigh the options. You gotta have a broad from time to time."

"I rely on the beast with five fingers," Arnie said. "And you know what, Angles? It never looks up at you and says, 'I love you,' or wants to be taken out to dinner or go shopping. And the momentary pleasure is the same, without any of the time-consuming, costly side effects."

I bet a hundred dollars to place on Go For Broke, but decided to watch the race from the rail up above the box seats. Risking money at the track is a serious matter to those of us who go to the races regularly, and the uninformed chatter of a neophyte on the scene can become a serious irritant, not to say hazard. Let Bedlington wallow in Melinda's charming ignorance, I said to myself; I'd watch the race alone and rejoin them afterward.

As I stood there, waiting for the horses to get to the post, I saw Melinda heading down the aisle to my right, perhaps on her way back from the ladies' room. Lonny Richards's girlfriend, the blonde with the wonderful legs, rose up out of a box near the finish line, waved excitedly, and came running toward her. They embraced and I could tell that the blonde was astonished to see her, though Melinda had her back to me and I couldn't make out her expression. They talked animatedly for a couple of minutes, then parted again and returned to their own seats. I was wondering idly where these two could possibly have known each other before, but in less than a minute the race went off and I focused my attention on the fate of my bet.

It was an easy win. Go For Broke got up by a nose and I was sure Jay had the Exacta, which paid over two hundred dollars for every five-dollar ticket. My own bet in the place hole returned a profit of a hundred and thirty, so I could go home a winner, and I said my thanks to Jay as I passed his happy box on my way to rejoin Melinda and Bedlington.

"Where have you been, dear boy?" he asked, as I showed up.

I told him about my minor coup and Melinda clapped her hands together in delight. "Oh, that's so great!" she exclaimed. "That's the horse I wanted to bet on, but Lucius wouldn't let me! It had the longest tail and I *loved* the way it bounced up and down! Oh, Lucius, you see? We should have listened to Shifty."

"He didn't tell us anything, Melinda," the plutocrat said. "You can't wager on these beasts on the strength of their looks, my dear. Someone has to explain the facts of life to you." He took her hand and stood up. "Shifty, we are on our way. Melinda will drive me home. I know you wish to linger here."

"Well, I might stay through the feature."

He reached into his wallet and handed me the usual crisp one-hundred-dollar bill. "Thank you, dear lad, it's been enlightening, if not exactly rewarding. I'll call you."

Melinda leaned forward and pecked me on the cheek. "Oh, Shifty, it's been such fun," she said. "I hope I didn't make a fool of myself. You were very sweet to put up with me. I get so excited. I think this is grand, really. Thank you, thank you!" She took Bedlington's hand to lead him out of the box.

"Melinda, who's that girl you were talking to?" I asked. "The one who came over to you just before the race. I was standing up there and I saw you."

She looked surprised, but covered it up quickly with a laugh. "Oh, Angel? That's Angel Price," she said. "Isn't that amazing? We knew each other in Milan two years ago. She was a model and I was modeling, too. We were staying in the same hotel. Isn't that wild? I mean, imagine seeing her here, of all places. She's an actress, she said. Wow, it's weird! She was pretty crazy and went out with a lot of wild guys, but she was fun. Hey, it's really a tiny world, isn't it?"

"You want me to phone you tomorrow, Lucius?" I asked, as they headed out.

"Certainly, dear boy," he called back, with a languid wave, then turned to Melinda. " 'Let's depart, dignified and stately.' "

"Oh, Lucius," she said, "you're wonderful."

"*Iolanthe,* Act One. A favorite of mine."

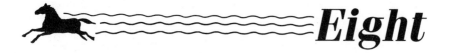 *Eight*

GETAWAYS

"I think you're the strangest man I've ever met," Amber said, as we sat on our blanket high on the slope of the hill, sipped mineral water, and gazed down at the smog-enshrouded towers of downtown L.A. "I mean, you have no feeling for nature at all."

"We could be at the races," I said, "in a setting easily as beautiful as this one and looking at horses. Don't you think horses are manifestations of nature?"

"Not in those circumstances," she said. "Horses belong in open fields, in prairies, not confined in little stalls and made to perform unnaturally for the enjoyment of a relative handful of degenerate gamblers."

"Oh, you're a hard woman, Amber. Is that why you won't come to the races with me?" I asked. "You think the animals are being mis-treated?"

"Yes, I know they are. I've been thinking about it ever since you invited me to go there," she explained. "So I called up the Humane Society and they told me all about it. I think it's disgusting."

"What is?"

"The way the poor horses are treated."

"Better than most humans, Amber. They're fed and groomed and taken care of when they're sick and all we ask them to do is run hard for us once every couple of weeks six to eight months a year. Is that so bad?"

"Would they do it if they didn't have to?"

"Would people obey the law, if they didn't have to?"

"A specious argument, Lou, and you know it."

"Amber, have you ever seen a Thoroughbred in action?"

"Only on film."

"If you had, you'd know that what a true racehorse wants to do most in life is run. It's as natural to him as breathing. And it gives him pleasure, it fulfills him, just as dancing does it for you."

"I think that's nonsense," she said. "Lou, you aren't going to tell me that horses would run races with each other if we didn't compel them to?"

"Not exactly, no, but—"

"I think it's criminal," she said. "It's an abuse of the animal's right to a life of its own. I believe in animal rights. That's why I'm a vegetarian."

"How do you know vegetables don't suffer?"

"What?"

"They're alive, aren't they? Just because you can't hear a tomato scream when you bite into it doesn't mean it isn't in pain."

"That's preposterous."

"Amber, life is a cruel business. We survive by using and eating one another. Think about that the next time you nibble on a lettuce leaf or snap off the head of a carrot."

"That's goofy. You are undoubtedly the most ridiculous and self-indulgent person I know," she said. "I don't know why I consented to see you again. You don't do anything worthwhile, you don't care what's happening to the environment, and you're indifferent to suffering everywhere. You're really almost evil."

"Oh, come on, Amber," I said, trying to take her hand. "I'm just one poor slob in a world of poor slobs trying to enjoy my life without hurting too many other people, that's all."

She snatched her hand away from me. "If we don't fight for justice and dignity against the polluters and exploiters," she said, "we have nothing."

"We have other people, Amber. We have love and pleasure and fun. Remember Voltaire."

"He was a man and a cynical one at that."

"He was French. He liked to eat well and he admired pretty women."

"You're a sexist, Lou."

"Sure," I admitted. "I love sex."

She turned to look at me in disgust. "What am I doing here with you? Why did I agree to see you again?" she asked herself.

"Because I'm so smart and funny and charming," I said, reaching up behind her ear to produce a tiny bouquet of violets I'd been waiting for the right moment to work into my act. I presented it to her. "And magic is my way of telling you I like you."

"Oh, Lou," she said, clasping the flowers in both hands and falling back onto the blanket, "you're hopeless."

"No, I'm full of hope," I said. "I just think the human condition is such that we need a few laughs to make it bearable. If that makes me a boorish exploiter, then I plead guilty. And is this fair? Here I am, picnicking with you in Griffith Park and arguing over matters beyond our control, when I could be sitting in a box at Santa Anita enjoying the most beautiful spectacle in the world, the living poetry of a magnificent creature expressing itself in action. You won't even give yourself a chance to enjoy it. And now I'd like very much to converge."

"Here? Don't be ridiculous!"

"All right, the hell with it," I said. "We'll just sit up here on this hill and argue. What are we arguing about? Why are we arguing?"

"Mainly because you make fun of all the things I believe in."

"I tease you a little, Amber," I tried to explain to her. "You have to let go sometimes, just let it all go. You do it in your dancing, you express yourself most fully. I do it with horses and magic, my two shields against the horrors of reality. Why can't you understand that? Is it so hard?"

I didn't really imagine I'd ever be able to convince her, but I was hoping I could get her at least to tolerate me. It wasn't only that I wanted to have sex with her either. The fact was that I actually admired her integrity and fierce commitment to all of her various causes. I found the intensity of her partisanship exciting and I wanted some of it to rub off on me, because I tend to accept things too much as they are and I am selfish. Mainly, what I wanted from Amber, in addition to the fleeting raptures of what she called convergence, was a feeling that I, too, could make a difference, however small, in the human condition. I'd lost it over the past few years, after some personal disappointments and because I long ago gave up any hope in the ability of mankind to make a better world. But I knew in my soul that people like Amber were on the side of the angels. It was important to try, if only I could get her to have a few laughs along the way. I'd even give up a couple of days a week at the track for her, if that's what it took. I mean, what the hell was I doing up here, in this big public park on a Saturday afternoon, when at least two horses I knew would win were getting ready to run at Santa Anita? Couldn't I make her understand the enormity of the sacrifice I was making on her behalf? What was the matter with this woman, anyway?

We sat there in warm winter sunlight for most of the afternoon, staring down over the acres of wooded hills, watching single files of mounted riders threading their way through the wilderness below us. No sound reached us except the call of birds from the surrounding branches of the trees, with only the occasional distant hum of a car engine. This was not the real wilderness, of course, but still I found myself wondering at the miracle of it, the survival of so much unspoiled beauty in the very heart of a heedless metropolis. Amber had been right. "It's not just another park," she had told me, when she had refused to meet me at the races and informed me she would see me only if I agreed to go with her on a hiking picnic into the park. "It's the real thing, Lou, right here in the middle of L.A."

And it hadn't been so bad. We'd packed a good lunch and hiked into the park from below, climbing up along the trails leading into the hills, then branched out on our own through brush and groves of trees until we'd reached this tiny open patch of ground, with its view down to the concrete city that from here seemed unreal, like a poorly focused projection on a huge screen. Amber had been here many times before; it was her secret hideaway and I suddenly felt privileged that she had thought enough of me to bring me here. We munched vegetable sandwiches and organically grown apples and drank mineral water and argued. Then, after the arguments, we found we were able to talk to each other, about this and that, small matters like movies and dance groups and the operas of Giuseppe Verdi and magic, pastimes unconnected directly to the salvation of the human race. She even talked to me about her job, confessing that she was bored by it and planned to move on to something else soon. "Mr. Flanders is nice," she said, "but there really isn't very much to do in that office anymore. I think I told you, he's the only active partner and there aren't many clients. In fact, we've lost a couple in the past year, since Mr. Coutts retired. Now Mr. Flanders seems to spend most of his time on the phone with brokers and investment people. It's easy for me, but it's also kind of routine. I'd like to work for the Sierra Club or the Wildlife Fund or Common Cause, so I've been looking around. I've written to all of them and I have a couple of appointments next week. I haven't told Mr. Flanders yet, but I will, if somebody offers me a job."

"Why don't you live off your income and then you'd have all the time in the world for your various causes?"

"I told you, Lou, I can't do that. It would be hypocritical."

"You know, the last totally honest person in the history of the world got himself nailed up on a cross."

"There you go again."

"Sorry, sorry, I didn't mean it."

When we ran out of light banter, we rested, with me lying flat on my back and Amber nestled in the crook of my arm, her head resting on my shoulder. My legs were still aching from the unaccustomed exertion of the climb, but it felt good to lie there in the sun with this odd but attractive person next to me. I kissed her and then, to my amazement, right there in the public park, with the blanket now pulled up around us, we converged. Except that this time it wasn't merely sex, but more like making love. We took each other in quiet, whispering, hurried tenderness, and then she fell asleep against me, as the sky began to fade above us. Good God, I remember thinking, maybe I'm actually going to fall in love with this crazy rich girl, even if she doesn't like or respect anything I do. I must be a sucker for women; I even forgave Amber that day for having lured me away from the track and my two live horses, both of whom, of course, won at nice prices.

When I got back that night, there was a message on my answering machine from my agent, asking me to call him at home. "I got you a Mexican cruise," he informed me. "It's a week on the *Panama Star*. You leave Wednesday afternoon from San Pedro, come back the following Wednesday evening. You do one show a night and you'll also work the dining room on your own. With tips, you could clear maybe fifteen hundred net. Okay? You're replacing a stand-up comedian with laryngitis, so I got to call them back right away."

I was in no position to turn the job down, because by this time it had become clear to me that my gig as Lucius J. Bedlington's driver had pretty much come to an end. He was seeing Melinda Kennedy every day and she was doing the driving, while also occupying most of his time. "You understand, dear boy, I have to help the child," he told me over the phone. "She doesn't know anyone and I have to see she gets settled and started on her career. I will call you from time to time, of course. Are you in serious financial straits?"

"No, Lucius, I'm fine," I said, and informed him about the cruise.

" 'Then away you go to an island fair that lies in a Southern sea,' "
he sang tunelessly. " 'We know not where and we don't much care,
wherever that isle may be.' Well?"

"Flanders would know," I said. "Ask him."

"Too easy, dear boy. *Gondoliers*, first-act finale. You really must try
harder."

I did see him once before I left, when Melinda couldn't come to him
because she was busy registering for film courses at some community
college in the San Fernando Valley. I picked him up at his place, as usual,
and we drove into Pasadena to look at apartments for her. "I wanted her
to move in here," he said, as we left the estate grounds in the Alfa. "I have
plenty of room, but she wouldn't. She said it wouldn't look right. I talked
to Derek about it and he was appalled that I'd even consider such an
arrangement, but then he's a lawyer and he's paid to be suspicious. He
even had the effrontery to ask me what I really knew about her." He
sighed. "Ah, well, she is young enough to be my daughter."

"She's young enough to be your granddaughter," I said.

He laughed. "Quite right, dear boy, but I'm feeling very sprightly
indeed these days."

"And maybe she is your daughter," I added.

"Just what Derek said," he answered. "I'm certain she's not, you
know, but I suppose I shall have to look into it seriously one of these days.
Meanwhile, there's no rush and I'm having the time of my life. She's a
breath of fresh air and she's changed everything."

"Everything?"

He gazed out at the passing scenery, while idly drumming the fingers
of one hand against the top of the car door. "Oh, perhaps not everything,"
he said. "Let's simply say it's all on hold, as it were." He chuckled. "Of
course it's driving poor Thanassis mad with impatience. Everything's
ready, you know. I was supposed to have departed this vale of despair to
eternal peace over a week ago."

"Well, that's good," I said.

"No, it's annoying," he corrected me. "I never would have imagined
it possible. This young person has rejuvenated me. I had truly thought my
life was over."

"It was a quick fix, all right."

"And, it turns out, she loves the races. She wants to go with me
whenever we can, especially when one of my horses is running. You
know, Shifty, I've never believed in any form of rebirth, especially of the
noisome Christian variety, but I have indeed been reborn and I'm
becoming a true believer."

"In what?"

"The incredible life force of the young in heart."

"Then the world doesn't look so bad to you anymore."

"Oh, it's a dismal trash heap, dear boy, but in the right company it can seem bearable enough." He glanced slyly at me and smiled. " 'Please you, that's the kind of maid sets my heart aflame-a!' *Princess Ida,* Act Two. Do you know what she calls me now?"

"No, what?"

"Bunny! Me, of all people! Bunny! Isn't that sweet?"

"Adorable."

We spent the rest of the morning looking at apartments, none of which Bedlington considered suitable for his protégée. "I want her not too far from me, where I can at least keep an eye on her," he explained, "but I will not have her living in a pigsty." He checked each one for cleanliness, turned on water taps, flushed toilets, peeked into closets, tapped on walls, tested shelves for dust, inspected the kitchen equipment, and inquired about the other tenants. Inevitably he'd uncover some glaring inadequacy, after which he'd inform the prospective landlord or his agent that he was a thief who should be in the used-car business or working for the government. Once I had to get between him and an irate, red-faced woman whom he'd denounced as an exploiting slut, because I was afraid she'd hit him with her cane. By the time I got him home again I wouldn't have been surprised to hear that a posse of Pasadena property owners was forming to come over and lynch him.

"Some of those places were okay," I said, as we drove through his front gate. "I mean, you could fix them up. And how much time is she going to spend there?"

"Not the point, dear boy," he said. "You don't understand."

"I understand. You want her to move in with you."

"Why not? I have six empty bedrooms. She could be very comfortable and it wouldn't cost her anything. Then I could have her around all the time."

"Lucius, Melinda's twenty-two years old," I said. "She's going to meet people, she's going to have friends, she's going to want a life of her own."

"She can do that. She can come and go as she likes."

"And what if she brings them home to you? You want the house full of bright young things?"

I parked under the porte cochere and Bedlington stepped out into the driveway. "I don't think you've grasped the essential point, dear boy," he said, turning to me with a cold smile. "Melinda enjoys my company."

"Well, sure, but—"

"*Bon voyage,* Shifty," he said. "Ah." He reached into his wallet and paid me off again. "Enjoy yourself, my lad. Call when you get back."

I saw Amber one more time before I left for Mexico. She took me to a health-food restaurant, a single small room with a tiny patio overlooking the Sunset Strip, where I ate the worst meal of my life. It seemed to be some sort of a curry made of flaccid vegetables embedded in chunks of gray rice. Dessert consisted of a rubbery yellow pudding that in retrospect made tapioca taste like ambrosia. "What the hell is this?" I asked, slapping at the gelatinous mass with a soup spoon. "Is it safe?"

"Everything here is organic and pure," Amber whispered fiercely, leaning across the table toward me so as not to be overheard by our waiter, a surly-looking hairy thug in his mid-thirties who was standing a few feet away from us. "You are ridiculous, Lou. This is probably the healthiest meal you've eaten in years."

"It may be the last," I said. "This kind of health food will kill you."

"Why do I tolerate you?" she asked, staring at me out of wide, incredulous eyes. "You're just saying these things to make me angry, aren't you?"

"Why would I do that, Amber?"

"This is rich in minerals and other nutrients and it's all been grown free of pesticides."

"What insect would eat this stuff?"

"You are impossible!" She stood up. "I'm going."

"Please sit down, Amber. We haven't paid the check. Or do you want me to do it?"

"No, no, I'm taking you."

She sat down and I beckoned the waiter over. "Check, please. Amber?"

"What?"

"Don't be mad. I'm just teasing, really."

"You make me so angry, Lou. You put down everything I do, everything I say, everything I believe in."

"Like gray rice? This is a belief?"

"It is gray because it hasn't been refined and had all the natural nutritious elements removed," she said. "What it looks like is not important. It's what it does for you."

"It does nothing for me. Hey, I've got an idea." I leaned over the table and took her hand. "Let's go somewhere and have dinner."

She angrily jerked her hand away from me and refused to say

anything else until the waiter returned with her change, after which she stood up and stormed out of the restaurant. "Something wrong?" the waiter asked.

"Nothing, I hope," I said. "Are you the proprietor of this place?"

"Nah. He's in the kitchen, him and his wife. They do the cooking. I just work here. I've only been here a week."

"Well, what was this rice dish we had?" I asked. "I mean, what was in it?"

The waiter shrugged. "Don't ask me, mister. I just work here. I'm an actor. I don't eat this shit."

I caught up with Amber out on the sidewalk, where she was standing by my car, waiting for me to take her home. When I opened the door for her, she got in without a word and sat there, arms folded, until I pulled up in front of the building. "Okay," I said, "I'm sorry. I thought it was a terrible meal, but I shouldn't have made such a big deal out of it."

She turned to look at me. "I don't think we should see each other anymore," she said, for the seventh or eighth time in our brief relationship. "You don't like anything I do, you don't believe in anything I value. I think we should just stop seeing each other."

"Would you like me better if I agreed with everything you said and endorsed all of your causes, Amber?" I asked. "Is that what you want from me?"

"We don't have a relationship, Lou. You can be so sweet, but you really don't approve of me."

"I thought it was the other way around. Everything I do or say pisses you off." She started to get out of the car, but I grabbed her hand and stopped her. "Listen, there are some things I can't do. One of them is eat gray rice. I can't pretend to like it. The next time you take me to one of these places, if I don't like the food, I'll keep quiet, I'll eat something else."

"Good-bye, Lou." She opened the car door.

"Listen, Amber, wait—"

But she was nearly at her front door by the time I caught up to her again. "Please, Lou, not tonight."

"But I'm leaving tomorrow. We can't say good night like this," I insisted. "We're arguing over nothing."

"It isn't nothing to me."

"Amber, I promise, no more cracks, no more jokes."

"You can't do that, Lou."

"No, you're right. Not all the time. But tonight?"

"No, Lou." She brushed past me and fumbled in her bag for her front-door key.

I came up behind her. "We don't have to converge," I said. "We can just talk to each other. Then, if you want me to, I'll go home. You realize I've never seen your apartment?"

"No, and I don't think you ever will." She found the key and opened the door. "Good night, Lou."

"I'll call you when I get back," I said. "Meanwhile, try to forgive me. I mean, gray rice—it's a new experience—"

Without even the hint of a smile, she gazed briefly and coldly at me, then entered the building and shut the front door in my face. That's one of the things I've never understood about women, I remember thinking, this congenital inability to accept an apology or to forgive a transgression, however minor. Or was I making an unfair generalization? A sexist one, undoubtedly Amber would have informed me. But then she was as guilty as I was of that sort of judgment on the basis of gender or any other category. We're a country of pigeonholers; everyone has to fit into a slot somewhere, properly labeled and identified, so that we won't have to deal with individuals in all their inconvenient complexities and delicate shadings. You play the races that way, risking money solely on the basis of class and groups, however statistically arrived at, and you get killed. And what is racing but a microcosm of life itself? Amber was clearly a system-player, I decided, and I didn't fit into her rigid little program. The thought saddened me and by the time I got back to my own place I had a bad case of what I call the getaway blues. It's a sort of miasmic depression that settles over me when aspects of my life are not going well, for any reason, and which I compare to the desolation of a racetrack late on getaway day, the last one of any meet. You get a bad case of the getaway blues and you wind up like Bedlington, wanting out for keeps.

I didn't call Amber again before I left. I had to depart for San Pedro in midmorning to board the *Panama Star* and get myself organized. I told myself I'd send her a couple of cheery cards from the stops the ship would make along the way and then try to see her when I got back. I wonder now whether it would have made any difference if I had called her. I suppose not. I was still awake at midnight and I actually picked up the phone to dial her number, but didn't. By that time she was dead. At least I hope she was.

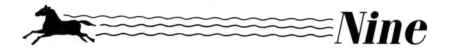 *Nine*

BAD TIMING

I heard about it first from Max Silverman, the manager of my apartment house. There was a note in my mailbox when I got back late the following Wednesday evening, asking me to drop in on him, and another one taped to my front door repeating the message and saying that the matter was urgent. I dropped my suitcases off without bothering to check my answering machine and walked across the darkened pool area to see Max, who lived in a couple of tiny rooms at the front of the building. The ship had docked a couple of hours late, due to a small engine malfunction that had developed on entering the harbor, and it had taken me another hour to clear customs, so that by the time I got home it was nearly midnight. Max, however, was awake; I could hear the plaintive sound of a violin concerto playing softly on his stereo. I rang the bell and also knocked, because Max, who was well into his eighties, was a little deaf.

"Ah, Shifty, how are you?" he said, as he opened the door. "You got my messages."

"Sure, Max. What's up?"

"Come in, come in," he said, stepping aside to let me pass. He was dressed in an old, tattered red silk bathrobe and slippers but was still wearing his favorite black beret. He hadn't shaved for a couple of days and looked mildly disreputable, with strands of gray hair sticking out from under his cap and his long, skinny arms protruding from the rolled-up sleeves of his robe like swizzle sticks. His teeth rested in a glass next to his favorite armchair, which faced the stereo and radio, an ancient machine dating back to the fifties that Max had embedded in a black-walnut cabinet and which he still referred to as his gramophone. It suited not only Max, but the rest of the room, which was cluttered with oddly assorted late-Victorian and Edwardian pieces and turn-of-the-century bric-a-brac that Max had picked up here and there during his travels around the world as a classical violinist, playing with various symphony orchestras and chamber-music groups. The walls were plastered with photographs, many of them signed portraits of famous performing artists of the time. In one corner rested a battered violin case, which contained, I knew, a valuable Italian instrument Max no longer played, because, he said, it had become painful for him to hear himself try. He lived essentially on his memories, propped up in his old age by the visible remnants of his active artistic past; but, unlike Bedlington, he had not given up on life, nor did he value material comforts. Over his bed hung a small Degas drawing of a dancer at the bar that he had acquired in Paris in the late thirties, the sale of which could have eased his existence, but he had consistently refused even to consider parting with it. He survived on his Social Security payments and a small pension, while managing the apartment building in exchange for his two rooms. "I have what I need, Shifty," he had once said to me. "I have food, a roof over my head, a beautiful thing to look at, music, and too many good memories. And I got my health. Can you tell me what else there is for an old man of my age?"

Max liked me. My devotion to horses made him nervous, because his favorite author was Fyodor Dostoyevski, who had ruined himself at the gaming tables, and Max was afraid I would follow the famous Russian down the tubes on the backs of too many losing favorites. But he forgave me even this vice, mainly because he also loved magic, and I'd drop in on him from time to time or invite him up to my place to try out a new effect or a move on him. "You stay away from the horses, Shifty," he'd say, "and you could be a great artist." But he rarely pushed me too hard and I never minded much when he did; he'd become a sort of surrogate uncle, disapproving but benign. He worried about me, but never needlessly, which was why I took him seriously.

"Sit down, Shifty. Here," he said, moving a mass of sheet music from the settee next to the stereo onto an adjacent table, already piled high with scores and books. "Sit. So how was the trip?"

"Fine, Max, it went fine," I said. "It was kind of a tough audience at first, a lot of blue-haired old ladies and retired bankers, mainly, but I eventually got them warmed up. Except for the other entertainers and the crew, I was the youngest person on board. You'd have fitted right in."

"What are you talking about? Bankers? What kind of music?"

I shook my head. "No, on second thought, Max, forget it. The closest anyone came to playing a classic was a medley the singers did from *Kismet*."

"*Kismet?* What is that?"

"Operetta, borrowed from Borodin, Max."

"Borodin? A third-rate musician in the original. What are you trying to do to me, Shifty? You want me to go on a cruise with old bankers and listen to Borodin? What did I do to you that you hate me?"

"Hey, Max, I don't hate you, just kidding. Anyway," I explained, "it was really boring, Max, but it was good money. So what's new here? What's the big urgent message?"

He didn't answer right away, but looked at me in puzzled dismay, then picked up the glass holding his teeth and headed for the bathroom. "Excuse me, I'll be right back." When he returned a couple of minutes later, his teeth were in place and he was holding a section of the *L.A. Times*. He paused in the doorway a moment, then walked over to the stereo and turned it off. "Debussy," he said. "Very nice."

"Come on, Max, what is it? It's so bad you have to put your teeth in to tell me?" He was so obviously ill at ease that I smiled at him, hoping to take some of the pressure off. "What's happened? They've outlawed horse racing in my absence?"

"The police were here," he said. "They want to talk to you."

"The police? What about?"

Wordlessly, he sat down, still holding the paper in his lap, and looked at me. "I guess I am not being very good at this sort of thing," he said at last. "I'm sorry."

"Max, what did the police want to see me about?"

"This dead girl."

"What dead girl?"

He tapped the newspaper and looked at me in anguish, his small blue eyes focused intently on me, as if he were afraid I might do something drastic. "You have heard nothing?"

"I have heard nothing, Max. I've been away, remember?" He didn't answer, but continued to stare at me, so I reached over and took the paper out of his lap.

The story jumped off the page and hit me very hard. A young woman named Amber Vivian Clark had been found dead in her apartment the previous Thursday morning by a cleaning woman who came once a week. She had been dead about thirty-six hours and was lying naked on the floor of her bedroom, her hands tied behind her back. Her throat had been slashed. The murderer had either had a key, come in with her, or had been admitted to the apartment, as there was no sign of a forced entry; but the crime itself had all the earmarks of a serial killing. "It looks like the work of the Westside Slasher," a spokesman for the police department had informed the press. The Slasher was suspected of having robbed and killed eight women of various ages during the past two years, all of them residents of the West Los Angeles area. Most of his victims had been sexually assaulted and all had had their throats cut. The women had all lived alone, two of the older ones in small houses, the others in apartments on the lower floors. In all of the previous cases, the killer had entered through a window and surprised his victims. This was the first time there had been no sign of a forced entry. The Slasher always left a mark in the form of a pentagram, but it was not known whether one had been found at this particular scene and the police would not discuss the details.

"Why would they wish to question you, Shifty?" Max asked. "You could not have done such a thing."

"I think I may have been the last person to see her alive, Max," I said. "We had dinner together that Tuesday night, before I left. Jesus, Max, I could have been with her."

"Then you would both be dead."

"Maybe not. If there had been two of us—excuse me, Max." I got up and went outside. I leaned against the wall of the building facing the pool and fought to get control of myself. It was late now and the water shimmered, reflecting the pale light of a half-moon, while a breeze rustled the fronds of the old palm trees that loomed above the building from the street side. Somewhere, out in that quiet city night, the pervert who had performed this atrocity was either sleeping peacefully in his bed or already mounting another assault on society. Clearly there was no justice and the quality of mercy was being strained everywhere. But then I had always known this, as most of us know it, as an abstract fact of life, a statistical presence. It isn't until such statistics are embodied in the reality of an event touching us personally that we begin to weep. Otherwise we should be crying out in anguish every moment of every day at the evil around us. Only the saints cry out for the universal suffering to stop and we get rid of them soon enough. No, there is no justice; there is only escape.

I turned around and walked back to Max's flat. He was standing in the door, his tall, thin, stooped old body and kindly face framed by the soft orange light from his living room. "I'm sorry, Max," I said. "I'll be okay. She was a very nice person. I only knew her a few weeks and not very well, but I liked her a lot."

"Yes, Shifty, I could see that. You want a cup of tea or cocoa?"

"No. No, thanks, Max. I'm going to go home. Do you have a name or a number?"

"Oh, oh, sure," Max said, groping in his pockets. "Wait."

And he disappeared into his flat, then came shuffling back holding a card out to me. "Here," he said. "When you got back, you should call, they said."

"Yeah, thanks." I took it from him and glanced at it.

"One very nice Negro man and a young one, two detectives," Max said. "Listen, Shifty, are you sure you are all right? You don't want to sit with me for a while?"

"No, Max, I don't. I mean, I really have to be alone right now. I mean, it isn't only that I liked her, Max. I think I liked her a little too much, even if she was a little nuts."

"Oh," he said, "it was like that."

"Yes." My God, I was crying, I realized. I turned away from poor old Max and went home to my empty apartment, where I could sit alone in the dark. I finally dozed off, still fully dressed, at about dawn.

The two homicide detectives at the West L.A. police station the next morning were courteous and efficient, even though I wasn't sure I had entirely convinced them of my innocence. I sat in a straight-backed wooden chair in a small, barren office and facing a desk behind which the younger of the two men interrogating me, a blond with a pale yellow mustache and light gray eyes, pecked at a typewriter as I talked. His name was Ken Harris and his approach to his job was solemn. He rarely looked at me, had little to say, and never smiled. I had the feeling that, if it had been up to him, I'd have been grilled into a confession. Luckily for me, most of the questions were asked by his older partner, a heavyset, big-bellied black man named Jude Morgan, who seemed to bulge inside his store-bought brown suit as if he had been stuffed into it. He carried a pistol in a shoulder holster and wore a small brown porkpie hat tilted back off his forehead. He had the stub of a spent cigar jammed into the corner of his mouth and chewed on it from time to time, shifting it back and forth like a wad of gum. He reminded me of a baseball manager trying to keep calm in his dugout while wondering whether to yank his starting pitcher. His dark face, under a full head of close-cropped gray hair, was unlined except for two deep creases from the bridge of his nose to his chin, and his eyes were those of a man in his mid-fifties who had seen far too many ugly scenes for one lifetime. His air of worn professionalism reassured me and I concentrated on answering him directly, while allowing Harris to get me down on paper pretty much on his own. "So that's about it," I concluded, after having provided a fairly detailed account of Amber's and my last dinner together. "I feel pretty rotten about this."

"Why? Why, rotten?" Harris asked, looking up from his machine.

"Because I really liked her," I said. "I hadn't known her very long, so I can't say I loved her. But if I'd been with her, maybe this wouldn't have happened to her."

"You had a fight that night, didn't you?" Jude Morgan asked from his post against the wall.

"Not really a fight," I explained. "More of an argument."

"The waiter in the restaurant heard you," Harris said. "He described it as a fight."

"What did you argue about?" Morgan asked.

"The food," I said. "Amber was a vegetarian and she was into health food. I thought the meal we had was one of the worst I'd ever eaten. I told her so and she got mad."

"You fought about the food?" Harris asked, as if I had admitted to masturbating in public.

"Well, yes. I—"

"Don't mind him, Mr. Anderson," Morgan said. "He don't know what food is. He thinks that meat-smelling bread they sell you at McDonald's is a meal, you hear? Don't pay him any mind. So what else did you argue about?"

"That night? Nothing. I wanted to go home with her, but she was still angry at me."

"But you argued a lot."

"Yeah, I guess we did, almost every time we saw each other," I admitted. "Amber had a lot of good causes she was committed to— wildlife, the environment, health, all good causes. I wanted her to ease up, enjoy her life a little more. I'd joke about it with her, but she'd get mad. She was a very serious person. Basically, I guess I admired her a lot." Suddenly, to my horror, I felt my eyes well up with tears again. I turned to look out the window and wiped them away. "Shit, I wish this hadn't happened to her." I looked back at Morgan. "How bad was it? Did he—abuse her?"

"Bad. You don't want to know the details, Mr. Anderson."

"No. Do you have any leads?"

"We have some prints we've been checking out," Morgan said, heaving himself away from the wall and easing himself down on the corner of the desk where Harris still sat, now leaning back in his chair, arms folded, eyes focused expressionlessly on me. "We'll need to get a set of yours before you go."

"Sure."

"We're also following up some leads, but I don't think they'll come to much." He blinked at me. "You say you've never been in her place?"

I shook my head. "No. We only went out together three times. Do you think you're dealing with this serial killer the papers write about?"

"Looks that way," Morgan said. "We don't know for sure." He smiled faintly at me. "What kind of magic do you do?"

"Sleight of hand, mostly."

"Like making stuff disappear."

"Yeah, that's right. Coins, cards, you know. Listen, Detective Morgan, this guy who did this to her, what did he do that was different?"

Morgan shifted uneasily inside his tight suit and scratched the back of his head. "I guess it's what he didn't do that bothers me," he said.

Harris looked at him. "Hey, Jude—"

Morgan cut him off with a wave of one hand. "Shit, Kenny, Mr. Anderson's got a right, I guess." Morgan looked at me again. "The Slasher leaves identification, in the form of a pentagram, usually drawn in black ink on the floor, the wall, or a piece of paper and left near the body. One or two times, he'd put it on the wall. Once he drew it in lipstick on a bathroom mirror. But always, somewhere, there'd be this pentagram. You know what that is, I'm sure."

"It's a magical symbol, a five-sided star," I said. "It's sometimes used in witchcraft or as a symbol for the devil."

"I figured you'd know, being as how you're a magician and all," the detective said, and then sighed. "Well, this time no pentagram."

"Maybe he was in a hurry."

"He had at least an hour, maybe more," Morgan said. "We figured the time of death at between eleven and eleven-thirty that night. And he could have hung around afterward."

"My God, he had all that time," I said, "and nobody heard anything?"

"Nope," the detective said. "And one other thing he didn't do—we're pretty sure he didn't take anything. The Slasher is also a thief."

"That's strange."

"Yes, it is. Just this once, see, he walks in like he's invited, does what he does and leaves. There's nothing missing. Her jewelry and checkbook and credit cards were in her bureau, her money was in her purse."

"You think maybe you're dealing with two serial killers?"

"Oh, I sure hope not," Jude Morgan said. "One of these loonies out there is bad enough. But two?" He shook his head sadly. "I sure hope not, Mr. Anderson." He blinked wearily at me. "Of course there are more similarities than differences, so it's probably the same guy. You planning on any more trips?"

"Not that I know of."

"Okay, you stay in touch, hear? Kenny will take you to get fingerprinted on the way out. And one other thing I would like."

"What's that?"

"I'd sure like to catch your act sometime," he said. "I got a grandson, he's just wild about magic and stuff. Maybe we could see you work sometime."

"Sure," I said. "Next time I'm at the Magic Castle or somewhere in town, I'll call you."

"I'd appreciate it."

I smiled at Harris. "You can come, too," I said. "You might enjoy it."

"I wouldn't count on that, Mr. Anderson," Morgan said. "Kenny ain't much on enjoying life. His idea of a good time is arresting people and putting them in jail. Very dedicated young officer. Wish we had more like him. You be good now, hear?"

"Fuck you, Morgan," Harris said, turning back to his typewriter. I waited until he finished and then followed him out, while Morgan sat there chewing on his cigar stub. I guess there's not much to do with guys like Harris. I mean, if I can't make them clap their hands in wonder and smile, I give up on them.

I went straight from the police station to Santa Anita. I needed desperately to clear my mind and nothing can do that for me more efficiently than a racetrack, where every day is a new beginning and nothing matters but the next race. I arrived about an hour and a half before post time, bought a *Form,* and sat down on a green bench near the paddock to do a little handicapping. I figured that if I tried really hard, I'd be able to forget about what had happened to Amber, at least for a couple of hours.

I wasn't able really to concentrate and the blocks of statistics on the page in front of me remained stubbornly indecipherable, just chunks of numbers on a sheet of paper. I folded up my *Form* and jammed it into my side pocket, got up, found a stretch of lawn behind one of the benches, and lay down in the sunlight. I hadn't had much sleep the night before and I soon dozed off, until the sound of male voices woke me up.

"So you like women with big, pendulous tits, Gino, is that it?"

"Hey, Dom, I didn't say that. I don't like them with big—what kind of tits?"

"Pendulous. Hanging down."

"No, Dom, I don't like that. You know I don't like that. You *know* that."

I opened my eyes. The two men named Gino and Dom were sitting with their backs to me on the bench a few feet away. I couldn't see their faces, but they were both heavyset, middle-aged men dressed in polyester slacks and sports coats and carrying *Racing Forms,* programs, and binoculars. Two veteran hard knockers, I surmised, arguing over women, loudly enough by this time to have roused me.

"So, Gino, you like broads with big, fat asses and thighs like oil drums, huh? You like that?"

"What are you saying, Dom, you know I don't like that," Gino answered. "Where'd you get this idea?"

"Oh, I thought you liked that."

"No, I don't like it."

"Okay, so you don't like it."

"No, you know I don't. You gone crazy or something?"

Dom didn't answer. I sat up and stretched. People were pouring into the track now through the main gates, buying programs and *Forms* and tout sheets and heading rapidly toward the grandstand. A crowd of beaders, two and three deep, lined the paddock railing, waiting for the horses entered in the first race to appear. There was a sense of expectation, of hurry in the air, the electricity of that pause in the theater before the curtain rises. It was twenty minutes to post time and I decided I'd better find Jay.

"So, Gino, you don't like women with big tits and fat thighs?" Dom asked.

"What the hell is it with you, Dom?" his friend answered. "I just told you."

"Okay, I got that," Dom said. "So if you don't like that, then how come you're fuckin' my wife?"

"What?"

"You heard me."

Gino stood up and leaned over his friend. "You gone crazy? What the hell are you saying? Me? Me fuck your wife? What are you, nuts? You gotta be nuts! I ain't even gonna talk to you no more. You're a fuckin' nut, you know that? A crazy man! I'm not even gonna talk to you! Fuckin' nut!" Red-faced and sweating, Gino backed away from his friend, then turned on his heel and stormed away, his binoculars hanging off his left shoulder and banging off his hip, his rolled-up *Form* clutched tightly in his hand like a club.

I stood up and Dom turned around and saw me. "Sorry," I said, "I couldn't help overhearing your conversation. You woke me up."

Dom looked at me sadly. He had a round, red-cheeked face with a small mustache and thin, arched eyebrows that swooped up his forehead as if they had been painted there. He looked like an old, fat frog squatting on a rock. "I was just asking," he said. "He didn't have to get so mad. Somebody's fuckin' her. I thought it might be him. Geez, thirty years I know him and he didn't even say who he liked in the double. That's friendship for you."

This is the kind of talk I seem to overhear only at racetracks and ordinarily it would have amused me, but today nothing seemed likely to raise my spirits. I left Dom to go on sitting disconsolately on his bench and went up the escalator into the grandstand to find Jay, whom I could at least count upon to keep me from betting recklessly and whose activities might provide additional diversion.

They didn't. Jay was glad to see me and his box was the scene of the customary comings and goings of his disciples and suppliants, engaged in their never-ending struggle with the pari-mutuel machines, but for once the action failed to charm me. I sat there pretty much like a stone, immobile in my depression, through the first six races on the card. None of Jay's entourage paid much attention to me, preoccupied as they were with the outcome of their wagers, but Jay noticed. During a lull before the seventh, when both Arnie and Angles had departed to bet and we were left alone, he turned to me. "So what's wrong, Shifty?" he asked. "I gave you a couple of good horses, but you haven't even made a move toward a window. You sick?"

"Yeah, I've got some sort of low-grade virus," I said. "It's kind of drained me." I didn't want to tell him about Amber, not now, perhaps never. There's not much room at the track for the vicissitudes visited upon us by the outside world and, besides, Jay and I were no longer as close as we had been, thanks to a falling out we'd had over an adventure with a horse in Mexico the year before.

"You taking something for it?"

"Time, just time, the old healer."

"Yeah." He leaned back in his chair and put his hands behind his head, looking very satisfied with himself. "Well, it's been a nice day for me," he said. "Two bets, two winners. I may risk a wager in the ninth. There's a speed horse in there I like. He's the lone F, out there in front all by himself going long."

"Sure. I hope you cash." I stood up. "I'm not doing myself much good here, Jay. I'm going home."

"Take care of yourself, Shifty. Oh, by the way," he added, as I started to leave, "what's your man Pickard doing with that cheapo in the nightcap?" I looked at him blankly. "The eleven horse. Charlie claimed him last week."

"What about him?"

"Take a look."

I did so. The animal Jay was referring to was a seven-year-old gelding named Sinful Slim, bought out of a race by Charlie for a tag of twelve thousand five hundred dollars and running in here for sixteen. "I don't know," I said. "Charlie claims cheap horses out of races, if he thinks he can improve them. He's probably just giving the horse a race in here, Jay. I wouldn't worry about him."

"I'm not worried," Jay said. "I wouldn't think of using him. The numbers are all wrong, the way the race comes up. But I thought Charlie didn't claim for Bedlington. He only has at least decent animals for him. And what's he doing putting Richards up? He never uses Richards. And who's Kennedy? Is that the Rose Bowl queen?"

I looked again, and this time more closely, at my program. Sure enough, there was Richards's name listed as the rider. And the owners of the beast were identified as Bedlington and Kennedy. "Must be. I don't know for sure, Jay," I confessed.

"You have to admit it's unusual."

"Yes, it is. I'll have to ask him about it."

It surprised me, all right, that Bedlington had obviously bought the horse for Melinda. She had clearly moved into his life in a definitive and ultimately unpredictable way. And whose idea had it been to engage Richards? Her friend Angel? Certainly not Charlie, who distrusted and disliked the jockey nearly as much as the people who had bet on him over the years. I'd have to find out about it, simply as a matter of interest, from the trainer. But not today and maybe not tomorrow. I was exhausted and emotionally drained. I drove straight home, fell into bed, and slept for ten hours.

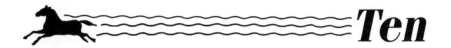

Ten

DOG DAYS

"Were you here when this horse ran for me?" Charlie asked, as we sipped coffee together at Clockers' Corner a few days later.

"Which one?" I scanned the animals galloping past us as they came through the gap, after the break, on their way out to the main track. It was about seven-thirty and overcast, with a winter chill and a hint of rain in the air. The riders were bundled up and the horses seemed to be steaming lightly as they moved out onto the racing surface for the last session of morning workouts.

"The bay colt with Lang up," the trainer said, "on the other side of the roan."

"What's his name?"

"That's Rudolph."

"Oh, yeah. No, I missed the race," I said. "I was on my cruise. How'd he do?"

"No good. Eighth, I think. I'll have to ship him down to Caliente to break his maiden," Charlie said. "Anyway, that ain't why I asked you. You know what Lang says to me when he comes back?"

"I imagine he had some excuse, right?"

"No, that ain't it," Charlie said, giving his cap a tug and settling himself comfortably against the rail to watch his horse break into a gallop as he moved up the track away from us. " 'I don't know what happened,' Lang says. 'The horse did everything right but run.' 'Oh, really?' I said. 'So what did he do right? Canter nice to the gate? Kiss you afterward?' Christ, I hate these jocks. And I hate these cheap horses even worse. This ain't a racehorse, this is a real bum."

"So if you don't like cheap horses," I asked, "then how come you're claiming them?"

"A man's gotta have some horses to run for him, Shifty," the trainer said. "You can't win races without horses and I ain't got any rich owners."

"You've got Bedlington."

"I guess he don't want to spend the money. Prices for good horses are up twenty, thirty percent this year."

"He never claimed before, Charlie."

"Well, I guess it's this girl. He wanted to buy a couple of horses for her. Anyway, what he does is, he calls me up and he says get me a couple of horses fast and he tells me he's got about fifty grand to spend. So I took this one that run the other day—"

"Sinful Slim?"

"Yeah. He's got an ankle, but I can control it for a while and maybe crank a race or two out of him at the right price. Last time was a gimme to make him eligible for the cheapest race they card here. I told the jock to let him run a little and then wrap up. Now I'll freshen him and work on that ankle, get maybe one good work into him, find a spot and let him run. He once had a little class and he's competitive."

"And the other one? What's her name?"

"Beatific. Oh, she can run. That's a real gambling horse, Shifty. She's got speed, and the guy I took her from, Whitley, he's been running her short. I think she wants to stretch out and she'll do better. Fact is, I'm planning to win with both of them, if I can keep 'em in one piece." He raised a hand to shade his eyes and help him focus better as he peered out across the infield toward his animal. "Look at that bum," he muttered. "He runs like a moose."

"You know, Charlie, it's strange," I said. "Three weeks ago, Bedlington was on the verge of committing suicide and all of a sudden he's acting like a teenager."

"You don't know the half of it," Charlie said. "He and his girlfriend, they're out here nearly every day now. Bedlington stays put in the Turf Club, mostly, but she's all over the place. Comes down to the paddock every time I got a horse running, asks me a whole bunch of dumb questions, wants to know everything about the horses."

"Horses in general?"

"Mostly just about his."

"What kind of things?"

"Oh, you know, Shifty, mostly about how they're doing and all. She don't know anything, but she talks like a gal who wants to gamble. You know she moved in with him, don't you?"

"No, but it doesn't surprise me," I said. "I know he wanted her to, but I wasn't sure about how she felt. She could be his daughter, literally."

"Yeah? That so?" Charlie drained his Styrofoam cup, crumpled it up and threw it into a nearby trash container. "Goddamn," he said, "he sure don't act fatherly to her. I can't believe that old man is so nuts about some chippie. I thought he was smarter than that."

"Weren't you ever in love, Charlie?"

"Every dog has his day," he said. "But I got over it." He began to walk back toward the stable area. "Come on, we're about through here. I got 'em all out early today."

"How's Mad Margaret doing?" I asked, as we strolled toward the gap and his barn.

"Not bad. She came back awful tired after that dumb race Lang rode on her. I'm gonna give her a couple of weeks more. You can't beat up on young horses like he done. Dumb jocks, I hate 'em all."

"So you're mad at Lang. Is that why you're using Richards now?"

"He ain't no worse than most of them," the trainer said. "No, it wasn't my idea, Shifty. It was Bedlington's. He said some friend of this girl's suggested it. It don't matter to me. He's as good as any of 'em."

"Oh, come on, Charlie," I protested. "You're not going to tell me Richards is as good a rider as Leavenworth and Singer and Medina? You know what they say about Richards, don't you?"

"About how he doesn't get horses out of the gate and all? Yeah, I know he pulls that stuff, but he can ride as good as anyone, if he wants to."

"If he wants to."

"He stiffs me one time and I'll take him off," the trainer said. "Mostly it don't matter who you put up, Shifty. Some horses you could tie a monkey on their backs and they'd win for you. Others, they won't run if you was to put a firecracker up their ass."

"Well, that's what you trainers think," I said, "but that's because you're an arrogant bunch. The fact is, I have a lot of respect for jockeys."

"I don't mind the good ones, the ones that get that little extra effort out of your common horse and make him win," he said. "Don't get me wrong, Shifty. I just blow my top sometimes, when I see the dumb things some jocks will do in a race, no matter what you tell them. One thing I don't never forget, though."

"And what's that, Charlie?"

"It's the only profession in the world where an ambulance follows you around when you're working," he said. "That's something to keep in mind, ain't it?"

"You going to ride Richards on all your horses now?"

"No, just Bedlington's. He's the owner and he gets to call some of the shots." The trainer chuckled softly. "Anyway, one bad move and he's off, if I get to say anything about it."

"You said some friend of Melinda's suggested Richards? Must be that blonde he's been dating," I said. "She and Melinda knew each other over in Europe."

"That so? Well, whatever the reason, it don't matter. The boy can ride, if he wants to."

"Boy? He's got to be in his mid-forties, Charlie."

"If they ride, they're boys to me, Shifty. Come on, let's take a look here."

I spent the next hour or so hanging around Charlie's barn, watching him and his small outfit work around his animals. His stable, a long, low sandstone building with a green roof, was tucked up in one corner of the backside, away from the main arteries along which horses and vehicles moved in irregular streams, so it was quiet. There were just the horses, most of them now in their stalls, sleeping, munching, or staring stolidly out at the world around them, and the men and women who cared for them. The atmosphere was relaxed but somehow intense, like that of an acting company on the road. Each human being had an everyday set of small tasks to perform, locked into routines made familiar by endless repetition, but also spiced by the unpredictability of the outcome. The men and women of this small, self-contained world were merely doing a job, functioning as stagehands and technicians at the service of the performers, the horses—the indifferent, dumb, magnificent-looking protagonists of the drama.

I had seen Charlie, in his role of director of this slightly lunatic enterprise, become cynical, foulmouthed, angry, exasperated by his world, but I thought of him as a happy man. He was in touch not only with mundane realities, such as the need to make money and the welfare of his company, but also with something less tangible and boring—an inherent nobility and integrity at the heart of the whole operation. For what does any real horseman ultimately desire from his curious, highly specialized pursuit? Only the realization of his dream, that somewhere down the line, maybe not tomorrow but someday, one of these players he tends and nurtures and fusses over will step out on a main stage somewhere and bring the house down. Is it only for the loot we are cheering when a Secretariat or a Ruffian wins a big race? Is it only because he earned more money than any horse in history before him that we clap for an ordinary-looking old gelding named John Henry, when he's brought back to the racetrack from time to time and paraded before the stands? Charlie knew what the secret was at the heart of the matter. "That old bum," I heard him say one day, when old John Henry jogged arthritically past us during an afternoon celebration at Santa Anita, "even when he got beat he thought he'd won. He didn't know what it was to lose."

"Some bum, Charlie," I told him.

"Yeah, he had a heart as big as a basketball." And he'd stood there and watched the old horse go by one more time. He'd been somebody's dream come true.

By nine-thirty or so, the work was over. The horses were all in their stalls, the grooms and hotwalkers had gone home, and Charlie and I sat in his tack room and talked some more. I don't even remember now exactly what we talked about, something to do with the way the world of racing turns, but certainly nothing of earthshaking importance. It helped to pass the time and I was still in a mood to seek oblivion, however temporary. "You know, Shifty," Charlie said later, as we got up to leave, "you're looking kind of beat."

"I haven't been sleeping too well, Charlie," I said, but I didn't tell him why. Every time I closed my eyes these days I saw Amber's face.

I had a couple of hours to kill before post time, so, on impulse, I drove into Pasadena and parked across the street from Derek Flanders's office. I hadn't spoken to him since getting back and hearing about Amber and he had not returned my six or seven calls. Each time I'd been answered by a male voice on a machine asking me to leave a message and I had done so, but to no avail. I felt a need to speak to him, for some reason, perhaps because the feeling had been growing in me that he knew something about Amber that I didn't know, some small bit of information about her that might let in a sliver of light and give me comfort. She had left so many unanswered questions dangling in the air between us. Not that I suspected Flanders of anything, but what if Amber hadn't been murdered by the Westside Slasher or some other serial killer? Who else in her life could have wanted her dead? Who could possibly have done such a thing to her?

I was sitting in my car, turning these considerations over in my head and wondering what I was going to say to Flanders that wouldn't offend him, when the front door opened and the lawyer himself appeared. He paused for a moment to say something to a pleasant-looking young man standing just inside the landing, then he turned and walked carefully down the short flight of steps to the sidewalk. He had a worn, dark brown leather briefcase in one hand and a set of car keys in the other. I got out of my car and walked across the street. "Mr. Flanders?"

He turned and peered at me, then nodded. "Hello, Anderson, how are you?" he said. "What are you doing here?"

"I've called you a few times since I got back," I said, "but I haven't heard from you."

"I know, I know," the lawyer said. "I've been really busy. I'm sorry." He glanced at his watch. "And I'm running very late now. I really can't talk to you."

"I just wanted to ask you about Amber."

"About Amber? What about her? It's a terrible thing, unbelievable. My God, what a world we live in, Anderson. I suppose you were the last person to see her alive."

"I assume that's why you gave my name to the police. You did, didn't you?"

"Well, of course. I knew you'd been seeing her and that you were having dinner with her that night. She told me so. Obviously, I had to inform them."

"Sure, I understand."

"I don't imagine you had anything to do with it, of course. Surely you understand that, Anderson."

"Yes, but I was wondering—"

"What? I really am in a hurry." He walked up to his car, the dark blue BMW sedan, and inserted a key in the door.

"Well, was there anyone in her life who could have done this to her? You see, Mr. Flanders, I didn't know her very well—"

"No one in his right mind could have had a motive to do such a thing, Anderson," he said, looking up at me. "It was clearly the work of some psychopath, probably this so-called Westside Slasher." He opened his car door. "Please forgive me, but I really must go."

"When can we talk?"

"I don't imagine we have anything to talk about, do we?"

"Maybe not," I said. "But I also wanted to ask you what you think of this business with Lucius."

"What business?"

"About this girl, Melinda Kennedy."

"Look, Anderson, Lucius is not only my oldest friend, he's my client," the lawyer said. "I can't talk to you about him now and certainly not out here in the street."

"Okay, sorry. I'm just confused and a little puzzled. You're not worried anymore about him, then?"

"Of course I'm worried about him. He's an unbalanced person, always has been. The way he's acting now with this girl may even be a sign of advancing senility or Alzheimer's or something. But I'm keeping an eye on it. At least it's kept him from killing himself, I guess we have to bear that in mind."

"What if she turns out in actuality to be his daughter? He's acting like he's in love with her."

The lawyer sat down behind the wheel, rolled down his window and looked out at me, as he started his car. "Anderson, you'll forgive me, but what my client does or doesn't do is really no concern of yours," he said. "I think it would be quite improper for me to discuss his affairs with you."

"You didn't think so a few weeks ago."

"That was then, this is now," he said. "I'm grateful for your help with Lucius and I appreciate your concern. If you see him and you think something else may be seriously wrong, I'd value your staying in touch, of course. Call me in a few days, if you like, and we'll talk then. I'm very busy these days, but I'm sure we can find some time. Until then, thanks and forgive me." And he drove quickly away from me.

He may have been in a big hurry and very busy, but something about his uneasiness and his very evident reluctance to talk to me at all troubled me. So I sat in my car for a few minutes to think it over, then I drove to a corner gas station a few blocks away on Colorado and called his office. This time a live male voice answered. "Coutts, Riley, and Flanders. May I help you?"

"Yes, hi. We've been expecting Mr. Flanders here, but he's late," I said. "Do you happen to know if he's on his way?"

"Yes, he is," the voice said. "Is this Mr. Freeman?"

"No, I'm his assistant. I usually speak to a Miss Clark. Isn't she there anymore?"

"No, sir. My name is Jeffrey, I'm temporary. I've been here a couple of days."

"Oh, I see."

"Mr. Flanders left here a few minutes ago," Jeffrey said. "He was running late, I know, but he's on his way. He should be there pretty soon."

I laughed. "I hope he doesn't get lost again. He had the wrong address last time. Do you want to check it, just in case? If it's still wrong, he may call in for it."

"Oh, sure. Just a moment," Jeffrey said. He came back on the line about thirty seconds later. "Hello?"

"Yeah, I'm here."

"Here it is." And he gave me an address on Seward, a street in Hollywood, not far from La Brea. "Is that right?"

"You got it. Okay, I guess he's just late."

"Well, he isn't *that* late, is he? It's only a few minutes after eleven now."

"I know, but we worry about him."

"Well, I'll tell him you called. May I have your last name?"

"Oh, don't bother. I'm sure he'll show up now. Thanks." I hung up before Jeffrey could ask me again.

I now had a choice. Either I could follow Flanders into downtown Hollywood, about half an hour away by freeway, and miss the first two or three races, or I could make a note of the address and check it out later. I sat in my car and thought about it. I asked myself, for instance, why I was suddenly acting like a detective in regard to old Flanders and I couldn't really come up with a rational explanation; obviously he couldn't have had anything to do with Amber's senseless murder. But I found myself still wondering why I had suddenly become such a nuisance to him, such an unwanted intrusion into his affairs. After all, I had put him back in touch with his old client and asked nothing from him. The whole idea had been to keep our loony aristocratic friend from easing himself snobbishly out of life and suddenly, with the appearance on the scene of Melinda Kennedy, there was no longer anything to worry about. I couldn't think of a lawyer in the world with a client like Bedlington who wouldn't have worried. Well, maybe he was worried; he just didn't want me in on it anymore.

All of this was pure speculation on my part, of course, but then I have a weakness for this sort of thing. Also, I always seem to get caught up in the middle of some sort of intrigue or find myself standing hip-deep in somebody's mess. Trouble seems to attach itself to me like a recurring virus and I just have to live with it. Then, too, I have to admit that I enjoy it. Ferreting out secrets and solving puzzles is what I do at the racetrack, which is a great training ground for life.

All right, I finally decided, I will sniff around old Flanders and I'll also try to stay in touch with Bedlington, whether he ever calls me again or not. I wasn't working and it would give me something to do. But all that could wait now. I had read the *Form* the night before and I really liked the card and for the first time since my return I felt like going racing. So I drove back to Santa Anita. In life, priorities have to be observed.

 *Eleven*

NO PAIN

I couldn't do anything wrong that afternoon. I sat in Jay's box, indifferent to the comings and goings of his entourage, and concentrated on isolating contenders from the total of one hundred eleven horses entered on the card. I couldn't miss. The winners fluttered up from the tangled under-brush of statistics in my *Form* like bright yellow butterflies. I hit the daily double for two hundred forty-eight dollars, a six-to-one shot in the third, a twelve-to-one long shot in the fourth, a three-hundred dollar Exacta in the fifth. I passed the sixth, because I almost never bet on anything at odds of less than two to one and I didn't think I could beat the four-to-five favorite in the race, which turned out to be an accurate assessment. In the seventh, a contentious sprint for a full field of ten down the hillside turf course, I risked two hundred dollars in the place hole on a five-to-two shot and doubled my money when he just got up for second by a nose, two lengths behind a ten-to-one outsider. By then I had about seventeen hundred dollars in profit in my pockets and I decided to wrap up for the day. The feature race had only six horses in it, with a pair of cofavorites who figured to go off at even money or thereabouts, and the ninth was a gallop at a mile and sixteenth for cheap claimers, the sort of contest Jay refers to as "the hospital handicap," a race in which most of the horses appear on the track bandaged to their eyeballs like Egyptian mummies and are suffering from various crippling infirmities. I decided simply to relax for the last two races and enjoy my winnings, so I folded up my *Form,* stuck it under my chair and grinned conspiratorially at Jay.

"A good day, Shifty, eh?" he said, eyeing me cautiously. He himself had had a couple of disappointments and was counting on the ninth to bail him out.

"Pretty good, Jay, thanks," I said. "You know how some days out here it all falls into place. This was one of them and I guess I was overdue."

"It's always a nice feeling," he said. "I had a good opinion myself out here, but I lost a couple of photos. Can't be helped. Not every day can be Christmas."

"Maybe if it could, we'd stop coming," I said. "It's the challenge of it that keeps us trying, isn't it?"

"One of the reasons, sure."

We were temporarily alone in the box. Angles had lost every race and had departed in a fury after finishing one-three in the Exacta in the fifth, while Arnie, a far more cautious investor but still a loser on the day, had retreated inside to one of the refreshment counters to nurse his soured stomach back to health with a bowl of soup. "I knew you were winning big," Jay said. "I can always tell. You sort of bounce in your seat when you get a winner. You've been doing that every race."

"Did I make it that obvious?"

"Only to me, because I know you pretty well," the handicapper said. "I think Arnie knows. Every horse you mentioned ran well. Angles and Fido and the others, they're so oblivious to the world around them they wouldn't know at post time if a quake hit and the grandstand came down around their ears."

"Well, I saw no reason to flaunt my successes in their faces," I said.

"Ah, track etiquette! For most of this gang out here, it's important not only to win but to flaunt it in people's faces. Unclassy, Shifty, distinctly unclassy."

Jay and I abided by a set of unwritten rules of behavior at the track that we had evolved together over the years. We considered it bad form, for instance, to exult in public over a big coup while all around us others were losing. Unless, of course, the losers were desperados like Fido or the

Weasel, players who were either arrogant about their expertise or celebrated for their indifference to suffering in general. "It's a pleasure to stick it to that guy," Jay told me one afternoon, after he'd loudly rooted in a long shot to nose out Fido's even-money favorite in a stakes race, causing the tout to bolt white-faced out of his box. "He's stiffed more suckers than Wall Street." "And you know, Shifty," Jay had said to me another time, "unless at least twenty percent of your operating capital is riding on some horse, it's really not appropriate to make a spectacle of yourself in rooting your animal home. Class is always cool."

I got up to go and cash and Jay smiled. "Don't blow it back on this race, Shifty," he said. "You can't beat the favorite. I do have a horse in the ninth."

"I'm through for the day, Jay," I said. "You go with luck, but you don't push it. Another good rule."

"Right. By the way, have you seen your millionaire?"

"Not recently."

"He's here, with the Rose Bowl queen."

"Where? In the Turf Club?"

"No. He's sitting in a front-row box just beyond the finish line. Angles saw them." Jay laughed. "Angles has a lot of unmentionable acts he'd like to perform on her and he ran through a few of them for our benefit earlier, when you were inside at the windows. I thought you might know."

"No, Lucius doesn't require my services much anymore, now that he's got Melinda to occupy his time. I guess I'll go say hello."

After I cashed my tickets and added to the sizable wad of bills in my pocket, I went looking for my plutocrat. I found him where Jay had spotted him earlier, sitting in a box with a formidable-looking dowager named Matilda Pond Worthing. I had seen her around the track for years and knew that she owned horses, mostly well-bred ones trained by an incompetent named Gerald Monkton, but I had never met her. She was a large, squarely built woman of about seventy with hard blue eyes, a tousled mane of dyed blond hair, and a prognathous jaw that looked strong enough to snap through steel cables. She was wearing a dark brown tweed suit, flat-heeled brown walking shoes, carried a large Gucci shoulder bag, and had a triple strand of pearls around her neck. Bedlington, in his light gray slacks and navy blue blazer, looked elegantly effeminate beside her, an impression confirmed when he introduced her to me and she seized my hand in a grip that made me wince. "Careful, Matty, you don't want to mangle the lad's digits," Bedlington said, as I withdrew my paralyzed fingers. "Those are the tools of his trade. He's a magician."

She looked at me disapprovingly. "Another of your odd entourage culled from the fringes of life, no doubt," she said, in a harsh, metallic voice echoing somewhere up behind her nasal passages. "Where do you find these people, Lucius?"

Bedlington grinned at me. "Don't mind Matty," he said. "Her manner is nasty, but she has a heart of tin." He turned to her. "Anderson here is the Mozart of magic. Mind your manners, Matty, or I'll have to take you over my knee, as I used to when we were growing up." He winked at me. "We're distantly related, second cousins or something of that sort," he explained. "Matty's ashamed to admit it. Sit down, Shifty."

"Ever since you began consorting with ruffians," she snapped, as I joined them, "and filling your house full of unsavory trash."

"I presume you're referring to my past indiscretions."

"You were always a dirty little boy, Lucius, and I suppose it's natural that you should grow up to become a dirty old man."

"You never liked any of my wives either, as I recall."

"I never understood why you had to marry all of them."

"Noblesse oblige."

"Oh, nonsense, really! And now this one! My God, Lucius, where did you find her?"

"She was a present from one of my exes, Matty, if you must know," he said, quite happily. "Pretty little thing, isn't she?"

"Yes, but who *is* she? What did you say her last name was?"

"Kennedy, Melinda Kennedy. Matty, you're becoming quite deaf."

"Don't shout, it's rude. Kennedy? Did you say Kennedy?" She recoiled in horror, as if she had caught him picking his nose in public.

"Oh, not those Kennedys, Matty," Bedlington hastily assured her. "Her father was an oilman from Texas—"

"Good God!"

"—but she herself was raised in Europe, mostly in Italy. She's really quite respectable."

"But who is she? What is she doing here?"

"Brightening my life considerably." He cleared his throat. " 'In the evening of my days, with the sun of life declining—' "

"Oh, shut up! That damned Gilbert and Sullivan! You can't be serious, Lucius? She's a child. Does she have any money?"

"I don't know. Some, I suppose. Her mother's remarried a number of times and all of the husbands seem to have done pretty well."

"Why don't you let me introduce her to my nephew, Rutherford?" she said. "She's just the right age for him."

"Rutherford? Nancy's boy? I wondered what had happened to him."

"He's now in his ninth and we all hope final year at Princeton, after which Langley will take him into the business."

"The bank?"

"Of course. What did you imagine? That he would be managing a fast-food chain or a discount clothing store? Langley *is* the Worthing Trust."

"Yes, I know. How is Langley?"

"Fine, never been better."

"I heard there was a little trouble, some sort of investigation—"

"Those Communists in Washington," she said angrily. "But we know how to handle them. Don't worry, Lucius, you aren't involved. At least I don't think you are."

"How could I be involved?"

"Exactly. Now about Rutherford, we have to get him settled. He's basically a good boy, he merely needs guidance, a strong hand on the tiller—"

"Which you will supply."

"Indeed. And a good marriage would help, especially if the child is wealthy enough to keep him in the Worthing style. His salary at the bank will be modest for a few years, till he fits in and gets the hang of things, and, as you know, Robert, the boy's father, never amounted to a hill of beans. Nancy's had a very hard time."

"I remember Rutherford. Has he managed to grow a chin since I last saw him?"

"Really, Lucius, what can you mean? The boy's no Adonis, admittedly, but he's extremely well-bred—"

"He's not a horse, Matty, and Melinda's not a brood mare."

"You're talking like a Red," she said, rising majestically out of her seat. "I should have known better. I feel sorry for you, Lucius."

"Don't go, Matty," Bedlington said, unruffled by her indignation. "I didn't mean to offend you."

She gazed down at him with unconcealed pity. "I am not leaving because you have offended me," she said. "Your behavior has always been offensive to me, but that is not the reason. You seem to have forgotten, if you ever did know it, that I own racehorses. One of them has just competed and I must find Gerald. Perhaps I'll see you later, perhaps not. I may call, Lucius, about this girl. You'll arrange an introduction, if she's suitable."

"Matty, I keep telling you—"

She cut him off with an imperious wave of the hand, like a Wagnerian opera conductor. "And I don't want to hear another word from you about it. I'll decide and that's settled." She sailed majestically out of her box toward the Turf Club.

Bedlington smiled at me. "Extraordinary, isn't she? Usually I try to avoid her, but today she spotted us in the Turf Club and insisted that we join her. She can't stand me, but she's obviously anxious to marry off her no-good nephew to somebody with money. I heard the business was in trouble."

"What sort of trouble?"

"Something involving bonds and some congressman or other. A sordid affair of some sort. I don't pay much attention to business, you know. I leave all that sort of thing to Derek."

"Well, she must drop a bundle on her horses," I observed. "Monkton's a crook who hardly ever wins a race. I know him. He's a magician, too."

"He is?"

"He can make any horse of his disappear at the eighth pole. Why does she use him?"

"I suppose because he's presentable in the Turf Club."

I understood what Bedlington meant. Monkton was in his early forties, good-looking, always fashionably and expensively dressed, even around his shedrow, where he never sullied himself with any form of manual labor. His true element as a horseman was the Turf Club dining room, where he could talk the game from behind his tinted lenses with his potential clients. He knew very little about horses, but he could train owners, which is how he had managed to survive over the years.

"The other reason," Bedlington continued, "is that Matty can't bear to be wrong about anything. And where would she go, if she fired him? She has bad horses, because Monkton picked them out for her, and no good trainer would want them in his barn, so she would have to start over. And how many real horsemen could she have a dialogue with? As you've probably surmised, dear boy, she's a formidable snob. Can you imagine her having an intimate tête-à-tête with Mr. Charles Pickard? No, it's easier for her to go on losing rather than admit a mistake."

"I hope her husband doesn't run his bank that way."

"Well, he's rapacious enough to be successful. Langley has impoverished several Third World countries with his loans. Enough is never enough for Langley."

Melinda Kennedy came hurrying up the aisle toward us as the horses entered in the feature appeared for the post parade. "Oh, Bunny," she said, "there's the most darling little gray horse with a long tail in here! I had to bet on him! Hello, Shifty, how are you? Oh, Bunny, he's so cute!"

She fell breathlessly into her seat beside him and gave his arm a quick hug, as she continued to chatter about her cute horse.

Bedlington blushed with delight. Outwardly, he maintained his aristocratic aplomb, but behind that cool, cynical exterior he seemed to have crumbled, like a pile of rubble hidden by a baroque façade. I was astonished. I hadn't imagined the extent of the inroads Melinda Kennedy had made into his life or the degree of influence she now seemed to exercise over him. When she rushed away again to bet on her horse with the fifty-dollar bill Bedlington had given her, I asked him how she was doing.

"Doing? In what way, dear boy?"

"Her film school."

"Oh, that. She's enrolled in some sort of workshop."

"Really? Where?"

"I don't know, dear boy. They have classes, mostly at night. Someplace in downtown Hollywood called Stage Two. It's very convenient."

"For what?"

"For me, dear boy. Her class meets three times a week and otherwise I have Melinda all to myself," he said. "She's an absolutely fascinating creature, don't you think?"

"She's very beautiful."

"Stunning. And so bright. She couldn't possibly be Isabel's daughter, of that I'm absolutely convinced."

"So whose daughter is she?"

"I haven't a clue, dear boy. Perhaps she was adopted, who knows?"

"Is that what Melinda told you?"

"She's hinted at it, yes."

"Lucius—"

He held up a warning hand and stopped me. "I know what you think, dear boy. Derek has already read me a lecture on the subject. I may just ask you to find out for me."

"Me?"

"Certainly. Why not? You wouldn't mind, would you, if I made it profitable enough for you?" He again held up his hand. "Hush, dear boy, here she comes. We'll discuss this some other time, all right?"

"Whatever you say, Lucius."

Melinda came back, her face pink with excitement. When the horses broke from the gate, she again jumped up in the air and began to scream for her favorite. Unfortunately, her cute gray with the long tail and the darling manner ran like a mule and came in last, fifteen lengths behind the winner. Melinda slumped back into her seat, her face a child's mask of disappointment. "Oh, that's so sad," she said. "What do you suppose happened?"

"The horse ran absolutely true to form," I explained. "He was a bum going into the race and he ran like the bum he is."

Melinda whirled on me. "Oh, Shifty, how cruel!" she said. "He's so adorable-looking. I just *knew* he was going to win!" She gazed soulfully at Bedlington. "Oh, Bunny, I'm so sorry. You shouldn't have let me bet on him at all. I suppose you knew he wasn't going to win either."

Bedlington put a consoling arm around her shoulders and kissed her on the forehead. "Now, darling, don't fret. It's only a horse race," he said. "And besides, you're supposed to be having fun out here. What's a few dollars lost here and there? I've been in racing for thirty years and I've never had a winning one."

Melinda quickly brightened, kissed him back on the cheek, and sat up very straight, like an eager little bird on a branch. "Anyway, that's over," she said. "Now we have to bet on the next race. My friend Angel tells me that this really cute horse in here called Wiggles should win. Lonny's riding him."

"What about it, Shifty?" Bedlington asked me. "Does this paragon of horseflesh have a chance?"

"Not in my opinion," I said. "He's one for thirty-one lifetime and utterly devoid of speed. But in this kind of a race anything can happen. Personally, I wouldn't risk a dime in here."

"Oh, you're such an old grouch," Melinda said, pouting adorably at me. "*I'm* going to go down and talk to Angel again." She bounced to her feet and skipped out of the box toward the paddock. With her mane of dark curls flashing behind her and her long legs, she looked like a nymph in flight. Ours were not the only pairs of male eyes following her progress.

"She's so adorable. 'Skipping hither, skipping thither, nobody knows why or whither,'" Bedlington said. "Well?"

"I haven't a clue," I confessed.

"*Iolanthe,* dear boy."

Wiggles looked terrible in the post parade. He sported heavy front bandages and his neck was coated by a lather of foamy sweat that his rider, Lonny Richards, periodically had to scrape off with his whip. But he ran the race of his life to finish second, with Richards pumping and slashing to bring him through a tiny hole along the rail, saving just enough ground to hold off the closing favorite, two lengths behind the four-to-one third choice in the contest. I noted with some interest that Wiggles, listed at fifteen to one in the morning line, had gone off at six to one, a significant drop in the odds. Somebody had liked the horse well enough to bet heavily on him, a fact doubly confirmed by a low Exacta payoff of seventy-eight dollars for every five-dollar ticket. "What should it have been, dear boy?" Bedlington asked, when I commented on the discrepancy.

"At least a hundred and twenty, normally," I answered. "Somebody liked this horse."

"But I told you," Melinda said, her face flushed with excitement, "Angel said that Lonny liked the horse a lot. They were all betting on him. I bet him across the board. Look!" And she held up a three-hundred-dollar ticket now worth about five hundred for us to contemplate.

"Who's 'they'?" I asked.

"Oh, Angel and her friends," Melinda said. "They all bet on Lonny when he tells them to. Angel is just making so much money. Oh, Bunny, isn't this fun? You're so sweet to bring me here. I just adore you!" She flung her arms around him, kissed him, and ran out of the box, presumably to cash her ticket.

Bedlington winked at me. " 'Oh, the happy days of doing! Oh, the sighing and the suing!' " he sang. " 'When a wooer goes a-wooing, oh, the sweets that never cloy!' Well?"

"Sorry, Lucius."

"*Yeomen,* Act Two."

He suddenly looked old and foolish to me. I got up to leave. "Shifty, please check with me in a couple of days," he called after me. "I'm quite serious about possibly requiring your services again."

"Of course, Lucius."

I took my time leaving, strolling contentedly out through the grandstand, my seventeen-hundred-dollar winning wad bulging reassuringly in my left front pants pocket. I stopped in the men's room at the far end and emerged a few minutes later to find Melinda talking animatedly with her old friend, Angel Price. They were so intent on their conversation that they failed to notice me, so I bent down over a nearby water fountain and lingered long enough to see Melinda suddenly reach into her purse and give Angel a couple of bills. She didn't seem happy about it either. The blonde took the money and dropped it into her shoulder bag, then walked away from her. Melinda, obviously angry, watched her go, then hurried back in the direction of Matilda's box. I straightened up and resumed my departure.

Whodoyalike fell into step beside me, as I headed toward the escalator. "God, I couldn't pick my nose today. How'd you do?"

"Not bad. How much did you lose?"

"You know that horse, Chinese Dentist?"

"Yeah, what about him?"

"That's how much I lost."

"I don't get it."

"Tooth hurty."

"Two hundred and thirty dollars?"

"You got it, Shifty. Maybe I should take novocaine."

Ah, the track, the track! I went out toward the parking lot, happily humming a little *Rigoletto* to myself. G and S is okay, but Verdi . . .

Twelve

DIVERSIFYING

Stage Two turned out to be a one-story, red-brick factory building set well back from the sidewalk and with a small parking lot in front. It stood halfway up the block from the nearest avenue, in an unprepossessing neighborhood of old wooden-frame houses and small commercial enterprises, flanked by ragged-looking front lawns, empty lots strewn with trash, and trees seeming to wilt visibly in the polluted air. Directly across the street, a tribe of gypsies occupied an old house with a front porch on which several sullen-looking men sat gazing disinterestedly at the passing scene, while their women and children were presumably out scavenging for a living. I parked directly in front of them, locked the Datsun for a change, as the occupants of the porch stared glumly at me, and rang the bell I found on the wall beside the front entrance to the workshop. No one answered, so I peered into the box office, which was closed, then walked up the alley to the right toward the back of the building, where I found a female mite dressed in jeans, sneakers, and a gray sweatshirt lethargically daubing paint on a canvas flat. "Hi," I said, "I'm looking for Ted Freeman."

She looked up, brushing an errant lock of hair back off her forehead. She was a pale-faced brunette with large, lustrous brown eyes, who looked as if she hadn't had a good meal in several weeks. "Oh, he's teaching now," she said, "but you can go in and wait." She aimed her wet brush back toward an open door directly behind her. "In there."

"Okay, thanks," I said. "Will he be long?"

The girl shrugged. "I don't know. You never know with him. I mean, if it's a tough scene—I mean, he can go on for hours, you know. He likes to hear himself talk."

"Shall I go in?"

She shrugged. "Sure, if you want. Just don't make any noise or he starts screaming."

I walked past her into a corridor whose walls were lined with posters of the company's past theatrical productions and photographs of workshop members in performance and rehearsal. I could hear the sound of voices coming from behind the wall to my right, so I kept on going toward the front of the building, found a door, and opened it.

"All right now, people," I heard an abrasive tenor voice call out, "I want the scene again from the beginning. And for God's sake, Bonnie, this time don't just play it, *be* it! Okay? Let's go!"

I tiptoed into the back of the room and sat down in the last row of about a hundred seats facing a small stage on which two young actors, a man and a woman, were playing a scene from some foreign play. The boy made a speech about the forests, to which the girl reacted by bursting into tears and rushing offstage. I thought they'd done pretty well, but the end of the scene was greeted by absolute silence from the twenty or so watchers in the room. I leaned forward toward a bushy-haired young man sitting two rows in front of me. "Excuse me," I whispered. "What's this scene from?"

He turned back and murmured, "*Uncle Vanya.* Boy, Ted is going to tear them to shreds."

"Why? I thought they were pretty good."

He looked at me in disbelief. "You're kidding? That was totally representational."

This apparently negative appraisal was soon confirmed by the voice I had heard earlier. It belonged to a plump, middle-aged man dressed in a light blue jumpsuit and basketball sneakers, who now arose from his seat on the aisle in the middle of the theater and ambled down toward the stage. He was bald on top, but sported a blond ponytail that covered the back of his neck, and his face was round, with a prim-looking mouth and small eyes all but hidden under tufted yellow eyebrows. The two young people on stage apprehensively watched him come toward them, as if expecting to be castigated. They were not to be disappointed. No sooner had the man reached the front row of seats than he launched into a high-pitched nasal tirade that tore them apart for their inadequacy. They had apparently committed every major histrionic sin since the birth of Thespis and he was not about to forgive them for a single one of them. By the time he had concluded, some fifteen minutes later, the girl had slumped to the floor of the stage in tears and her ashen-faced partner in crime had retreated several steps backward, as if about to be shot without a blindfold for his act of treason to art. "Any questions, people?" the man now asked, turning back to the audience.

A very thin, intense-looking young girl with an acne-scarred face and lank, dull brown hair stood up. "Ted, what I don't understand is why she runs out of the room after his speech about the trees," she said.

"What don't you understand, Lisa?"

"I mean, why she's so upset," Lisa said. "He's just talking to her about trees and stuff."

"She's in love with him, Lisa," Ted said. "She can't stand it."

"Yes, but why doesn't he react—"

"That's one of the many things wrong with the scene," Ted said. "He doesn't love her, not the way she feels for him. He just wants to get into her, see? But, of course, the way Bonnie and Jeff played it, you wouldn't know that. It's all surface crap, just playing the lines, unmotivated horseshit. Jeff and Bonnie know what I'm talking about, don't you, kids?" He turned back to his actors. "Right?"

"Yeah, sure, Ted," the boy mumbled miserably, while the girl on the floor just nodded dumbly, the tears drying on her cheeks.

"All right now," Ted continued, "if there aren't any other questions, we're going to take the scene from the top one more time, only this one's an improv. Jeff, I want you to play this guy like a frustrated schoolteacher, okay? You want to fuck her, but you're too shy, too timid to make a move toward her, got it?"

Jeff nodded. "Sure."

"And you, Bonnie, we've got to get some sex out of you. You've got to want to be laid, you've got to really come on to him, make him see you as a sex object. It's the only way you can think of to get him to be aware of you, got it? Let her craving come out of the scene, out of what she *feels*, not only what she does, and certainly not what she says, okay? You find a way to do that. Fuck the lines, the lines are bullshit. What I need is the truth of what's really going on here. Find the truth under the text and the lines will take care of themselves, got it?" The girl nodded dumbly and rose unsteadily to her feet. "Okay, kids, take five. When we come back, I want the scene the way Chekhov *felt* it, not the way he wrote it. I don't want words, I want truth, I want reality, I want *essence*! Got it? Okay, go for it." He turned and headed quickly back up the aisle toward me.

I stood up. "Mr. Freeman?"

"Yes? Who are you?"

"My name's Anderson," I said. "I'd like to speak to you a minute."

"Sure, come on back to my office," he said. "Or you can wait till the class is over at twelve, whatever."

"Well, I may do both."

"Come on then."

I followed him back to a small office at the front of the house. It contained a battered wooden desk piled high with correspondence, newspapers, magazines, books, and manuscripts. The walls were covered with more posters of Stage Two productions, most of them of various classics, as well as blown-up clips of favorable reviews. One side of the room was lined with bookshelves full of theatrical reference works and collections of plays. A large orange cat lay sleeping on the padded swivel chair behind the desk. Ted Freeman picked him up and set him down on the desk itself. The cat opened his eyes briefly, yawned, and went right back to sleep. "Sit down," Freeman said, pointing to the only other seat in the room, a straight-backed wooden chair in the corner, facing him at an angle. "You an actor?"

"I'm a magician," I said, "but I've been thinking that I need to join a good workshop."

"I don't work on nightclub acts," Freeman said. "That's show biz."

"I know, I gathered that," I said. "But I get some acting parts, mostly in TV. And I thought I could develop my acting talents, if I have any."

"Everybody has talent," Freeman said. "You just have to clear the underbrush away to find it, to get to the heart of it. This isn't just another bullshit workshop where the actors do scenes for the casting directors at the studios, that crap you see every day of the week on TV. This is a place where we go for the subtext, the truth at the heart of the drama. I don't want acting, I want *being*. Do you understand?"

"I think so," I said. "I watched this last scene."

"Bonnie and Jeff? A couple of very talented kids, but they're still acting, they're still playing the words." He leaned over his desk, extracted a mimeographed form from under the orange cat and handed it to me. "Why don't you fill this out and leave it with me after class or drop it off the next time you come. It'll give me an idea of your background and experience. We'll set up an audition for you. Do you have a scene prepared?"

"No. I can show you a few moves, but the dialogue is mostly improvised patter to go along with my act."

"I'll need a scene. Can you prepare something in a week?"

"Sure."

"You can let me know when you're ready and we'll set an audition time. Meanwhile, you can start attending the classes, if you like. The beginners meet on Tuesday and Thursday nights, from seven to ten. We also have body movement, dance, mime, speech, and martial arts. It's five hundred a month, if you take the whole package, which I strongly urge everyone to do, if you want to be a complete creative performer; or three hundred just for the acting workshop. Then you can audition for our productions. We do four a year, mostly contemporary versions of the classics. But you'll be at least six months away from being able to participate in those, I'm sure. The scene work is the heart of what we do here and that's what you should concentrate on for now." He stood up and shook my hand. "Well, nice having you with us," he said. "You're welcome to drop in on any of our sessions this week to help you structure your participation here. Now we'd better get back to class."

I followed him out of the office and into the auditorium, where his actors sat, expectantly awaiting his return. "By the way," he asked, as we headed down the aisle, "how did you hear about us? Our *Variety* ads?"

"No, Melinda Kennedy told me about you," I said.

He stopped long enough to glance back at me. "Really? How do you know her?"

"Through Lucius Bedlington. We're racetrack acquaintances."

"Is that so?" he said, looking oddly ill at ease. "How strange."

"Why strange? She is a member here, isn't she?"

"Oh, yes," Ted Freeman said hastily, "yes, indeed. Very promising young talent, one of our most dedicated young artists. Well, let's get to work here." He turned back to his class. "All right, Bonnie? Jeff? Let's go now, let's find the essence, let's go for the truth!" And he sat down in the first row to watch, as the room became very quiet. I eased myself into an aisle seat, about halfway back.

The scene began with Jeff alone on stage, staring out into the wings. Slowly he turned toward us and said, "All these fucking trees, meaningless crud." He grabbed his crotch. "My balls ache, I'm hard for her. I know she wants me, but if I give her the old beef and cream treatment, she'll fall in love with me, the bitch, and I can't marry her. What does she expect from me? Why can't she just open her legs and let me split the uprights? What is all this love shit?"

Bonnie came on stage and confronted him. Wordlessly, she began to undress, deliberately removing one garment at a time and dropping it carelessly on the floor at her feet until she was naked. Jeff watched her, then took her by the shoulders and pushed her to her knees. "Get down, bitch, I know you want me," he said.

Bonnie stretched out beneath him, on her back, her arms raised imploringly toward him. Slowly, Jeff descended toward her, but, just as he was about to lie on top of her, he looked up. "This is as far as we've gotten with the scene, Ted," he said. "We decided to attack it this way, but I don't know if it works."

"Kids, that's wonderful," Ted Freeman said. "That is the finest improv on that scene I can imagine. You are playing the essence now, not the surface bullshit."

With the same garrulity with which he had dismembered their performances earlier, Ted Freeman now proceeded to lavish praise on his actors, who listened to him intently, their faces aglow with delight. Bonnie sat up, still naked, hugging herself, while Jeff knelt beside her, hands on his thighs, shoulders hunched under the cascade of praise pouring his way. Clearly, it was sheer rapture for both of them. Twenty minutes later, when it was finally over, Ted Freeman clapped his hands and said, "That's it for today, kids. Thanks and I'll see you Monday." He got up and moved quickly up the aisle back toward his office.

Bonnie turned her back to us and began to put her clothes back on, while the rest of the class, chattering and joking with one another, prepared to leave. I waited until the bushy-haired young man I'd spoken to earlier passed me, then I followed him out into the street. "Hi," I said, "I'm Lou Anderson. My friends call me Shifty. That was a terrific class."

The boy looked at me and grinned. "Yeah, it was pretty intense, even for old Ted," he said. "I'm Barney. You an actor?"

"I'm a magician," I said, "but I do some acting."

"Yeah? That's cool. You gonna sign on?"

"I'm thinking about it. Melinda Kennedy's a friend of mine and she recommended it. You know her?"

Barney shook his head. "No. She new?"

"Yes. She's in the film classes."

Barney looked puzzled. "Film classes? We don't have any film classes. You sure you got the right place? Stage Two is strictly an acting workshop, with the emphasis on stage work. Ted thinks TV and movies are mostly commercial crap. Of course we'd all starve to death without it, but he's right. The stage is the only medium for an actor to really find himself, stretch himself to the limit. You must have the wrong workshop."

"Maybe I do."

"What's this girl's name?"

"Melinda Kennedy. Ted knows her."

"Yeah? Well, maybe I've seen her around."

"You'd remember her, if you had."

"A real looker, huh?"

"Yeah."

"Well, maybe I'll get to meet her. But you must have misunderstood her about film classes here."

"Yeah, I guess I did. You know anybody named Angel?"

"Angel? Angel Price?" He looked as if he'd bitten into a rotten piece of fruit. "Yeah, sure. I used to date her. She's a cunt."

"That doesn't tell me much about her."

"She's like poison, man. You don't want to know her."

"She's a member of the workshop?"

"Yeah, I met her in class. She used to be Ted's girl, maybe she still is. I haven't seen her around for a while, which is okay by me. Forget her, man. She'll tear you up."

"Okay, just asking. She's a friend of Melinda's."

"I feel sorry for Melinda. I'll see you around, man."

"Yeah. Thanks." I started back toward my car.

"Hey, and look out for Ted," Barney called after me. "He'll tear you up the first time you do a scene for him. Just don't take it personal. He's gotta break you down to make you find yourself."

I thanked him again and walked to my car. The gypsy men were still out on their front porch across the street and seemed not to have moved an inch. Ted Freeman would have loved them. They had boiled life down to its very essence.

I made Santa Anita by the middle of the card that day, but I shouldn't have bothered to show up. The only horse I really liked went off as the eight-to-five favorite in the seventh and was annihilated coming out of the gate by a nondescript animal that swerved in toward the rail, then he was fanned wide as he was making a move on the turn for home and finished a dismal fourth. I made only three bets, lost them all, and gave back a couple of hundred from my previous day's winnings.

I didn't see either Lucius or Melinda, which was all right with me, because I hadn't decided what, if anything, to tell him about my visit to Stage Two. Jay and I went for dinner to a small French bistro in a part of old Pasadena that was being restored and gentrified. Unlike me, Jay had had a good day, having hit a triple for over a grand, so I let him pay for the meal, which turned out to be tasty but overpriced. We spent a leisurely time chatting about this and that, mostly on matters relating to our mutual obsession with horses, and I was pleased. We were becoming good friends again, as we had been before the debacle in Mexico.

It must have been about ten-thirty when we parted and I started to drive home. I wasn't sleepy and I was feeling a little restless, so I stopped in at Dudley's, a bar and restaurant on Little Santa Monica in West L.A. that had recently become a favorite hangout of mine. It was owned by an ex-jockey named Robert Dudley, an English-born journeyman rider who had hung up his tack a couple of years earlier after a bad spill at Hollywood Park that had shattered his right leg. He was an affable guy, with a long, serious face, a prominent, slightly hooked nose, and black hair slicked back and parted in the middle. He walked with a pronounced limp, but never complained, perhaps because he was doing better with his restaurant than he ever had as a rider. It consisted of a long T-shaped room, with a bar on the left, along the full length of the stem, and eating booths on the right. The head of the T contained more tables on a raised level slightly above a brightly lit pool table, which seemed to be always in action. Track posters, blowups of famous races, jockey silks, pants, boots, helmets, whips, and other racing memorabilia hung on the walls, and the bartenders, Luis and Pablo, were both ex-exercise boys. It was a popular place that attracted sporting types and pretty people.

Tonight was no exception. I had to push my way past a noisy young crowd at the bar before I could find a seat toward the very end. I ordered a beer and looked around. The inner room was a little emptier, but the pool table was in use. A couple of shiny-faced, intense-looking Latino kids dressed in jeans and black windbreakers were leaning on their cues, staring in dismay at the shabby-looking old man who was imperturbably beating their brains out. Arnie Wolfenden, attired in a long gray duffle coat, with a blue cap pulled down low over his forehead to shield his eyes, was shuffling wearily around the table making impossible shots from every angle. His pool cue flashed like a rapier over the green felt cloth as the balls rattled or dropped gently into the pockets. It took him about ten minutes to clear the table, after which he gazed silently and sadly at the kids, who reached into their pockets and handed him a pair of twenty-dollar bills. "Man, where'd you learn to shoot pool like that?" one of them said. "You couldn't sink a shot twenty minutes ago."

Arnie didn't answer. He simply shrugged, put his cue up on the rack and walked slowly toward my end of the bar. He looked as sad as if he'd just witnessed a painful rite of passage. "Arnie, don't tell me you're hustling children now," I said. "Do you need the money that badly?"

"I'll have a beer," he said, shuffling up to me. "They wanted to play, Shifty. What could I do?"

"Come on, Arnie, you hustled them."

"Shifty, if it doesn't cost them anything, they won't learn," he said, shaking his head. "Education is expensive. Think of Harvard."

For the next hour or so Arnie and I talked horses. He had been having a poor meet, but he'd also been around long enough to know that eventually he'd pull out of it. Arnie was a scuffler; he'd been around racetracks most of his life and he'd never held a job, honest or otherwise. "There's always fresh," he'd say, meaning that somehow from somewhere enough money would always materialize to keep him in action. When the luck turned, he'd always repay his debts and then he'd begin to save against the inevitable losing streak down the road. In a pinch he could always hustle a little pool, too, as he had tonight, although he could no longer go up against the real tough players anymore. It was a question of stamina, not skill. "I can't stand around a table too long now," he once said. "I broke down one day making a run for a window. I got shut out, too, or I'm up fifty grand."

"You don't bet no money," Angles Beltrami had said. "How could you ever be up fifty grand?"

"Angles, you don't grasp the principle," Arnie had told him. "You don't need money at a racetrack, you need winners."

I enjoyed talking to Arnie almost as much as I did to Jay. Wise old horseplayers rank right up there with Socrates, as far as I'm concerned, and I've always liked to bask in their expertise. The time passed quickly with Arnie and I was so absorbed in his discourse on the human condition that I failed to notice the presence in the room of the very person I'd been thinking about off and on all day.

Angel Price was sitting on a barstool up toward the front. She was wearing a very short, tight miniskirt and a blouse cut low in front, spiky-heeled pumps, gold hoop earrings, and overlapping layers of gold chains around her neck. She looked lethal. Jack Leone was standing next to her, with a drink in his hand and a cigarette dangling from the corner of his mouth. I pointed them out to Arnie.

"I wish I knew what was going on there," he said. "The rumor is that there's a group of wise guys who have been cashing tickets on Richards lately. You notice how he's suddenly riding like a demon in some races? In others he's his usual self, a stiff. The only problem is, I have a hard time reading him. Is he here?"

"I don't think so, I don't see him," I said. "This is pretty late for a jock."

"He doesn't come out too many mornings," Arnie said. "I'd say you have to have considerable sangfroid to put that guy up on your horse. That's French, Shifty."

"*Merci,* I'm glad you told me. I think I'll go talk to her."

"The story is that it's Jack Leone she's mostly with," Arnie said. "He may resent the intrusion."

"I'll charm him off his stool."

I strolled up to Angel Price just in time to hear Jack Leone say, "We'll wait ten more minutes. If he don't come, we'll blow."

"I'm here," I said, smiling. "Hello, Jack, good to see you. Angel, I'm Lou Anderson. My intimates call me Shifty. I'm a friend of Melinda's."

Angel Price gazed at me without a flicker of recognition or acknowledgment. "Beat it," Jack Leone said.

"I thought you were waiting for somebody."

"We are. It ain't you."

"Why are you being so unfriendly, Jack? I just want to buy you and Angel here a drink. I've been cashing a lot of live tickets recently on your boy Richards. I just thought I'd express my gratitude."

"I said beat it."

"How do you feel about it, Angel? Do you have an opinion?" I reached around behind her head and plucked a tiny bouquet of violets out of the air for her, one of my most successful icebreakers. "Here. For you." I offered it to her, but she seemed confused, unsure how to react.

"How did you do that?" was all she said, in a small, lost voice from a distant shore.

"Magic. How else?"

Jack Leone thrust himself between us and pushed me away from her. "Hey, asshole, I asked you nice. Now I'm telling you. Get the fuck out of here!"

"Wow, Jack, what's the matter with your mouth?" I peered closely at him. He backed up a step. I suddenly flicked my left hand out sideways, causing him to jerk his head to the right, while my right hand swooped into his left jacket pocket and emerged with a small baby's shoe. "Hey, here it is," I said. "You've had your foot in your mouth all day. No wonder you couldn't talk like a civilized human being."

Jack Leone obviously had no sense of humor. "What the fuck—" he began, then again shoved me away from him with both hands.

"Okay, okay, Jack, I'm going," I said, as our little contretemps had begun to attract the attention of the people around us. "Take it easy. Sorry to have bothered you. Just wanted to say thanks and hello, that's all. See you around." I returned to my seat next to Arnie.

"I don't think you impressed them," he said. "Something lacking in your approach, perhaps."

"Well, we don't know how she feels about it, Arnie," I said. "She's stoned. Jack just isn't the friendly, outgoing good guy I had hoped for. One of your tougher audiences."

"I'll let you buy me another beer now," Arnie said. "I presume you're holding."

"I am indeed."

I ordered two more beers. No sooner had we been served than the person Jack and Angel had been waiting for appeared. He was a large, burly-looking man of about fifty dressed in a black suit, a white shirt, and pink tie, somebody's driver. He did not approach them, but stood quietly inside the entrance until Jack spotted him, after which he left. Jack took Angel's arm, helped her off the stool, salvaged her coat from a hook on the wall, and draped it around her shoulders as he guided her out into the night.

"So what do you make of that, Shifty?" Arnie asked.

"I'd guess that old Jack seems to have more going for him than one broken-down, crooked jock," I observed. "If I didn't know him to be a person of the highest integrity and morality, I'd say he was doing a little pimping and perhaps a little dealing on the side."

Arnie sighed. "That's what you have to do in business these days, Shifty," he said. "Diversify."

Thirteen
CONFESSIONS

Two days later, Melinda Kennedy confessed everything to Bedlington. She had come out of her bedroom at about eleven o'clock to find him still sitting in his living room and sympathizing on the phone with Pericles Thanassis, who had called again to complain about the thoughtless manner in which all of his meticulous arrangements for his client's demise had been upset by repeated delays and postponements. "My dear Pericles, I must apologize for the miracles of modern medicine," she heard Bedlington tell him, just before hanging up. "My departure has been indefinitely put off by a new procedure I can only describe as an excess of happiness. A check is in the mail."

"Oh, Bunny," she said, running into the room to give him a hug, "is that the funny little man who keeps calling from the funeral home? Whatever can he want?"

"Me, my beloved. Until recently I was at the top of his hit list."

"You? What do you mean?"

So he told her and in some detail. She listened, presumably amazed, then fell sobbing into his arms. He consoled her. "I haven't the slightest intention of going through with it now," he assured her. "Come, come, my dear, there's no need for all these tears. You've changed all that. You've brought something entirely new and fresh into my life. Come now, no more tears. Let's plot our day. What is it to be? The races again? The new Greek antiquities exhibit at the Getty? A picnic in the hills? I have Scopes alerted and I believe he's already making up a picnic basket— moldy goat cheese, a duck pâté, an unpretentious claret. What is it to be?"

But she had been unable to stop crying. She broke away from him to run out of the room, then returned a few minutes later, after having splashed water on her face, to confront him. She was very pale, he recalled when he told me about it, but very determined, even desperate in her resolve. She stood motionless in the doorway, as if poised for a quick getaway.

"I'm not the person you think I am," she announced, in a dark little voice of doom. "Oh, Bunny, you must believe me. I didn't mean for all this to happen. I didn't know."

He started to rise out of his chair, but she motioned desperately for him not to approach her. "Don't, please," she said. "Let me finish. It's very important to me. Then if you want me to, I'll go."

"Go, my dear? Why would I want you to go?"

"Bunny, you don't know anything about me."

"I know you're not my daughter."

"You do?"

"Yes. I called Isabel a week ago, in Rome. She told me. At first she babbled away about this and that, her usual lunatic rambling—the woman is deranged—but eventually I got her to admit it."

"You did? How?"

"I told her a few inspired lies," Bedlington said, "about having had a blood test and not being an A-positive, as she had claimed I was— actually I am—and about having spoken to my sawbones, who told me about HLA typing and a DNA probe and all that sort of rot, and she fell for it. She admitted having cooked the whole thing up, dear child. So if that's what's troubling you, forget it. I couldn't go on not knowing, given the way I feel about you. So that's cleared up."

"Is that all she said?"

"Oh, you know, simply that she wanted to make sure you'd be all right. She was worried about you, wanted you well taken care of and all that."

"Then she didn't tell you the real reason?"

"Is there something else?"

"Yes. Oh, God! Oh, Bunny, I'm so terribly sorry!" She came over and sat down on the edge of the sofa, facing him, leaning anxiously in toward him, her hands clasped softly in front of her as if in supplication, her face pale with grief. "I'm not Isabel's daughter either," she said.

"No? Who are you, then?"

"Kennedy *is* my real name, Bunny, but my parents live in Raleigh, North Carolina. My dad's retired now, but he was in the army. He was a warrant officer. He was a career military man and we moved around a lot. That's how I happened to live in Europe and learn Italian and all that. He was stationed in Naples for five years."

"I see. So?"

"I met Isabel through Filippo," she continued. "I worked as an actress in two of his pictures."

"Then she cooked this whole thing up as some sort of joke, is that it?"

The girl shook her head, then bowed it, as if afraid to look at him. "Oh, Bunny, you're going to hate me so much," she murmured, "so much. And I care for you such a lot. I never imagined—I never dreamed . . ."

He reached out to comfort her, but she shrank from him, as if she felt herself too unclean to be touched. "Melinda, my dear," he said, "sooner or later you'll have to tell me everything, won't you?"

She nodded miserably, but kept her eyes averted from him. "She called me up one day," she said. "I hadn't seen her or Filippo for weeks, not since the wrap party. I'd been working as a model in Milan and I'd been home only a couple of days."

"So you do live permanently in Rome."

"Yes. I have a little apartment just off the Via Veneto, up near the Villa Borghese. You know, the park—"

"I know Rome quite well. Go on."

"She presented it as just another job. She told me all about you and how she'd been married to you and all and about how you were in a kind of big depression and you were going to kill yourself and all that, only she said you weren't dangerous or anything, and she said it was a question of getting your mind off yourself and how you'd always liked pretty girls and everything. I thought she wanted me to have sex with you or something, so I said no, I wouldn't do that, but then she said no, it wasn't like that, that I was going to pretend to be your daughter and that anyway you were too old now for all that sort of stuff and I didn't have to do anything I didn't want to and I could leave anytime I wanted to if it got too difficult and all, and the way she presented it the whole thing amounted to a kind of a lark and a free trip to L.A., where maybe I could get my career going in the movies and TV and like that, and I'd have all my expenses paid and it would be like another acting job, that's all."

The words had all come pouring out of her in a single cascade of sound, tumbling over each other like a stream over the edge of a waterfall, and now she sank back in her seat exhausted and pale, one hand over her eyes, too appalled by her own confession to look at him. He came over and sat beside her on the sofa and gently put an arm around her. Her head rested against his shoulder, but she still couldn't look at him. "Did she offer to pay you?"

Melinda nodded. "Ten thousand dollars plus the expenses," she said, in a low, choked voice. "Oh, Bunny, I'm so ashamed."

They sat together in silence for a couple of minutes, while slow tears ran down her cheeks and Bedlington sorted through the implications of what she had just told him. "It was Derek, of course," he finally said, with a sigh. "The old fool."

"Bunny, I didn't realize—I didn't know—I mean, you've been so wonderful to me, you're such a wonderful man," Melinda said. "I've never known anyone like you. I had no idea what I was getting into, what would happen to me. I thought it was all going to be such fun and that you'd be nice and all, but nothing like the person you are. Nobody warned me. Oh, God, Bunny!" And she suddenly bounded out of his arms and fled up to her room.

He let her go, then walked over to the phone and called me.

Derek Flanders was waiting for us in his office that afternoon and actually seemed pleased to see us, though he was obviously a bit put off by my presence. "I insist on Anderson being with me, Derek," Bedlington said, as we entered and before the lawyer could protest. "You've become such a devious schemer and unconscionable liar that I'm going to insist on a witness being present every time we meet from now on."

"What are you insinuating, Lucius?"

"Insinuating? I'm accusing you directly of being a bald-faced liar and schemer on a Borgian scale," Bedlington thundered. "You should have been a politician. You have a genius for mendacity."

"Please sit down," the lawyer said calmly. "You might as well be comfortable while you're shouting at me." He smiled at me and indicated the seats facing his desk. "Mr. Anderson, please."

I sat down, but Bedlington refused to do so. He leaned with both hands on Flanders's desk and thrust himself forward pugnaciously, as if he might bite off the lawyer's head. "What in hell did you mean by daring to meddle in my private life in such a manner? If you weren't my lawyer, I'd sue you."

"So you've found out about the girl."

"Of course I've found out. Did you think I wouldn't? Did you manage to convince yourself that this farcical charade would simply play itself out and disappear, like a bad Broadway-bound show dying of incompetence on the road somewhere? What is the matter with you, Derek? How did you imagine it would end?"

"Pretty much like this," the lawyer said, "with you shouting angrily at me. I thought it might go on a bit longer. I hadn't counted on your becoming quite so infatuated with the girl. Or she with you, for that matter. Where is she?"

"Sobbing her heart out in her room. Where did you think she'd be?"

"I don't know," the lawyer said, quite cheerfully. "I imagine she'll get over it. It must have been a strain on her, poor thing. I warned her about you."

"Oh, you did."

"Yes. But she's very young. She didn't believe that anyone her age could be charmed out of her pants by anyone as ancient as you. I tried to prepare her. You *are* a menace, Lucius—a man of devastating wit and erudition, with enough *savoir-faire* to bowl over the Queen of England. You've always been able to have any woman you wanted. She wasn't able to cope with you."

"Oh, cut the crap, Derek."

The lawyer smiled and leaned back in his chair. "Ah, Lucius, these young people today, what do they know? Nothing. Wham, bam, thank you, ma'am. They've never known what it's like to be courted by a real gentleman, showered with tasteful gifts, flattered day and night by small attentions, treated with consideration and respect. No wonder she was overwhelmed by you. I should have anticipated it."

Bedlington slumped backward into the chair behind him, as if suddenly deflated by his friend's praise. "I'm finding this very tiresome, Derek," he said. "Would you mind not launching into a catalogue of my presumed virtues and accomplishments? I know perfectly well what I am and who I am and, as you know, the view no longer pleases me at all. I've lived a selfish, self-serving, and ridiculous life built largely around the futile pursuit of women."

"You loved it."

"No, I loved *them* and I paid for my infatuation with my whole life,"

Bedlington said. "I probably could have amounted to something." He glanced fiercely up at his old friend. "And now would you mind telling me exactly what you meant to accomplish by all this?"

The lawyer shrugged. "It worked, didn't it?"

"From the beginning, please."

"Well, the basic idea was to get your mind off yourself," Flanders explained. "The only thing that's ever worked with you was women. You'd talked yourself into believing that that part of your life was all over, so you became increasingly morose and eventually suicidal. You decided there was nothing in life worth living for, so you set about organizing your own death as if it were some sort of elaborate costume ball. Most people wouldn't have believed you'd go through with it, but I knew better. I knew you'd do away with yourself with the same élan and snobbish indifference to the world at large that you've always displayed. I had to find some way to stop you. And the only way I could think of was to find a beautiful young woman who could give you a renewed interest in life. I knew you wouldn't even let her get near you, unless I could think of a way to get your immediate attention. I wasn't sure either that her sexual attractiveness would do the trick, since you'd convinced yourself you had turned into a living fossil no beautiful woman would look at twice. I wondered if your prostate had given out or something, so I checked with Dr. Merrill's office and he told me you were in great shape generally. That was when I decided to call Isabel. It was her suggestion to pass this girl off not only as her daughter, but possibly yours as well. A great idea."

"Oh, great. I didn't know you were still in touch with her."

"I wasn't. But I'd known her pretty well during the years of your marriage and right after, when we had to settle your divorce. She was quite reasonable, I remember, and she always had a great sense of humor. She laughed all through the settlement."

"Why wouldn't she? She got half a million."

"Then I'd read about her from time to time. She was always in the news somewhere, you know—*People* magazine, the gossip columns, TV entertainment news, society chatter. I have a weakness for that stuff, so I knew about her marriage to Fracasso and that struck me as a possibility. So I called her. She was in New York and I flew out to see her. She loved the idea. She thought it would be a great joke to play on you."

"Ha ha," Bedlington exclaimed mirthlessly.

"It was Filippo who came up with Melinda," Flanders continued. "She'd had small parts in a couple of his movies and she had just the right background for the job. After he talked to her on the phone, I flew to Milan to see her, where she was finishing up a modeling stint, then I went on to Rome with her to meet Isabel and to finalize the whole deal. It was a snap. The money was right for her, she'd been thinking about coming to the States anyway, so it all just fitted in perfectly. Best of all, she wasn't married and she'd just broken up with her boyfriend, who'd been an assistant director on Filippo's movie, so there wouldn't be any complications on the emotional end. As I said, it was easy."

"And all those documents Isabel showered on me?"

"A snap," the lawyer said. "The birth certificate's genuine—Kennedy's her real name—so that gave us a good start. She had some childhood snapshots and it was no problem having them doctored so she'd appear in a couple of them with Isabel. The work was carried out by the same group that executed the medical and dental certificates. Filippo uses a fantastically corrupt firm of Neapolitans, who specialize in that kind of thing. Being an international movie tycoon means having to move people and things around sometimes more expeditiously than can be done through regular channels."

Bedlington stared at his old friend. "You know, Derek, I'm amazed," he said. "I've known you practically all of my life and it turns out that I don't know you at all. I never could have imagined you'd be capable of cooking up such a nasty scheme."

"It worked, didn't it?"

"All too well."

"You'll never go through with it now, no matter what happens to this girl."

"Nothing's going to happen to her. I'm going to marry her."

"Oh, don't be a fool, Lucius. Give her some money, that's all she wants, and send her on her way."

"You miscalculated, Derek. The child is in love with me. You played a cruel trick on both of us, but it backfired."

"What trick? It was a business arrangement. She's been paid and very handsomely. Now let her get back to her own life."

"The point is, dear boy, that I'm also very fond of her. I see no reason to give her up." He stood up. "By the way, who picked up the tab for this caper?"

"I did, of course. You don't imagine I'd ask you to pay for it?"

"Why not? You've always charged me a fee before."

"Let's say I decided to make you a present of my services this time."

"Very generous of you, Derek." He started for the door. "Come on, Shifty."

"You're not really going through with this?"

"Of course I am. And why shouldn't I? You made your point. You showed me I still have some serviceable years left and I intend to make the most of them."

"Wonderful," the lawyer said sarcastically. "I'll draw up the papers and give you a call in a couple of days."

"What papers?"

"Surely you haven't forgotten, Lucius, that we live in a community-property state," the lawyer said. "She'll have to agree to sign the same waivers all your other wives had to sign. Maybe I was wrong. Maybe you are growing senile."

"Melinda and I haven't discussed matters yet. I suppose we have much to talk about now."

"If she really cares for you, Lucius, she'll agree. If not, I'd suggest that she might be trying to use you."

Bedlington paused grandly in the doorway, gazing pityingly back at his old friend. "What would you know of love, Derek?" he asked. " 'Brightly dawns our wedding day. Joyous hour we give thee greeting!' "

"Yes, but remember—'all must sip the cup of sorrow, I today and thou tomorrow,' " the lawyer shot back.

"Ah, Derek, well done, dear boy," Bedlington said, smiling faintly. "I suppose I should forgive you, even if I'm not sure you meant well."

" 'This haughty youth, he speaks the truth whenever he finds it pays,' " Flanders said. " 'And in this case, it all took place exactly as he says!' "

Bedlington laughed and walked out of the room. I looked back at Flanders. "You guys are both more than a little crazy," I said. "What was that?"

"*The Mikado,* of course," the lawyer answered glumly. He did not seem overjoyed about the way the conversation had ended.

Bedlington had very little to say during the drive back to his house. Mostly, he hummed snatches of G and S to himself. As I parked the Alfa at his front steps, he peeled off another of his hundred-dollar bills and dropped it in my lap, then bounded briskly toward his front door. Scopes appeared like an apparition at the entrance. "Oh, thir, thank goodneth you're back," he said, putting out a bony arm toward the wall to keep himself from toppling over. "Mith Kennedy hath packed her bags and inthists on leaving, dethpite my every effort. She'th called a taxthi, thir."

"Never fear, Scopes," I heard Bedlington say, as the door closed behind him, " 'for here is love and here is truth and here is food for joyous laughter . . . !' "

I knew that one. *Pirates.*

*   *   *

I had planned to spend a quiet evening at home, working on some basics and studying the *Form,* but I couldn't seem to relax. The trouble was that I couldn't quite believe in what was going on. It all made sense, if you happened to live in a comic-opera world, which evidently suited both Bedlington and Flanders. But the tale seemed ragged around the edges to me, like a brightly colored but badly woven coat with loose threads left hanging here and there, dazzling to behold but liable to come apart at the seams at any moment. As a magician, I deal partly in illusion and misdirection is one of my basic techniques; I know it when I see it. The trouble was that in this case I couldn't isolate the source or understand the impetus for the performance. I was a professional in the field and I was being fooled. It bothered me.

At about eight I dropped in at Dudley's for a cup of soup and a hamburger. Business was slow that night and I had no difficulty getting a booth across from the bar. As I was sitting there, sipping a light beer and waiting for my order, the owner limped past me. I stopped him and invited him to have a drink with me.

"Hello, Shifty," he said, slipping into the seat across from me, "how's the magic game, eh? Treating you better than the horses, I hope."

"I'm between engagements," I said, "but the horses are being kind to me these days."

"Killing them, are you?"

"Not exactly, Bobby, but I'm winning," I said. "Sometimes it's hard for me to believe some people have to work for a living."

Dudley laughed. "You know, all those years I rode I don't think I ever cashed a ticket on my own winners," he said. "Every time one of my owners bet for me, we'd lose, and whenever I won we'd be empty-handed."

"There's a message in there somewhere, Bobby."

"Yes. And I've always remembered what Eddie Arcaro once said. Ever see him ride?"

I shook my head. "Before my time, I'm afraid."

"Mine, too, but I've seen film. He was smashing. Anyway, he said that if he'd known how much money he could have made booking the action in the jocks' room, he wouldn't have bothered riding. I was never one of the lucky ones, Shifty."

My food order arrived and I ate, while Dudley and I talked about betting coups. We both agreed that they were not as prevalent in the game as most horseplayers tended to believe. "Jockeys and trainers know their own horses," Dudley explained at one point, "but they don't know the competition. Most of them don't even read the *Form*. I once rode a horse for a chap, came in fourth or something, and after the race he said to me, 'You had a hole there on the rail. Why didn't you go through it?' I had to explain to him that unfortunately the hole was moving faster than I was."

"Some guys specialize in putting over horses, though," I said. "They live for it. You been watching Lonny Richards lately?"

Dudley shook his head. "No, Shifty, I don't go racing much anymore. I'm awfully busy running this place. Oh, I might go once or twice a meet now, but that's it. I've got Ellen and the kids and a pretty full life away from the track."

"Lonny a friend of yours?"

"No," he said, shaking his head. "He tried to put me over the rail once coming down the hillside at Santa Anita a few years ago and we had a dandy little scrap in the jocks' room afterwards. We both got ten days for that one and things remained cool between us after that. He's not my sort of chap at all. He used to do some things I disapproved of and for a while there he got into drugs. I gather he's clean now."

"Maybe. I saw his man Leone in here the other night."

Dudley nodded unhappily. "Oh, yes, Jack comes in here frequently these days. Always has some girl with him. Not a nice man."

"You talking about the blonde, Angel Price? The one with the legs?"

"Yes, that one, too."

"I thought she was dating Richards."

"Lonny doesn't come in here, so I wouldn't know. But I've seen Jack with a lot of girls."

"She was stoned on something."

"Wouldn't surprise me, Shifty."

"Do you think he's dealing?"

"Not in here. I run a pretty tight ship. If I catch anyone dealing or using, out they go."

"I thought maybe she was hooking for him, too."

"I wouldn't know about that either," Dudley said. "I certainly wouldn't put it past him. He seems to have lots of money to spend and he surely can't be earning it from Richards, can he? He must be doing something. I keep an eye on him, you know, but I've never seen anything overt, or I'd ask him to leave. The one thing I don't want is trouble with the police. If you lose your license in this state, it's very hard to get it back. And this place is all I have, Shifty."

"You said 'a lot of girls.' Who else besides Angel?"

"Oh, several, at least. Though, come to think of it, she's been around more than the others lately. He had two of them in here the other night.

This blonde, Angel, and a really rather spectacular-looking brunette. They made quite a pair, left here around midnight with a large group of people, mostly men. They came in very fancy cars, I heard from my valet-parking people."

One of the waiters came over and called him to the phone. He excused himself and disappeared toward the back. I finished my dinner and got home by ten o'clock. I dreamt of Amber and woke up before dawn in an icy sweat.

Fourteen

ANGLES

"What's the matter, Charlie? You don't look happy," I said, as I brought the trainer his first coffee of the morning. "We got a horse in trouble?"

"We got a trainer in trouble," he said, taking the container from me and hazarding his first sip, the steam from the hot liquid blowing up into his eyes.

"Who?"

"Me."

"You mean both these horses in here today are stiffs?"

He shook his head. "No, they're both going to win."

"So what's the problem?"

"Neither of them should be running yet," he explained. "The filly's maybe a week away and I'd like more time to work on Slim's ankle. It's pretty bad."

"So why are you running them?"

"Because if I don't run the filly today, there ain't another race for her until the next book, maybe three weeks from now," the trainer said, as we walked to the rail at Clockers' Corner to watch the horses go by. "She drew an easy field and she ought to win, but they wouldn't let me put a bug boy up on her, so I got to carry the weight. Slim, he shouldn't be running at all, but I guess I asked for this when I claimed them two. It goes with the territory."

"Who's they, Charlie?"

"Oh, Bedlington and whoever's telling him what to do these days. That girl, I guess."

"I thought you always called the shots."

"I used to, Shifty, till the old man got talked into investing in gambling horses. Now all these people want to do is cash tickets. My guess is they're going for the Pick Nine today."

"There's a nice payoff," I said. "The pool is up over four hundred thousand."

The trainer nodded unhappily. "That's what I mean. I'm not a horseman anymore, I'm some kind of conditioner for a bunch of betting junkies."

"It's got to be Richards and Leone and their group."

"Don't tell me, Shifty, I don't want to know," Charlie said, seeming to sink into himself, his cap pulled low over his eyes, his shoulders hunched into his blue windbreaker, and his arms resting on the rail. "All I got to do is worry about the goddamn horses. That's tough enough. If I got to think about who's betting on them and how much money's up, I'll start doing things I shouldn't be doing." He suddenly looked up as Tim Lang rode past on a good-looking chestnut filly and his expression brightened.

"Who's that?" I asked.

"Mad Margaret. She's doing pretty good."

"She looks great. When's she running?"

"Next week. She'll win."

"You putting Lang up again?"

"Sure, why not?"

"After what he did to her the first time?"

"That's one mistake he won't make again," the trainer said. "With a new boy, I wouldn't know what to expect."

"Sometimes the logic in racing escapes me, Charlie," I said. "It seems to be one of the few areas in life, outside of politics, where incompetence is rewarded."

"Don't worry about it, Shifty," Charlie said, his gaze fixed on the filly as she moved away from us up the track.

"She working?"

He nodded. "Three-furlong breeze."

"So how come Bedlington let you ride Lang on this horse?"

"Because I insisted," Charlie answered fiercely. "This filly's got a chance to be a real nice horse. If he don't let me call the shots with her, then I got to say good-bye. The rest of his string, I don't care who he wants up. But Richards don't come out much in the mornings and he don't know this filly like Tim does. I ain't takin' no chances with her."

Mad Margaret worked in 35.3, well in hand, with Tim Lang riding high and keeping a tight hold on her. She looked wonderful out there, with her neck bowed and her muscles rippling under her gleaming coat in the cool, bright air of early morning. When she came past us again a few minutes later, Tim Lang sitting confidently in the saddle, his face reflecting the pleasure of an anticipated victory with her, Charlie hurried away after him toward his stable. "This one I do myself, Shifty," he called over his shoulder. "I don't even trust Eddie with her. You coming by the barn?"

"Maybe later. Anyway, I'll see you at the races, Charlie."

I watched him leave, then fished my program out of my side pocket. It was a Friday, a day I tend not to go to the races, because of the horrendous weekend getaway traffic one encounters going home and because, even if I'm not working regularly at the Magic Castle, I like to drop in there and need to spend the afternoon preparing for it. The Castle is a place to stop by and try out new moves and I had a few I'd been working on, but you can't just show up, pick a spot, and expect to dazzle the folks. Not with all those pros around and a reputation to live up to. No, you have to prepare and you have to pace yourself and you need the support of your peers. Magicians are generally supportive of each other, but arrogance is repaid with indifference, slipshod work with harsh criticism. I knew the rules and I abided by them. But the night before, no sooner had I returned home from Dudley's and snapped the *Form* open for a quick look at the entries, than I knew I would not be going to the Magic Castle the following night.

Now, with my program open in front of me, I reviewed the possibilities. I wasn't even thinking about the Pick Nine, because it's such an idiotic bet. You are supposed to try to pick the winners of all nine races, a task compared to which scaling the Empire State Building à la Kong is a cinch. It is only worth chasing when the pool becomes huge, as it usually does, and when there is a mandatory payoff, which occurs at Santa Anita only after the pool has reached half a million dollars or more. Otherwise, to win you have to pick all nine races; if you're a small bettor, you might as well play the lottery. No, it was Charlie's two horses I wanted to concentrate on.

Sinful Slim, with Richards up, was entered in the first race. He had drawn the two hole in this gallop for cheap claimers going a mile and one-eighth, was lightly weighted and figured to win, if his suspect ankle held up. He'd be no better than the third choice in the contest, perhaps at three or four to one. Beatific, the filly stretching out in the ninth, had drawn the outside post at a mile. She'd have to use her speed to get position by the clubhouse turn and not get fanned too wide, but she was the only animal of the eight in the field who figured to fire early. She ought to clear, I reasoned; then, if Richards could give her a breather down the backside, she should have enough left to fight off the closers and win, probably at good odds, five or six to one. She was moving up in class and had never run long before, so she would be overlooked in the betting. At least that was the way I was thinking, as I leafed through my program, only to have my speculations interrupted by a nasal voice in my ear.

"I know something you don't know," it said.

I turned around. Maury Levine, all five feet six inches of pasty flesh, bulbous nose, and rotting teeth, was grinning broadly at me. He had on dirty blue corduroys, scuffed Nikes, a food-stained red-and-black lumberman's shirt, and a wrinkled brown sports jacket with patched elbows, worn open to reveal the outthrust of his sizable paunch. He was smiling hideously. "Hello, Mooch," I said. "I doubt it."

The smile remained stiffly in place, but his piggish brown eyes were serious. "I'm not kidding," he said. "I know something you don't know."

I leaned in toward him. "Why would you tell me, Mooch?" I asked.

"You got twenty dollars?"

"Not worth it, Mooch."

He turned my reply over in his head a few times, as if surveying a small but baffling puzzle. "Okay," he said at last, "give me ten and I won't tell you."

I laughed. "My God, Mooch, you must be desperate."

"I'm tapped, Shifty," he said, glancing unhappily away from me toward the track, where the horses moved past us in the bright, clear light like figures out of an illustrated mythological saga. "And they threw me out of here yesterday. I can't even get in today to make a bet."

"What did you do, Mooch?"

He shifted his weight unhappily from side to side, as if about to break into a little soft-shoe. "Ah, I was standing next to this old guy during the fourth and he's got two dollars on the favorite and he beats me out a nose at the wire and he starts cackling like a chicken about what a great handicapper he is and I'm standing there with a bill on the loser, my last one, and it would have paid a grand easy. What do you expect?"

"You told him off?"

"Not bad, Shifty. I mean, I've done worse, you know? I only called him an asshole, only there's this security guard there and he complains to him about my foul language, so they throw me out. Shit, I should have kicked him in the ass, the old fart. I mean, I'm tap city and this stupid senile old bastard is jumping up and down 'cause he won three dollars and eighty cents. What would you have done?"

"I would have been unhappy."

"Exactly, you got it, Shifty. I was unhappy, the dumb bastard. So they threw me out." He suddenly leaned forward and grabbed my lapel. "But listen, Shifty, I do know something. Give me ten bucks, I'm desperate."

"One time, Mooch," I said, reaching into my pocket. "One time only." I handed him a ten-dollar bill.

The Mooch stuffed it into his trouser pocket and glanced quickly around, then took my arm and pulled me over to a corner under the grandstand, out of sight of the hundred or so watchers in the area. "Richards has got three mounts today," he said, in a low conspiratorial voice. "He'll win with the first one."

"I thought he might win with the last one, too."

The Mooch shook his head. "No chance, Shifty."

"Are you telling me he's going to stiff Charlie's filly in the ninth? Why would he do that?"

"They don't think she can win from out there, Shifty," the Mooch explained. "Too tough. She's got to break good, not get rushed too early, get the rail on the turn, set easy fractions, and have enough left for the drive. It's too risky."

"So it's easier to stiff her," I said. "But why? With this kind of money in the pool, if Richards and Leone and their guys could anchor their Pick Nine with singles at each end, they could go deep enough in the other races to maybe win the whole thing. So why would they do this?"

"For ten bucks you want me to lay it all out for you?" the Mooch answered. "You want me to take you by the hand and show you?"

I reached into my pocket again, peeled off another ten from my roll and handed it to him. Although we were completely alone, he paused long enough to take still one more look around, then jammed both hands into his pockets, as if to make certain the two bills I had handed him were still safely in there. "You may hear something about it," he said. "Not early, not after the second or third, but later. They're going to go so deep in the other races that they're sure to be alive for all of it, you follow me?"

"So far, sure."

"Watch, listen," the Mooch said. "After the fifth or sixth, watch what they do. You'll pick it up, Shifty, I promise you. It'll be all over the track." He started to move away from me.

"How many people are you telling this to, Mooch?" I called after him.

He turned around. "Me? You crazy? You think I want to die?" He started to move away again. "Thanks for the twenty. If I win the first, and I think it's a lock, I'm back in action."

"You betting with a bookie?"

"Nah, I'll get a friend of mine to run it for me. I'll be out in the parking lot." He paused in his flight just long enough to look back at me one more time. "Shifty, I hate this fuckin' place, you know that? I wouldn't even come here, if it wasn't the only action in town." And he disappeared around the corner of the grandstand.

I was standing at the paddock rail about twenty minutes before the first race when Jude Morgan came up beside me. He was wearing the same brown suit and the same brown porkpie hat he'd worn the day he and his partner had questioned me regarding Amber's death and he emanated the same air of tired professionalism that had struck me then. "Hello, Anderson," he said, "you know anything about these horses in here?"

"A little," I said. "I think the two horse, Sinful Slim, is going to win the race."

"That so? He sure don't look like much."

I had to agree with Morgan. Sinful Slim was a skinny roan with bandaged front legs and a small, square head. Seemingly uninterested in his surroundings, the old gelding docilely allowed Eddie to lead him around the ring, plodding along, head down, like an old customs clerk going back to work. "He's got a bad ankle, but he'll run his race," I said. "The trainer's a friend of mine."

"The price isn't much," Jude Morgan said.

"Five to two? It's all right, if he wins. He's an old hard knocker and he'll be tough in this field." I looked at Morgan and smiled. "Detective Morgan, I didn't know you were a horseplayer."

"I guess we didn't discuss it. I get out here a few times. Used to go with my daddy. How's the magic business?"

"I'm not getting rich, but it's what I do. It's fine."

"That the trainer over there?" Morgan asked, pointing at Bedlington.

"No, that's the owner. Charlie Pickard's the little chunky guy with the cap."

"That sure is some pretty lady with them."

I had to agree with him. Melinda Kennedy looked terrific. She was wearing high-heeled black pumps, a short black skirt, a white blouse, a black square-shouldered suede jacket, and a single strand of pearls. Her long, curly hair fell gracefully over her shoulders, framing her oval face and large eyes; she looked like a Renaissance Madonna I had once seen, radiant with happiness at the miracle of life. She had her arm through Bedlington's and clearly now owned him.

When the jockeys appeared to take their mounts, I spotted Jack Leone, directly across the ring from me. He was alone, his glittery gaze focused on Richards, who, I noticed, seemed to be looking around for someone. Angel Price, I guessed, but she had apparently failed to show up. As the horses filed out through the gap toward the track, Leone faded back into the crowd. With the jockey on him, Sinful Slim seemed to have woken up; his head came up and he bounced a bit, like an athlete on the sidelines, waiting to go into the game. I decided to bet on him.

"You feeling lucky?" Morgan asked, as we headed for our seats.

"I don't know. Maybe I'll get lucky."

"Hey, like my daddy always said, if you ain't got luck, what have you got?"

We went up the escalator together and walked into the grandstand, heading for the pari-mutuel windows. "How much you gonna bet?" Jude Morgan asked, as we joined a short line of bettors.

"I'm stepping out, Jude. A hundred dollars on the nose," I said, "which is a big bet for me."

"I guess you show-biz folks make more money than us law-enforcement boys," Jude Morgan said. "Ten dollars, that's my limit. How can you afford to bet like that?"

"I need the money," I said. "This horse is going to win, Jude."

I could see greed seep into his thinking, corrupting his conservative style, so that by the time he reached the window, right after me, his resolution had broken down. "Fifty to win on the two horse," he said, turning away in disgust with himself as he shoved the ticket into his breast pocket. "Hey, Anderson, if this horse don't win, I'm gone."

"What you guys need to do is get a union, strike for a raise."

"Yeah, sure." He stood there, looking unhappy. "Let the hoodlums loose on the public. Great idea, Anderson."

"Come on, let's watch this together," I said, as we headed out. "We can root him in."

It was like stealing, I reflected, as I watched Sinful Slim get a perfect trip. He broke alertly, tucked in comfortably along the rail in third around the first turn, a couple of lengths behind the leader, waited while two other animals made abortive moves on the last turn, then swung out to the middle of the track at the head of the lane to get running room, responded to Richards's whip, and blew past the leaders to win easily by three lengths. He paid $7.80 for every two-dollar ticket. I grinned at Morgan. "See how easy it is?"

He grunted, which I guess is about as close as he can come to a laugh. "Don't bullshit me, Anderson," he said. "I know about this game. My daddy taught me and he died broke. What else you got today?"

"Nothing till the ninth," I said, "and I'm not sure about that one. It's a tough card. Meet me at the paddock before the race, if I don't see you earlier, okay?"

"Okay," Morgan said, "and thanks for the tip."

"My pleasure. Anything new about who killed Amber?"

He shook his head. "Nope. It's a bad one, Anderson. But he'll do it again and someday, maybe, he'll make a mistake."

"Do you think it was the Slasher now?"

The detective shrugged. "I'm not convinced, but everybody else seems to be and I can't establish a motive. So?" He smiled, but not with pleasure. "You got any ideas?"

"Me? No. But I still think about her. She keeps me awake some nights."

"Become a cop, Anderson," Jude Morgan said. "You won't sleep good ever again."

It was Angles Beltrami who clued me in. He came to Jay's box after the fifth with some interesting information. "Get this, guys," he said, hurrying into his seat directly behind Jay. "The word is out that there's a potentially winning ticket up for sale. It's a big one."

"How big?"

"Huge, over fifty grand."

I looked at my program. Leone and his group, whoever they were, must have bought a Pick-Nine ticket in which they had every possible contender from the second race through the eighth. Now, knowing that Richards would stiff Charlie's filly in the ninth, they were shopping their action around, hoping to pick up sucker money for a bet they knew they wouldn't win. I explained my reasoning to Jay, but added, "They risked a lot of money for this play. There's something wrong with it, even if they do know Richards won't let Charlie's filly run her race."

Jay nodded thoughtfully. "You're right," he said. "They're in for a lot of money already. No real long shot has won yet. Still, unless the favorites win the next three races, which seems unlikely, they could be going into the ninth with the only live ticket. Or there might be several. Anyway, the ninth has five live horses out of the eight entries. They have Beatific, Richards's horse, singled, so it looks like they might have a big shot, especially because Leone is Richards's agent and he'd tout Beatific as a good bet. Still, this early I'd say they couldn't get more than twenty, thirty thousand for a fifty percent share, which I presume is what they'd be selling."

"The angle's obvious," Beltrami said. "They oversell it, pick up three, four times that much. They know the ticket's a loser."

Jay shook his head. "No, Angles, there's something missing. It's a risky play at best and all they could do is maybe get their money out. If they decided going in that their boy would stiff the filly in the ninth, why buy such a big ticket?"

Arnie looked up from his *Form,* which he had been studying with the contemplative gaze of a Talmudic scholar. "What if they have a mutuel clerk involved?" he asked.

I stared at him. "Arnie, that's it!"

"What do you mean?" Angles asked.

"They buy the ticket early," Jay explained, working it out as he went along, "then, before the first race, they take it back to the clerk they bought it from. They cancel it and get their money back."

"So?" Arnie asked.

"So once the ticket has been cancelled, the clerk is supposed to keep it," Jay continued, smiling faintly. "But if he doesn't, if he gives it back to them, there's nothing on the ticket to indicate it's invalid. The computer would spit it out, but Leone and the boys, as far as everybody else is concerned, would have in their hands what looks like a live ticket for sale."

"A nice way to pick up a quick forty or fifty grand," Arnie observed, "at no risk. Wish I'd thought of it myself. Do we know a crooked mutuel clerk?"

"More, Arnie," Jay said. "Much more. The ticket's dead. They can sell it off for as much as they can get to as many people as they can get to and at no risk."

"Unless the filly wins," I said.

"How can she win, if Richards is going to strangle her out of the gate and then rush her wide around the turn?" Angles asked. "What a deal! These fuckin' crooks!" He suddenly brightened. "Hey, you know what?

I can box the other four contenders in that race and nail the Exacta!" He bounded to his feet. "I'm going to check this out a little more. I want to make sure."

I got up and wandered into the betting area under the grandstand, where the horsemen hang out. Almost immediately I spotted Jack Leone, standing at a corner of one of the bars and surrounded by a group of heavy hitters. I bought myself a coffee and hung around to watch. During the ten minutes or so I lingered, I saw seven or eight people come and go, watched the group form, dissolve, and re-form, as the negotiations continued. Some sort of business was definitely being transacted and it was fevered, not unlike a corner of a commodities exchange where traders are dealing in quick speculations.

"Well, magician, how's it going?" Jude Morgan asked, coming up beside me. I had been concentrating so hard on the action around Leone that I hadn't seen him. He looked relaxed and confident, a winner.

"Pretty good," I said. "You?"

The detective actually smiled, an occurrence so unusual that it made his face look as if it had cracked. "Ain't lost a bet, not since you got me started. What do you have?"

"Nothing, really, Jude. But don't bet on Richards's horse in the ninth. It's definitely a no-go."

"Nothing else?"

"No, nothing but underpriced favorites the rest of the day."

"Then I'll take off," he said. "I shouldn't be here anyway. You stay good, Shifty, hear?"

He ambled away, his tiny hat jammed onto the back of his head, and I returned to my seat for the sixth, which was won by an obvious choice, at even money.

I would have left, too, but I wanted to witness the outcome of Jack Leone's big coup, so I sat there in the box with Jay and Arnie and watched two more favorites come bouncing in, then I got up again and went back under the grandstand. Leone and his group had vanished, but I spotted Angles, leaning against a post and watching the odds blink the numbers for the ninth. Beatific had been bet down to two to one.

"What's the story, Angles?" I asked, coming up behind him. "You heard anything?"

Angles whirled on me. "It's all over the fuckin' track, Shifty," he said. "The word is they sold off pieces of the ticket for maybe a hundred grand." His eyes glittered with fierce elation. "Goddamn thieves! I'm gonna get mine now, see?" He patted his pants pocket. "I figured the angle. I got two hundred in Exacta boxes, using four horses." He laughed, but without pleasure. "You don't figure the angles on these bandits, you got no chance, Shifty, none."

"Ladies and gentlemen, your attention, please!" the announcer's voice suddenly cut in over the public-address system. "Trainer Charles Pickard, please contact the jockeys' room immediately! That's trainer Charles Pickard . . ."

"Now what? They shot Richards?" Angles said. "I tell you, Shifty—"

I didn't wait to hear him out, but hurried down to the paddock. It was about twenty minutes to post time when I got there, but the horses had not yet entered the walking ring. Bedlington and Melinda Kennedy were standing in the center of the patch of green and seemed unconcerned. "Ah, Shifty," Bedlington said. " 'Welcome, gentry, for your entry sets our tender hearts a-beating.' *Ruddigore*. How are you, dear boy?"

"Fine, Lucius. What's going on?" I asked, as Melinda Kennedy turned one of her dazzling smiles on me.

"What do you mean?"

"Is something wrong?" Melinda asked.

"Didn't you hear the announcement asking Charlie to contact the jockeys' room? That usually means there's going to be a change of riders," I explained.

"What? Really?" Melinda said. She was still smiling, but her expression now seemed forced and her eyes were stony. "It can't be. Nobody can ride this horse but Lonny. That's what Angel says."

"By the way, where is Angel?" I asked.

"I don't know," she said. "It's the strangest thing." She gazed immediately up at Bedlington and clung to his arm. "Oh, Bunny, what's happening?"

"Nothing at all, my dear," he reassured her. "One rider is much like another, Charles assures me. A substitute will be found."

"Yes, but Lonny—oh, Bunny, I'm so worried."

He patted her reassuringly, as if she were a small, nervous poodle. "Don't fret your pretty head about it. Charles will handle it. That's what he's paid to do, my very own."

The horses were filing into the paddock, with Eddie leading Beatific in last. Charlie didn't show up for another couple of minutes, then came hurrying up to us as the jockeys began to move toward their mounts through the small crowd in the ring. Richards was not among them. The trainer was out of breath and looking a little pink around the jowls. Before we could ask him anything, the announcer's voice blared out the news. "Ladies and gentlemen, your attention, please!" it said. "Please take note of a late change of riders in the ninth race. Number eight, Beatific, will now be ridden by Carlos Medina. Carlos Medina now up on number eight, Beatific . . ."

"That dumb boy got himself into a fight," Charlie said.

"Who, Charles?" Bedlington asked.

"Richards. Actually, it was Lang who started it," the trainer explained. "I guess Tim was pissed off about Richards taking your horses away from him and he must have said something. Anyway, Richards took a swing at him and busted his hand. They had to pull them apart."

"He struck him, Charles?"

"He missed. Lang ducked and Richards hit the metal locker. They'll both get days, but Richards can't ride anyhow. He busted his hand up good."

"Well, Charles . . ."

"Oh, my God," Melinda said, looking very pale. Over her shoulder, I spotted Medina, a small, trim figure trotting toward us from the jocks' quarters in Bedlington's pink-and-black silks.

"What's wrong?" I asked Melinda. "Carlos Medina is a better rider than either Richards or Lang and he suits this filly perfectly. He's good out of the gate and he won't rush her. He's a great judge of pace. Maybe she'll win."

"Is that right, Charles?" Bedlington asked.

"You heard him," Charlie said, as Medina now joined us. "Carlos, how are you?"

"I'm good, *señor*," the jockey said, now turning to shake hands with us. He was short, like most jockeys, but with big shoulders and muscular arms. With his copper-colored, angular face and high cheekbones, he looked like a Mayan warrior plucked out of an ancient frieze. He had been one of my favorite riders for many years, always among the top ten in earnings in southern California, and I had never known him to do anything but his best on whatever animal he rode. I figured we were lucky to get him, because he usually worked only for the very biggest stables and the richest owners. He was in his early forties, reportedly very well off, and he only took a few mounts a day now. He must have liked Charlie to have agreed to ride Beatific, because Charlie had no important horses and only a small stable. No one awed him and nothing impressed him, not even Melinda Kennedy's spectacular good looks. He was a happily married Latino, with his major conquests behind him in all areas. When Melinda was introduced to him, he merely nodded, quickly released her hand, and looked toward Charlie for instructions.

"Carlos, this filly has speed and I guess you know there isn't much to run early with her in here," the trainer said. "Get her out on the lead, if you can, then I don't have to tell you the rest."

No sooner had he finished than the paddock judge called for the riders and Eddie held the filly still on a tight lead while Charlie gave his boy a leg up. Then the field began to move out toward the track. In the saddle, Carlos Medina suddenly looked ten feet tall to me. "She's going to win this race," I said calmly, my gaze focused on Melinda. "I'd bet on her, if I were you, Melinda."

"Shifty's right," Bedlington said. "Come, my dear." He began to lead her back toward the Turf Club.

I lingered long enough to note the pained, pinched expression on Melinda's face, then I clapped Charlie on the shoulder. "See you in the winner's circle," I said. "Want me to make a bet for you?"

"Me?" Charlie answered in mock amazement. "Bet on my own horse? Do I look that crazy, Shifty?"

I laughed and trotted away from him toward the grandstand. I wanted to find Jack Leone, if I could, just for the sheer perverse pleasure of the occasion, but he had disappeared and no one I asked had seen him or Angel Price. Two minutes before post time, I bet a hundred dollars on Beatific to win, at odds of seven to two, and walked to the rail above the first section of boxes to watch the race.

It was a beautiful thing to see. Medina broke the horse perfectly from the outside and asked for a little early speed, while the longest shot in the race, breaking from the one hole, scrambled hard for the lead. Medina didn't try to go with her, but took hold of Beatific and let the long shot go, so that he was able to tuck in and sit second around the first turn behind a fast quarter of 22.3. At the half-mile marker, the leader began to fade, after running the half in a zippy 46.2., Beatific, in second, about two lengths back and clear of the rest of the field, now moved to the front. She was running easily still, with Medina sitting chilly, until, as they hit the last turn, two horses made a run at her and came up alongside. Through my glasses I watched Medina go to work. He seemed to flatten out along the filly's back, his long arms beginning to pump high up on her neck as he asked her for whatever was in her.

Beatific responded and shot to the lead again, opening up three lengths on her pursuers around the turn. At the head of the stretch, she was still running hard, but at the eighth pole she began to tire, with three horses closing determinedly on her. At the sixteenth pole, she began switching her tail back and forth, eager to pack it in, but Medina wouldn't let her. First he banged her right-handed, his whip flashing above her flanks, then switched hands and stung her left-handed once, all the time still flat along her back and neck, arms extended, head down. The filly found one last burst of energy and lunged over the finish line, a winner by two heads and a neck over the three closers.

A group of about ten people rose up as one from a row of boxes directly below me and began jumping up and down, hugging each other and screaming with delight. Elsewhere, farther down and to my left, I spotted two other groups of celebrants, a total of about twenty people. All of them seemed overjoyed. I waited, then followed the largest of the groups to one of the Special windows, where holders of big tickets have to sign IRS forms before they can collect their winnings. About thirty people eventually showed up, all chattering and smiling and kidding around, waiting for the race to be declared official before trying to collect their huge payoff.

The atmosphere changed abruptly, however, when the track announcer revealed that no one had picked all nine winners and that, therefore, the bulk of the Pick-Nine pool would carry over to the following day, with twenty-one holders of tickets picking eight winners each collecting about a thousand dollars apiece.

People around the Special window began shouting at one another and at the mutuel clerk serving them. Someone said, "Where's Jack? Where's Jack Leone?" Two or three young men, their faces white with rage and dismay, began looking for him. Two middle-aged men took swings at each other. A woman hit someone over the head with her handbag, another woman screamed and fell down, a third one fainted and was dragged unceremoniously to one side. Several security guards lumbered creakily toward the action, as knots of bemused observers paused to witness the carnage. I stayed long enough to hear one long, anguished female wail, the call of someone in genuine despair. "Oh my God, Leonard, how could I have let you do this to me? You promised! You promised, you dirty son of a bitch!" And the big, lethal-looking handbag flashed overhead once more before descending with a solid thump on someone's, presumably old Leonard's, luckless head.

I took my time strolling out of the track toward my car. I had no intention of getting caught in the rush hour, so I was going to sit in the old Datsun for a while, until the parking lots emptied, turn on the radio to pick up the news or a little light music before grabbing a bite to eat somewhere and heading home. I needed time to sort the day out in my head, which by then had become as confused as the Cretan Labyrinth; somewhere, back there in the maze of blind alleys and double switches, the Minotaur lurked, but who or what was he and wouldn't it be dangerous to find him?

I couldn't make connections, that was my trouble, and it didn't cheer me up much to tell myself that I'd had a nice winning day either.

On my way out, I passed the Mooch. He was standing by the tall iron fence near the main grandstand entrance, his pudgy hands clutching the railings, his face a sweating study in pure loathing. "Did you see that, Shifty?" he screamed. "Did you hear what they did? They stiffed at least fifty people, I heard, at least fifty of them poor bastards!"

"What do you care, Mooch?" I asked. "You won your bet, didn't you? And I'm not even going to ask for my twenty dollars back."

"Are you kidding me?" he said hoarsely. "Are you kidding? I bet it all back on the two horse in the ninth and got beat by a head."

"How could you do that, Mooch? When Medina got the mount—"

"Nobody warned me!" he screamed. "I hear it on the PA and I'm out here and I can't get nobody to run my bet! I'm stuck! I hate this fuckin' place! I ain't coming back, no, sir, not even when they let me in I ain't coming! Hey, Shifty, wait—I got the winner of the fourth tomorrow! You got a fin?"

 *Fifteen*

FAILURES

The body of Angel Price was found late that night, around two A.M., by one of her neighbors, a gay young man who lived with his older roommate directly across the way from her. The building, located on a narrow, winding street in West L.A., was a two-story, California-Tudor structure built around a dusty-looking small garden. It was occupied mainly by singles and young couples on their way up in the professions who couldn't yet afford to buy a condo or a house of their own. Most of the tenants knew and watched out for each other, but no one had heard or seen anything that might have led anyone to believe Angel Price had been the victim of a crime. "I hadn't seen her for a couple of days," the young man told a TV reporter, "but I didn't think anything of it. When Larry and I came home, I noticed that her door was slightly ajar, so I knocked to make sure she was in and was all right. I never imagined anything so terrible could have happened to her. God, it's just awful! Larry and I are going to move. This city is simply becoming a jungle."

Angel Price was naked, but her mouth and eyes had been taped shut. She had been tied spread-eagled to the bed frame and had been sexually abused, after which her killer had carved a pentagram on her stomach, then slit her throat. The reporter informed his viewers that it had almost certainly been the work of the notorious Westside Slasher, another in the growing list of atrocities perpetrated by this psychopathic cultist, rapist, and killer. In the background of the scene, as the reporter delivered his stand-up account, I caught sight of Jude Morgan, looking very glum and sadly professional as he watched the corpse of Angel Price, encased in a body sack, being wheeled toward a waiting ambulance.

I was sitting in my kitchen at the time, watching the news of the morning unfold on my TV screen. It was about eight-thirty, I think, and I hadn't yet gone out to get the paper. I flicked the set off, finished my first cup of coffee, and telephoned the West L.A. police station. Detective Morgan had not yet come in, but I left a message for him to call me, then I walked out to the front of my building to pick up my *L.A. Times*.

Max Silverman, dressed in a tattered red silk bathrobe, slippers, and a black beret, was sweeping up around the pool area. "So, Shifty, you know the news?" he said, looking disgusted. "Is this a world to live in, I ask you? Parking tickets they can give, prostitutes they can arrest, but criminals? Never. So how are you?"

"I'm fine, Max. Yes, it's terrible." I didn't really want to talk about it with him, so I kept on going, picked up my *Times* and headed back toward my place.

"Oh, Shifty, I forgot," Max said, leaning on his broom. "A young lady brought a letter for you yesterday. Did I give it to you?"

"No, Max, I don't think so."

"Wait, I'll get it." He leaned the broom against the diving board and shuffled toward his apartment. "A very good-looking young lady, Shifty, a regular beauty."

"Dark, about five-six, long curly hair, nice figure?"

"That's the one," Max said, grinning. "You young people, so complicated. She writes you a note. Why didn't she telephone?"

"Maybe she did, Max. I probably forgot to put my machine on."

"So if your agent calls—"

"He gets mad at me. He likes to be mad at me. I can't afford to work anymore, Max," I said. "I'm making too much money betting horses."

Max scowled. "Ah, you are crazy, like all gamblers. You will ruin yourself. It is a sickness."

He disappeared briefly, then came shuffling back holding a small pink envelope in his hand. "Here," he said, thrusting it at me. "Does this girl know you are diseased?"

"Oh, yes, Max, she does," I said. "She's also sick."

I left him shaking his head and muttering to himself as I went back to my place. Once inside, I opened the envelope, which was undated and addressed simply to Lou Anderson, and read the note. "Shifty, please call me, I must talk to you," it said. "It's urgent. Melinda." And there was a phone number that was not Bedlington's.

I called the number, but got no answer, then I went back to my kitchen, poured myself another cup of coffee, and turned to the sports section. On the racing page there was a lead story about a coup involving an invalid Pick-Nine ticket that thirty-two people had tried to cash at Santa Anita. It had been cancelled prior to the first race and illegally returned to its buyer, a jockey's agent named Jack Leone. No one had seen or heard from Leone, who was well-known around the track, since before the ninth race, but the pari-mutuel clerk who had carried out the transaction, a middle-aged man named Dennis Lipsky, had been suspended and was being questioned by the authorities. Lipsky claimed that it must have happened by chance, because dozens of such tickets are punched in and out of his machine every day; and he was being backed up in his version of events by several members of his union, all of whom claimed that they, too, could have inadvertently returned an invalid ticket to a bettor, who might have carried out a number of other transactions at his window and confused the clerk into returning it.

I thought about that for a few minutes, after reading the story twice, but I quickly decided that Lipsky must have been in cahoots with Leone, if only because of the size of the ticket; no one could have carelessly bungled a transaction involving that much money. It had cost over forty-eight thousand dollars. A terrific coup, if only Beatific had lost the race, as she was supposed to.

While I sipped my coffee, I tried to get a feel of the play, like a gambler at a craps table who can't yet determine whether the layout is turning hot or not. There were so many possibilities, but they seemed unconnected; it was like trying to handicap a stakes race in which all the contenders had come from out of town to run for the first time against each other. No foundation all the way down the line, as some character in an old Saroyan play used to put it. I got up and went into the bathroom to wash up and I was in the shower when the phone rang. I jumped out, threw a towel around myself, and hurried to my bedside to answer. It was Jude Morgan. "Anderson?" he said. "You got a horse for me?"

"No, Jude, not today. I may not even go. The card looks tough."

"So what can I do for you, my man?"

"First maybe I can do something for you."

"Yeah? What's that?"

"I can tell you some stuff about Angel Price, the girl who was murdered last night."

"Not last night, Shifty. She'd been dead at least twenty-four hours. What do you know about her?"

"Can we have a cup of coffee together, in about half an hour?"

"Sure thing. You want to come by the station?"

"Are you trying to depress me?"

He laughed. "Okay. There's a restaurant called Dolores, on Santa Monica, corner of Purdue. I'll meet you there. Now what can I do for you?"

"Ever heard of the Worthing Trust?"

"Only that it's a bank."

"Okay, well—there's some sort of investigation going on regarding it, maybe in Washington."

"Not my thing, Shifty."

"I know, but you have a frauds division or something. You could find out fast for me, couldn't you? I just need to know the basics."

"Sure, why not? I'll call downtown."

"I'd appreciate it."

"You got money in this bank? Lot of 'em in trouble, you know."

"I heard. No, no money. But I have a friend who may have, lots of it."

"I'll let you know. See you."

As soon as he'd hung up, I tried Melinda Kennedy again and this time she answered, sounding a little out of breath. "Oh, Shifty, I'm so glad you called," she said. "I just have to see you."

"What's wrong?"

"Please, Shifty. I need to see you."

"Where are you?"

She gave me an address off Baldwin, up into the foothills above Santa Anita. "It's just a little place of my own," she explained. "I rented it a few days ago. I just had to have someplace to be by myself, you know? I need to think things over. Lucius is so possessive and I don't know what to do about him."

"I thought you were in love with him."

"It's so complicated," she said. "Please. I've got to see you. I'm frightened, too."

"What about?"

"You heard about Angel?"

"Yes."

"Isn't it terrible? I got home last night from my workshop and found out about it on TV. I can't believe it."

"Your workshop?"

"Yes. We're in rehearsal with a piece. Oh, Shifty, please come. I have to see you."

"You going to the races?"

"No, not today. Lucius and I are going to lunch at the county art museum, but I'll be at my place by four. Can you come then?"

"How about after five? I'll come straight from the track, okay?"

"Yes. Oh, thank you. You're so sweet. Bye." And she hung up quickly, as if afraid I might change my mind.

Dolores is a twenty-four-hour coffee shop, with a counter on the left as you enter and a triple row of booths on the right extending back to a more formal eating zone at the rear of the premises. Jude Morgan was sitting alone in a corner booth, where we'd be able to talk freely without being overheard. He was dressed in a gray suit that looked as wrinkled and out of shape as the brown one and his hat rested on the seat beside him. He looked worn, but full of some sort of dull anger, like a factory worker trapped in a hateful assembly-line job from which he could see no escape. He made no effort to smile at me when I arrived, but nodded once as I sat down and looked at me out of cool, cynical eyes, as if nothing I would say to him could possibly surprise him. "You don't look happy," I said, after I'd greeted him and we'd ordered black coffees.

"Anderson, there isn't a hell of a lot to be happy about," he said. "Just a typical working day. You know, there ain't enough dynamite in the world to blow up all the folks who don't deserve to be here."

"Well, at least you had a good day at the track."

"Yeah." His expression softened slightly. "It's the one place I can go where I can put all this other shit aside. Say, you're a pretty good handicapper, my man. How come you know so much?"

"I need to supplement my income, Jude," I explained. "Close-up magic is not exactly an overpaid profession. Besides, can you think of a better way to spend time than hanging around a racetrack?"

He grinned. "I never met a horse yet I didn't like better than my fellow man," he said. "Speaking of which, what have you got for me? You knew this girl?"

"Yes. Not well, but I've seen her around. Did you read the sports section this morning?"

"Yeah, but real quick. I was late getting to work, on account of I didn't get much sleep last night. They got me up around four, after the call came in about the girl. What's her story?"

I told him about Jack Leone's attempted betting coup and his subsequent disappearance.

"What's that got to do with this girl?" he asked, a little impatiently. "You ain't telling me he killed her?"

"Are you convinced it was the Slasher?"

"That's what they're saying."

"What are you saying?"

He shrugged and his face seemed to draw itself down, as if pulled into place by the deep lines on either side of his mouth. "It don't matter what I'm saying," he said. "I haven't got much to go on."

"I don't expect you to give me details—"

"You wouldn't want to hear them."

"—but I'd bet there are discrepancies here, just as there were with Amber."

"Where'd you learn to talk English, Anderson? Some fancy private school?"

"I'm from the East, Jude. I even studied geography."

"My God, you don't say."

"Am I right?"

He nodded. "Yeah, but not so's you could build a case around it. I'm the only one who seems to notice them. Small things, but they're different. So then, are you telling me that this guy Leone killed her? If he did, why? And are you saying he also killed your girl? Did he know her? Why would he do that?"

I shook my head. "Hey, wait a minute, Jude, I don't have any answers either. I'm just a concerned citizen, that's all."

"Yeah? Well, tell me what you're concerned about."

"Angel Price was a working girl, which is what nice people like me call hookers," I explained. "She was an actress who belonged to a workshop in Hollywood named Stage Two and she fooled around with at least a couple of guys there, including Ted Freeman, who runs the place. She was Lonny Richards's, the jockey's, girl and she also worked for Leone, running bets and stuff for them. Leone is Richards's agent and they've been pulling off some nice betting coups the past couple of months. As an old horseplayer, you know that Richards is a crook, but he can really ride when he wants to. Besides her acting gigs, if she had any, and running bets at the track, Angel prostituted herself for Leone. I'm pretty sure he had her addicted to some sort of drug—"

"We'll find out in the autopsy."

"—and I'd bet he rented her out for parties or to guys with lots of money to spend on sex. She had a terrific body."

"It's not so terrific now."

"I didn't see her at the track yesterday," I continued, "and I noticed that Richards was surprised she wasn't there, because he was looking all around for her. She used to come to the paddock before the races he rode in and he'd flash her some kind of sign, after which she'd go off to bet, probably for him as well as for her. At some point Leone began using her in all these other ways as well. I don't know if any of this is helping you."

"I don't know either, Anderson," Morgan said, with a sigh, "but it sure is interesting. Maybe we'll ask Mr. Leone a few questions. But why would he kill her, do you think?"

"I haven't a clue, Jude," I admitted. "You're the detective. Maybe she double-crossed him. Then I thought, hey, maybe one of Leone's clients killed her. Maybe one of them is the Slasher. Though that wouldn't explain Amber, would it?"

Jude Morgan leaned back in his seat and spread his arms along the top of the booth, as if to have a good stretch. He smiled. "Anderson, you got a hell of an imagination, you know that?"

"You have to find Leone first."

"Well, I guess we can find out where he lives, anyway, and do a little snooping around."

"Good thinking, Detective Morgan," I said. "I'm heartened to know that the public weal is in such competent hands."

"The public what?"

"It's an archaic way of saying well-being."

He shook his head. "Damn, but you're a smart son of a bitch. Where'd you say you were educated?"

"Long Island. I had a terrific English teacher and she made a big difference. Tell me about the Worthing Trust."

He reached into an inside jacket pocket and produced a computer printout that he dropped on the table in front of me. "It's all yours," he said. "It's kind of interesting. What's going on?"

"I'm trying to save a friend of mine a lot of money," I said. "I don't think he'll believe me, if I can't show him some documentation."

"Fair enough. Read it on your own time, I've got to get back." He dropped a crumpled dollar bill on the table as he slid cumbersomely out of the booth.

"Thanks, Jude. I'll call you if I hear anything else."

"You do that, Anderson," he said. "Better still, keep picking them winners."

"Whenever you want to go to the races, just call me. If I don't go myself, I can at least tell you whatever I know."

"Maybe we ought to go into it together for a living," he said. "It sure beats the hell out of what I do."

"Too tough, Jude. You need a fall-back position at the track."

"No, Anderson, what I need is a few laughs."

"Those I can guarantee you. Winners? Well, they only come in streaks."

"My daddy laughed a lot," Jude Morgan said. "He didn't have one damn dime and he drove my poor momma up the wall, but he sure had fun. He had more fun in a week than I've had the last ten years. I'll see you, Anderson."

After he'd gone, lumbering out of the restaurant like an old elephant moving reluctantly back into its cage, I ordered another cup of coffee and a tuna-salad sandwich and began to read about the Worthing Trust and its colorful owner, Mr. Langley Worthing, outspoken defender of free enterprise and fearless investor of other people's money.

The address Melinda Kennedy had given me turned out to be that of a square wooden cottage behind a patch of ragged lawn at the very end of Munro, a short, narrow street off Baldwin. Behind it the mountains loomed, darkly menacing in the late-winter chill, and a single street lamp cast a pale glow over the eight or nine other early-California bungalows in the immediate neighborhood. The whole area had the look of a movie set in the nineteen-thirties, as if frozen in time, a throwback to an era of abandoned hopes. I parked the Datsun in front of the house and looked for a bell. Before I could find it, Melinda Kennedy opened the door. "Hi," she said. "I'm so glad to see you, Shifty."

She gave me a quick hug and ushered me into a tiny living room sparsely furnished with two wicker armchairs, a settee, and a coffee table. Soft rock music emanated from a portable stereo in one corner. The whitewashed walls were bare, but several framed posters were stacked upright beside the stereo, presumably because Melinda hadn't yet decided where to hang them. The only light came from a single floor lamp next to one of the chairs, and a picture window at the rear of a dining alcove looked out on a small backyard overgrown by weeds and bushes. "This is nice," I said. "How'd you find it?"

"Angel knew about it," she said. "She knew I wanted a place of my own and she had a friend in real estate out here. All the houses on this block belong to an estate that's tied up in litigation, so they rent the cottages out on a month-to-month basis. If they ever settle it, I suppose they'll sell the whole parcel to some developer, but it may be a while. Anyway, it's perfect for me right now. Want a drink?"

"Sure. What have you got?" I sat down in one of the wicker chairs as Melinda headed for the kitchen.

"Not a lot, I'm afraid," she said, disappearing around the corner. "Some so-so red wine, a California Chardonnay that's not too bad, a light beer and—oh, a bottle of Jack Daniel's that I found here when I took possession." Her head peeked out. "I really haven't had time to get settled, you know."

"A small Jack Daniel's on the rocks," I said. She disappeared again and I could hear her rustling about for ice cubes. "Who'd you say administers these houses?"

"It's a bank," she called back. "The Worthing Trust. Why, you interested? One or two of these places come up for rent from time to time. Nobody stays very long because they're so small and pretty primitive, but they're darling, I think." She reappeared, pausing to hold up a plastic glass full of cubes and booze. "All right?"

"Looks lethal to me."

"Good. I'll get myself a glass of wine." She disappeared again briefly, then reemerged with our drinks, handed me mine and sat down on the settee at right angles to me.

She looked fairly devastating in the soft, pink glow of the room. She was barefoot and wearing only a tight pair of cut-off jeans and a black T-shirt that did little to hide her breasts, which appeared to be unfettered by a bra. She wore no jewelry, but her face had been carefully made up and her long, curly hair cascaded to her shoulders, framing her pale, lovely face and eyes that looked dark green in the dim light. She saw me appraising her and smiled. "I'm sorry," she said. "I really didn't have time to get dressed. I've been trying to get this place cleaned up."

"Are you planning to live here?"

"I don't know, Shifty. I'm so confused. That's why I need to talk to you."

"Obviously, Lucius doesn't know about it."

She shook her head and looked away from me. "No," she murmured, "but I just had to have a place of my own. Lucius is so in love with me it's—well, suffocating. Oh, that sounds so unkind, so ungrateful. I'm so sorry." She glanced sideways at me, like a wild animal aware of another presence but afraid to put any trust in it.

"Are you going to marry him?"

She turned to stare at me. "Boy, Shifty, you're very direct, aren't you?"

"Look, Melinda, I don't really know what goes on between you and Lucius and maybe I don't want to know," I said, "but you send me a little note, you plead with me on the phone. What's going on? You said you were afraid. Of what?"

"My God, Shifty, poor Angel. I mean . . . I don't know . . ."

"You think someone's trying to kill you, too?"

"No, of course not. It's just that when something that terrible happens to a friend of yours, well, it's scary. Do you think I'm being silly?"

"No. But you're safer in Bedlington's house than you are in this place. It's pretty isolated."

"I know. I'm not planning to live here or anything. I just needed somewhere to get away, to be by myself."

"You haven't answered my question, Melinda."

"Which one?"

"About marrying Lucius."

She looked at me in silence, her body poised on the edge of her seat, her hands cradling her glass and her lips half-open as she gazed at me. "You really don't know, do you? And if I tell you, you'll hate me."

"Why would I hate you?"

"Shifty, I love Lucius, I really do," she said. "He's such a wonderful old man. He's taught me so many things in just these few weeks. But I—I don't love him like a lover. He's—he's old, Shifty, he's so old . . ." Again she looked away from me. I could see a tear beginning to course slowly down one cheek.

"You've made love to him, right?"

She nodded slowly. Now a small sob escaped her. She continued to look away from me. "I . . . I don't know what to do."

"Just tell him exactly how you feel," I said. "Don't tell him he's old, but tell him you don't love him that way."

She turned toward me. Tears streaked both cheeks. She raised a hand to brush them away. "He won't believe me," she said. "He won't believe me now. And if I leave him, he'll kill himself. You know he will."

"So to keep him alive, you'll give your body to him and perhaps you'll also marry him," I said. "That seems like a sensible exchange. He's very rich."

"How can you be so insensitive, Shifty? I thought you were my friend."

"I didn't know we were friends," I said. "I thought we were just acquaintances."

"You know better than that, don't you?" she said. "I've seen it in your eyes. I see it now."

"Really? What exactly do you see, Melinda?"

"That you want me," she said, "maybe just as much as I want you." She put her glass down on the coffee table and leaned across it to kiss me. Her mouth was open and warm and I suddenly realized that she was right; I did want her, but out of pure lust, not love, not even affection. I returned the kiss and finally she broke it off. "You see?" she whispered, pulling back and smilingly snuggling into a corner of the settee. "You see? I knew it."

"What do we do now?" I asked.

"You put your drink down and then we go into my bedroom and make love," she said.

"And Lucius?"

"We'll worry about all that tomorrow, Shifty," she said. "Right now I need you. I want you." She swung her legs to the floor, stood up, and extended her hand toward me.

"All right, Scarlett," I said, "lead the way."

She took my hand and led me into the bedroom. The room was empty except for a large mattress, made up as a bed, resting on the floor. The only light came from the open door into the living room. I stood with my back to it and faced her as she turned toward me. Her eyes suddenly seemed monstrously large, like those of a big cat, and her pale features seemed blurred, indistinct, except for her open mouth and its two rows of gleaming, perfectly aligned teeth. I had a wild moment in which I felt I was about to be devoured. Then she moved in on me again and this time her kiss was as lustful as mine. Her arms went up around my neck and she pressed herself into me. "Mmm, I could mount you right here," she whispered. "Do you want me to do that?"

"Maybe we'd better get undressed."

"Here, let me do it first. I want you to look at me," she whispered. "Then I'll undress you."

I stood in place and watched her remove her shirt. Her breasts were full and they looked very white, like small moons, in the half-light. Slowly she wriggled out of her jeans, stepping lightly away from them toward me, her hands outstretched. "Don't you think we'd better talk a little business first?" I said.

She paused, a foot or so from me, and seemed to be hanging there in space, like an interrupted dream. "What do you mean?" she asked. "Business?"

"You're a terrific actress," I said, "but I don't know what you charge for these services. I haven't got the kind of bucks Jack Leone's clients like to throw around. Am I getting a discount rate?"

"You . . ." she hissed.

I didn't see it coming; she must have struck like a snake. I felt her nails tearing at my face, raking away skin from my left temple and cheek. I ducked away from her and she lunged for me again, but this time I was ready for her. I stepped to one side and kicked out with the ball of my left foot. It caught her on the right leg about knee high and sent her sprawling to the floor. She screamed, holding her leg at the joint. "You cocksucker!" she shouted. "You motherfucker! I'll kill you! I'll kill you!" She tried to get up, but couldn't. "You've broken it! You bastard! I'll kill you!" Holding her leg, she began to crawl toward the mattress.

I didn't wait to hear anymore, partly because I was afraid her screams might have aroused the neighbors, whoever they were, so I walked quickly out of the room. When I reached the front door, I paused long enough to look back. I couldn't see her, but she had stopped cursing and shouting; the bedroom was silent. I wondered whether I ought to make sure she hadn't fainted or something, but my decision was made for me. The first bullet quite literally singed my cheek and embedded itself in the wall beside my head, sending chunks of wood and plaster flying. The second one missed by a wider margin, hitting the wall between the door and the stereo.

I decided to become a moving target and went into a crouch as I got the front door open, then scurried in a zigzag, like an escaping hermit crab, out onto the sidewalk. I ran around behind my car, got the door open, and scrambled into the seat, my key already in the ignition. I spun the car into a quick U-turn and headed off down the street. No one apparently saw me go. In my rearview mirror, I could see the open door into her living room, but no sign of her. I had to suppose she was right, that I had broken her leg, but I couldn't pretend to be sorry about it. She must have had the gun under the mattress and I figured that that kick probably saved my life.

Sixteen

MORTAL COILS

I drove down to Baldwin, turned left, made a U-turn, and parked about fifteen or twenty feet up from the corner, beyond a circle of light cast by a street lamp and under the branches of a big pine. From there I could easily keep track of every car going in or out of Munro and see who was driving. I was pretty sure Melinda would be unable to get out of there by herself and I was curious to see who would come to her rescue. I was willing to bet it wouldn't be Lucius Bedlington, since he obviously had no idea that she had a place of her own and whatever explanation she came up with might strike him as a little odd. She wouldn't risk it. So I snapped the lights off in the Datsun, turned on the radio to the news of the day, tilted my seat back, and tried to relax. I thought it might take some time. The scratches on my face had stopped bleeding, but, as I waited, I kept my handkerchief pressed to them to make sure.

Over the next hour, three cars of people coming home from work turned into Munro and only one car came out, an ancient Ford station wagon driven by an elderly couple. At about eight, just as I was beginning to wonder if I'd adopted a sensible strategy, a rust-colored Toyota sedan came speeding up Baldwin, abruptly slowed down, then made a sharp turn into Munro. I was almost certain that the driver was Ted Freeman. I caught a glimpse of his pale, fat face in profile and recognized the long, yellow ponytail. I left my lights off, but raised my seat up and waited.

About twenty minutes later, the Toyota showed up again, with Melinda Kennedy in the front passenger seat, which had been tilted back, probably as far as it would go, so she'd be able to stretch her leg out. The car stopped at the corner, then turned quickly down Baldwin, speeding toward Santa Anita. I followed at a discreet distance, as it turned left on Colorado, then made a long loop around the track, and pulled into the emergency entrance of the Arcadia Methodist Hospital, on Huntington Drive, a short block east of the Turf Club entrance.

I didn't think I needed to follow them inside, so I kept on going, circling the track. The parking lots lay empty, miniature Saharas in the moonlight, while beyond them rose the great, black bulk of the old art-deco grandstand. I turned up Baldwin, heading back toward the freeway, past the barns where the horses slept or stood patiently awaiting the start of a new racing day, their heads thrust out of their stalls, their innocent, curious eyes probing the dim lights illuminating the shedrows for clues to the meaning of their lives. I doubted they would find any, but I remember envying their innocence that night. They, at least, lived existences uncomplicated by motives of greed and envy and hate. I remember thinking, as I drove, that I, on the other hand, was spinning on the edge of a hidden whirlpool of emotions, into which I couldn't see clearly yet and the depth of which I had only begun to fathom. I could still feel the sting on my cheek of the bullet fired at me out of the darkness of that empty bedroom and my head throbbed dully where Melinda's nails had gouged small chunks out of my flesh.

I drove straight home, parked on the street outside my building and went inside to pick up my mail and messages and to wash up. The mail consisted exclusively of solicitations and bills, which I dropped on my kitchen table without opening, but there was a welcome message from Happy Hal Mancuso on my answering machine. "Shifty, you hopeless degenerate," it said, "I have two weeks for you at the Pair O' Dice Inn in Reno, beginning April seventh, if you ever want to work again, which I doubt. I don't know why the hell I waste my time with you. You'll work the lounge two shows a night and you can also do your number in the dining areas on your own, optional. With tips, you ought to clear fifteen hundred a week easy, but I need to know by Monday, at the latest. I figure you ought to be broke again by now, you poor sap, so this might straighten you out, though I doubt it. I need the commission, so you better take this or I'm through with you, you bum. Where the hell have you been? I checked the Castle and they said you haven't even been in there recently. Are the horses running at night now? You're sick. I don't know why I waste my time with you." It was the sort of message Hal knew would warm my heart. He loved me, I could always tell. At least I wasn't some lousy rock singer or dirty-mouthed lounge comic, the only acts Hal seemed to be booking these days. I made a note to call him back in the morning and went into the bathroom to clean up.

Melinda had really quite literally nailed me. There were three slash marks above my right eye, on my temple, and two more on my right cheek. They weren't deep and they had stopped bleeding, but I put some antibiotic ointment on them just to make sure I hadn't been poisoned, then washed up and changed into clean clothes, combed my hair again, and headed back to my car. I was ravenous. Amazing how a little adventure can stimulate the gastric juices.

I went to Dudley's, where I sat in one of the booths across from the bar and ate a rare hamburger steak under a mound of sautéed sweet onions, french fries, and a salad with a garlic-vinaigrette dressing. I drank two beers and a coffee and spent part of the time chatting with Bobby Dudley, who wanted to talk about Jack Leone's failed betting coup and speculate on where he might be hiding. "I can't imagine what he'll do now, can you?" the ex-jockey said. "His boy Richards and Lang got ten days each for their scrap and the stewards are talking to Richards about Jack."

"Of course he denies knowing anything about it," I said. "I'd imagine the cops will want to talk to Leone about Angel Price, too."

Dudley's eyes opened wide. "Good God, you don't think he had anything to do with that, do you?"

I shrugged. "Who knows, Bobby? Maybe one of his customers is the Slasher. It's a possibility, anyway, wouldn't you say?"

Dudley shook his head. "Incredible business, isn't it? I never liked Jack much, even in the days when he was just a jockey's agent. Rather an arrogant man, not to be trusted."

"You got that right, Bobby. By the way, this is a wonderful steak. Who's cooking for you these days?"

"My wife," he answered, with a grin. "My chef quit on me a week ago and Ellen's filling in."

"Hire her permanently," I advised him. "Pay her whatever she wants. The onions alone were worth the price of the meal."

"I'll tell her," he said. "She'll be pleased. By the way, what happened to your face?"

"My gentle approach to seduction was misinterpreted by a lady I was out with," I explained. "She took exception to my suggestion that she ought to undress and abandon herself to the carnal romp. A bad miscalculation on my part."

"Indeed. Who was she?"

"It doesn't matter. I'm better at magic than love, Bobby."

"Who isn't?" he said. "I've been married for twenty-five years and I still never know whether we're going to make love or not."

"You still do that? After twenty-five years?"

"Oh, yes," he said. "Once a season, lad. I especially enjoy the one in the spring."

It was well after eleven o'clock when I left Dudley's. I still wasn't sleepy, but I headed for home, intending to spend an hour or two at my table, dealing cards and practicing moves. Not only did I need the work, but I'd always found it the best way to clear my mind of the day's rubbish. After a while, I'd be able to get up from it and sleep. Art is not only a tonic, but a great release.

This time I drove into the carport under the building, parked in my slot and walked up the back stairway to my apartment. As I reached the pool area and started across the near end of it toward my front door, I sensed rather than saw my attacker. He came at me from out of the shadow of the building, from a corner half-hidden by a six-foot philodendron to the right of the diving board. He was dressed in black, so that all I could see before he was on me was a long, pale face the color of milk, the eyes hidden under a heavy, dark brow, and the flash of a long blade held waist-high in his right hand.

I had no time even to cry out. I was able to parry the first thrust with my left hand, the blade slicing across my palm. He tried to grab me with his left arm as he lunged again, but I ducked under it. He recovered quickly and struck a third time. The knife went into my left side, two-thirds of the way down to my waist, as I turned to escape him. "Fire!" I shouted. "Fire! Fire!"

He was quick, I had to concede, but I was quicker. I just had time to grab his wrist with my right hand as he moved in again, and push the blade aside, while I reached up to his face with my left hand, stuck my bleeding palm against his jaw, and drove my fingers hard into his eyes. He grunted and staggered back a couple of steps. While he was still off-balance and trying to clear his sight with his left hand, the knife in his right one jabbing blindly ahead of him, I moved to his right, poised myself on my left foot and kicked out hard with my right one.

It caught him just below the knee and he fell, hitting his head on the edge of the diving board, the knife still in his hand. He grunted again and began to heave himself to his feet. "Fire!" I screamed. "Fire!" Then I kicked him again and he went to his knees. I picked up one of the folded aluminum chairs stacked by the board and hit him across the nose with it, with the full force of my whole body behind it. He fell backward into the water and sank. "Fire!" I screamed again and at last I could hear movement above and around me, saw lights flashing on, heard doors slamming, feet running, voices calling out.

I concentrated totally on my assailant. He came up gasping and thrashing about, the knife no longer in his hand. I suddenly realized that he couldn't swim and had fallen into the deep end of the pool. He got a hand on the edge of it and I brought the chair down on it, reveling in the satisfying crack of his knuckles as the metal bar struck them. He screamed and let go, then began to thrash about as his head went under again. "Fire!" I yelled, then abruptly sat down. I wasn't feeling very well.

Of the next few minutes I retain only scattered impressions. I see Max, his wispy white hair in wild disarray, his robe open, barefoot, and holding his violin case in his hand. I see a blur of faces, all vaguely familiar to me, but which I can't precisely place, like the half-remembered features of people from my childhood. I see the top row of apartments and the landing that runs the full length of the building and encircles the pool area and figures running back and forth on it and up and down the stairs. I hear voices, too, people shouting, a woman's scream, the sound of a siren whooping in the distance. In the pool, I sense rather than see a great thrashing about of bodies in the water, but whether it's a struggle of some sort or a rescue, I can no longer tell. Something is hurting quite a lot and one face swims close up against mine, that of my overhead neighbor, a furniture-store owner, who seems deeply concerned about me and whose lips seem to be saying something, but I'm not sure exactly what. And finally I'm looking at the night sky and I can feel that I am in motion and that someone is pressing something on my left hand, immobilizing it, and I am moving steadily now through a sea of faces and then I am in the dark and all alone with myself and it is suddenly very quiet.

"You were fortunate," the doctor said, leaning in over the side of my bed so I could see him. "You have lost some blood, but we do not think the wound has punctured your lung."

"How do you know?"

"We took an X-ray, of course," he answered. "We will take another one tomorrow morning to be sure."

"Then what?"

"Then you may go home, if you wish." He smiled faintly, but it didn't seem natural to him. He had a round, dark face with black eyes and a small, pinched mouth. I gathered he was Indian or Pakistani. A thick mop of dark hair threatened to overwhelm his forehead and he peered out at me from behind very thick eyeglasses. He looked like a night creature caught in a sudden shaft of light and he spoke with an accent, very precisely, rolling his r's and clipping his t's and p's.

"Where am I?" I asked.

"Cedars Sinai," the doctor said. "You are going to be all right. The bleeding has stopped. We do not think you need a transfusion. We have taken three stitches. Is there anyone who should be notified? Your own doctor?"

"My agent," I said. "He's going to be very angry if I can't work. What's the matter with my left hand?"

"That took six stitches," he said. "It was a bad cut, but it will be all right. You should try to keep it elevated for a day or so, which is why we have rigged you up this way."

"How bad is it?"

"Not bad. Largely superficial. No tendons severed. You should have full use of it in several weeks, at most. There will be a scar, of course. Again, you were fortunate."

"I wouldn't take this kind of luck to the track," I said. "Can you think of some other term?"

He blinked uncomprehendingly behind his thick lenses. "I probably will not see you tomorrow," he said. "If the second X-ray is positive, you may leave us in the afternoon. You will want to spend a few days at home before resuming your normal life."

"Thanks. I really appreciate what you've done for me. However, there really is somebody who ought to be called. It's important."

"Your wife?"

"My luck is not good there either. Detective Jude Morgan, at the West L.A. police station."

"I will give instructions—"

"It's very important," I said. "Please call him yourself. Be sure to leave a message, if he's not there."

"I am very busy—"

"It's a criminal matter, very important."

"Ah, well, then I will do it. But you must rest now. Try to sleep."

"Sure, but call him. Jude Morgan, West L.A."

I did sleep, right through the night until the following dawn, when they woke me up and took me back to X-ray.

Jude Morgan showed up at about eight, as I was sipping a cup of tepid tea and nibbling on a piece of dry toast. He came in unannounced, dressed in the brown suit this time and with the hat on the back of his head. I was lying in the end bed, nearest the window. The first bed was occupied by an old man who seemed to be growing plastic tubes out of every conceivable aperture and who, I had gathered from the nurses' chatter, was not expected to make it through the day. He was unconscious and his mouth was open. The middle bed was empty. Jude Morgan walked up to me and sat down in the only chair, with his back to the wall. He didn't seem surprised to see me either. "For a guy who leads the kind of life you do," he said, "you sure seem to get into a lot of trouble. Tell me about it."

I gave him a full account of the attack, but not about the little scene with Melinda Kennedy. "There's more," I concluded, "but it's all pure speculation."

"Go ahead, speculate."

"It would only confuse you, Jude," I said. "If I can figure it all out, I'll clue you in."

"That's nice, Anderson. That's very thoughtful."

"I always want to be sure my information is accurate," I said. "When I give a friend a tip, it's because I know something."

"That surely is nice of you. I'm deeply moved, my man."

"What happened to the guy who stabbed me?"

"We're holding him. He's in worse shape than you are. He's got a broken hand and he isn't breathing all that great. Took in a lot of water, which wasn't all that good for him. He might make it, then again he might not. Did you do all that to him?"

"Yes."

"This guy weighs maybe a hundred and eighty, hundred and ninety pounds. You a Black Belt or something?"

"No. A few years ago I read a book called *Every Woman Can,* about self-defense for women."

"For women."

"Yes. The lady who wrote it, Mary Conroy, is a little blond person who also teaches courses in self-defense. I took one of her classes and I work out with her occasionally. Useful stuff."

"For women."

"For men, too, Jude. I don't have a lot of heavy muscles, you may have noticed. Who's the guy who attacked me? Do we know?"

"Yeah, we do and it's kind of interesting. He's a hood out of New Orleans named Gus Rougier, better known as the Blade. Supposed to be real good with a knife. He's done time, quite a lot of it, once for rape and once for manslaughter. He killed a guy in Baton Rouge for somebody else, cut his throat, but he copped a plea and did only three and a half years. He's not cheap, but he'll work for about ten thousand dollars plus expenses. I'm thinking once again that I'm in the wrong business."

"How long can you hold him?"

"Long enough, I guess. We're checking some stuff on him. So tell me, Anderson, why would a man with a big knife come all the way from Louisiana to cut up a little old magician who never did nobody no harm? My partner, Mr. Harris, is real curious about that. Wants to ask you a lot of dumb questions."

"Try to keep him away from me, Jude," I said. "He depresses me."

"I know how you feel," Jude Morgan said. "He kind of depresses me, too. But I can't keep him off of you forever. Give me a time."

"I get out of here this afternoon, but I may have to take it easy for a few days. Then I have to try and set something up."

"What?"

"A meeting I'm going to insist on."

"You think you can?"

"I'm good with words, Jude, and I'm fairly inventive. Haven't you noticed?"

"What in the hell happened to you?" Charlie Pickard asked, as I came walking across the grass toward him. "Were you in an accident?"

"You could say that, Charlie," I answered.

"Looks like your head hit the windshield, but what happened to your hand?"

"It's cut, but I'm told it'll be all right. Otherwise I may want a job. Need a good hotwalker?"

"Always, but you don't fit the bill. You ain't even got two hands."

"I can do more with one hand than most people can do with two. Where's Bedlington? I kind of figured he'd be here, with this colt of his running today."

"He's coming," Charlie said. "I talked to him this morning and he said he was. He's kind of upset. His girlfriend got in some kind of accident, too. Broke her leg or something. Ain't you driving for him anymore?"

"I don't think so," I said. "I've been calling him at home, but he wouldn't come to the phone. Maybe he's mad at me."

"What about?"

"How should I know, Charlie? But the rich are never wrong. By the way, how's this animal going to run?"

"Better even than last time," the trainer said. "He loves the turf and this is the same group he ran against before. And I got a bug boy up, on account of Lang is still out, so he's carrying a feather."

As he spoke, the horses emerged from the saddling stalls and headed for the paddock. Dummkopf, Bedlington's big-footed, placid four-year-old, led the way, head down, with Eddie holding him on a loose lead. He had drawn the rail in the ten-horse field and was listed on the tote board as the favorite, at two to one. As usual, he seemed uninterested in the proceedings and two to one isn't my kind of price, but he wasn't the real reason for my presence. I'd been trying for two days to get hold of Bedlington, while my wound healed, and I'd figured that Melinda must have said something to him to keep the old man from talking to me. When I saw Dummkopf listed among the Santa Anita entries in the fifth that Sunday, however, I'd taken myself out of bed a day early, dressed and come out. I even took the precaution of wearing a jacket and tie, just in case I had to chase him into the Turf Club. I had to see him, or I'd have to turn the whole matter over to Morgan prematurely.

While Charlie was giving instructions to his rider, Juan Palestrina, the meet's leading apprentice, I thought I caught a glimpse of Bedlington, standing by the rail near the gap, but I couldn't be certain. Perhaps he had spotted me and decided he still didn't want to talk to me. I waited until the horses began to move out, then walked back toward the grandstand with Charlie. "Funny about Bedlington," he said. "He was supposed to be here. I think this colt's going to win easy, if the boy will wait on him and not go too wide."

I bet the eighty dollars I had won so far that day on Dummkopf to win and watched him lag way behind the leaders at the start of the race, then come with a big rush around the last turn and through the stretch to win going away, despite having gone wide. He paid six dollars even, which made me a comfortable winner for the day. I didn't wait to cash my ticket, but took advantage of the usual post-race crush of people moving to and from various parts of the track to sneak into the Turf Club past an usher who knew me and had benefited in the past from a couple of tips of mine.

I found Bedlington sitting with Matilda Pond Worthing at a small table about fifty feet beyond the finish line. I walked up to him with a big smile on my face. "Congratulations, Lucius," I said. "Why didn't you come to the paddock?"

He gazed coldly up at me. " 'And all third persons who on spoiling *tête-à-têtes* insist, they'd none of 'em be missed,' " he said, " 'they'd none of 'em be missed.' "

"Do you actually allow your servants to come into the Turf Club?" Matilda Pond Worthing asked. "Is there no place sacrosanct from the rabble?"

"I'm sorry to bother you, Lucius," I said, "but it's very important that I talk to you. I've been calling you for two days at home."

"Was it to discuss Melinda's impending action?"

"What action?"

"The one she intends to take against you for attempted rape."

"Good heavens!" Matilda Pond Worthing exclaimed. "Who *is* this awful person?"

"I doubt very much that she'll take any legal action against me," I said. "I didn't attack her. On the contrary, she tried to seduce me, then tried to kill me."

"Preposterous!" Bedlington exclaimed. "Outrageous!"

"Lucius, what *is* this person saying? Shall I have him removed?"

"I see she managed to inflict some damage on you," Bedlington said, approvingly. "Probably saved her, didn't it?"

"No, the damage was inflicted by someone else."

"And wholly merited."

"Lucius, all I want you to do is read this," I said, reaching into my pocket and placing the envelope containing the computer printout Morgan had given me on the table in front of him. "You'll find it interesting."

"Indeed? What's in it? Your criminal dossier?"

"I have no criminal record, Lucius," I said. "It's nothing about Melinda either, not directly."

"Why should it be of the slightest interest to me?"

"Because it chronicles in some detail the misadventures of your bank, the Worthing Trust," I said. "I've known you long enough to suspect that you pay very little attention to your financial affairs. I also have a strong feeling you're overcommitted there and that you may not be as rich as you think you are. Regardless of what you feel about me at the moment, Lucius, you'd better pay attention. They're robbing you blind."

"Lucius, I find this intolerable," Matilda Pond Worthing said, rising majestically to her feet. "This man is clearly a criminal and an agent of the Comintern. I shall summon the authorities."

"Hey, wait!" I said to her. "Look what you've done!" I reached down to her chair and removed a small rubber frog, which I now held out to her. "You've been sitting on my frog." It suddenly jumped out of my hand toward her. She shrieked and tottered back into the aisle. I caught the beast and stuffed him quickly into my pocket. Matilda Pond Worthing, her face pink with rage, steamed away from the table.

"Undoubtedly to summon reinforcements," I said. "Call me, Lucius, call me tonight. I can tell you a lot more and I know you'll want to, after you've read that."

I could tell that he was amused by my little scene with the frog, but he was struggling with his composure. "What is the meaning of all this, Shifty?" he asked.

"If you think about it," I said, "you'll realize that Melinda is lying. We're just a couple of victims, Lucius. You more than me."

" 'Whene'er I spoke sarcastic joke replete with manner spiteful,' " he recited glumly, " 'this people mild politely smiled, and voted me delightful.' "

"Which one?"

"*Princess Ida.* You're hopeless. What did you mean, 'seduce'?"

I didn't answer, mainly because I didn't want to hang around long enough for Matilda Pond Worthing to return with the security guards I was sure she was busily rounding up, but, as I left, I saw Bedlington pick up and pocket the envelope. Now I had to hope he would call me and then set up the meeting I wanted.

Seventeen

SAD SONGS

Derek Flanders was not happy to see me. When his new secretary, a small, birdlike creature of indeterminate age appropriately named Miss Finch, ushered me into his office, he did not even bother to rise from his chair to greet me. "What are you doing here?" he asked, his face flushed with anger. "Who asked you to come here?"

"What's the matter with you, Derek? I did, of course," Bedlington said, waving me into a chair beside him and facing the desk. "Hello, Shifty. How are you? You look like a ghost."

"I'm feeling like one," I said. "Probably lack of exercise."

" 'Gaunt vision, who art thou that thus with icy glare and stern relentless brow, appearest, who knows how?' "

"*Ruddigore?*"

"Excellent guess, Shifty, my lad," Bedlington said. He seemed to be completely at ease, elegantly dressed, as always, the picture of worldly charm. His eyes were focused in mild amusement on his old friend, as if he and I were engaged in some sort of practical joke, with the lawyer as our chief victim.

"This is really no time to play games," Flanders said. "I thought you had something serious to discuss, Lucius. I have a very busy day ahead of me and I only consented to see you because you said it was urgent. What's going on?"

"Well, I was struck, as I'm sure you were, by the story in yesterday's *Times*," Bedlington said. "I mean, on the front page, too. It must be a very sizable debacle. Very flattering picture of Langley, I thought. Makes him look positively distinguished, with all that silver hair. And he seems to have lost a lot of weight since I last saw him. When was that? Oh, seven, eight years ago, at least. I remember him as a plump little boy, with an unpleasant way of whining about anything he didn't like and a conniving manner about getting his own way in everything. I didn't realize you'd been seeing so much of each other, Derek. I bump into Matty at the races, of course, but she never mentioned it. Probably doesn't know anything. How deeply involved are we in this mess?"

"Nothing to worry about, Lucius," the lawyer said. "Nothing we can't set right."

"Specifics, please, Derek."

The lawyer shifted uncomfortably in his seat and cleared his throat. It had begun to rain outside and it was dark in his office, with the only light filtering into the room through the branches of the old trees in the garden outside his windows. Flanders's face was in shadow now, as if a small cloud had passed over it. "I don't see why we have to discuss these private business matters in front of a stranger," he said.

Bedlington leaned toward him. "Stop it, Derek," he said. "I called the bank this morning and was told that my accounts were frozen. I can't even get to my safety deposit box. Am I correct in assuming that you've tied up my entire estate in the Worthing Trust?"

"Lucius, it's a complicated matter," the lawyer answered. "I was going to call you about it, of course, but we've been working very hard to get things back on track. The government, in its usual blundering fashion, came into the picture just as Langley was about to resolve some of the problems he's been facing and just as two of the major investments were about to turn around and become profitable. The takeover bid for Bayou Petroleum was essentially a sound one—"

"Financed by junk bonds sold to investors in the lobbies of Worthing branches, is that correct?"

"Yes, but—"

"And these reckless investments for speculative acquisitions are, of course, uninsured by any agency of the federal government. Is that correct?"

"Well, yes, but—"

"And so now you're trying to defend what the papers are calling possible criminal activities by telling me that, if only Langley had had a little more time free from the regulators and the government snoops and the S.E.C., it would all come out just dandy in the end. Is that what you're telling me, Derek?"

"Lucius, it's a far more complex situation than it may seem," Flanders insisted. "You mustn't leap to conclusions based essentially on sensationalized media accounts. It's going to take time—"

"You're lying to me, Derek." Bedlington reached into his inside pocket, produced the bulky envelope containing the computer printout I had given him at Santa Anita and tossed it onto the desk. "I know exactly what Langley and his swindling cohorts have been up to," he said. "Bayou Petroleum is one of his many disastrous investments. What did they find down there in the Louisiana swamps, chewing gum? And what about these other shrewd ventures—office-building construction in L.A., Houston residential real estate, resort development in Panama and the Philippines, a recycling plant in South Dakota, a proposed toxic-waste disposal firm in Palm Springs, and other equally disastrous enterprises. Is there a single investment that has shown even the possibility of a profit at some future date? Couldn't he have invested in Peruvian cocaine or arms for China?"

"Lucius, you really don't understand—"

"Shut up, Derek, I understand perfectly," Bedlington said. "What I do fail to grasp is how I could have been such a fool as to trust you to manage my affairs all these years."

"You must give me time—"

"Not another minute, Derek, not one second. All I need to know from you is the full extent of my involvement in these schemes. I hope you aren't going to tell me that every penny I possess is committed to the Worthing Trust."

There was a long, uncomfortable silence in the room. I could hear rain spattering on the roof and against the windowpanes, the rustle of a stiff wind through the branches of the trees outside. Derek Flanders sat frozen in place, as if impaled on his chair.

"Well?" Bedlington asked. "All of it, Derek? Right? All of it?"

The lawyer nodded. "But you see, Lucius . . ."

This time Bedlington did not interrupt him; he merely leaned back in his chair and stared at his old school chum, as if he suddenly found himself confronted by some sort of loathsome insect, a look to turn its object to stone, and the lawyer faltered, then fell silent. " 'The criminal cried, as he dropped him down, in a state of wild alarm,' " Bedlington murmured. "Shifty?"

"I don't know, Lucius. *Yeomen?*"

"No, I didn't mean that. *The Mikado,* actually," he said. "You'd have known, right, Derek?"

The lawyer didn't answer, didn't move. His face seemed to have disappeared in the shadowy light, the features simply to have dissolved; he occupied space, but had ceased to exist.

"Tell him, Shifty, tell him what you told me last night."

"Some of it is speculation, Lucius," I said. "I don't know all the facts."

"Never mind. Out with it."

"All right." I took a deep breath and plunged in. "Why don't you begin, Flanders, by explaining to Lucius what your real motive was in recruiting Melinda Kennedy."

"I thought I made that perfectly clear," the lawyer answered, apparently suddenly feeling himself on firmer footing. "It was a way of keeping you from doing away with yourself. And it worked, didn't it?"

"I suggest that you had another reason," I said.

"Oh, really?" Flanders said, his voice an almost tangible sneer. "Are you going to accuse me now of pandering to Lucius's penchant for young girls? As if I'm to blame for keeping you alive, Lucius? I'm finding this very tiresome—"

"Do keep quiet, Derek," Bedlington said. "It's perfectly clear to me why you did it. It's so you could go on managing my property. You had my power of attorney, which, by the way, I've revoked this morning. You'll be hearing from my new lawyers in a day or two and you'll have to do some meticulous accounting. It would be comforting to think that you had only my continued welfare at heart, but Shifty has managed to persuade me that you clearly had other motives. Perhaps only one—greed. I suppose I should have noticed that your firm seems to be moribund. I never hear any phones ringing in here and that should have tipped me off, shouldn't it? I wonder how you hit on Langley. Promised quick returns, I imagine. Get in, get out, make a fortune with my capital and I'd never know. Unluckily for me, I never paid much attention to my affairs these last few years. I trusted you to administer my estate conservatively and I paid you a tidy retainer to do so. I surmise that you must have been desperate. Old Coutts was always the real brains of this firm, I knew that. But I trusted you, Derek." He heaved himself to his feet. "Well, no need to belabor points. I imagine I'll be able to salvage something from the shambles. I have the house, I have my paintings, and, of course, my priceless G and S collection." He turned to me. "Not much point dragging this out, Shifty. If you'll drive me home . . ."

I ignored him and kept my eyes fixed on the lawyer. "I wonder when it all began to turn sour on you, Flanders," I said. "It was only money, after all, and I'm sure your old friend Lucius here, your partner in the G and S game show over the years, wouldn't have let you go completely under, if you'd leveled with him. Why did you do it?"

"I don't have to account to you," the lawyer said. "Get out."

"You're going to have to account for more than money," I said. "How about the murders of Amber Clark and Angel Price?"

I heard Lucius gasp. "What?"

I looked at him; his face was a white mask, disbelief and horror stamped on it as if he had been physically struck. "I told you that I don't know all of it, Lucius," I said, "but we do know quite a lot."

"We?"

"Friend of mine, a detective at the West L.A. police station," I said. "A professional hit man named Gus Rougier, better known as the Blade, was the man who attacked me the other night. That was after Melinda invited me to her secret little hideaway up here off Baldwin, donated for the occasion, I'm sure, by Flanders and his friends at the Worthing Trust. The idea was to seduce me. I guess there was a general feeling I was becoming a pain in the ass just by hanging around and asking too many questions. I'm not convinced, really, that Melinda wanted to kill me that night, though she did have a gun under the mattress. When things turned ugly, she certainly wasn't averse to using it. Not a very good shot, I guess, or I'd be dead, under a headline that read something like 'Magician Murdered in Empty Cottage,' or perhaps, 'Actress Fights Off Rapist, Shoots Him Dead.' Good juicy headlines. Almost as sensational as the ones the Westside Slasher gets, right, Flanders?"

The lawyer did not answer. He was so quiet, so still that he might as well have stopped breathing. Bedlington, ashen-faced and looking suddenly very old, moved gingerly toward a chair, put a hand out against the armrest and gently lowered himself into the seat, as if afraid he might crack and fall to pieces. "Go on, Anderson," he said in a strange, hoarse voice. "Is there more?"

"Quite a lot more."

"Where's this man now?"

"Rougier? In custody," I said. "Permanently, I hope. But he's very good at making plea bargains. He's a convicted rapist and killer, who has done time for both crimes, but he was out because he turned state's evidence against the businessman who hired him to kill a journalist in Baton Rouge, Louisiana, eight years ago. It was a swindle involving Bayou Petroleum. He served only forty-two months for that job, while his ex-employer got life. How did you find him, Flanders?"

The lawyer remained silent, a disembodied presence in the room. I looked at Bedlington. "Are you okay, Lucius?" I asked.

The old man nodded. "Go on," he murmured. "I want to know."

"I imagine you found Rougier through Langley's Louisiana connections, the ones involved in the Bayou takeover," I continued. "He's not cheap, but he had the right qualifications. The subtle, even brilliant, touch was finding someone who could consistently execute a copycat killing. I mean, there's a lot of random violence in our society, isn't there, much of it directed at women, so you could have hired someone locally to get rid of Amber. Still, being able to make it look like the work of the Slasher was a nice added touch. Amber lived in the correct part of town and the newspaper accounts of the Slasher's operating methods were adequate to the task. Rougier got a few things wrong, things he couldn't have known about, because the police didn't report every gruesome detail about these killings, but he got the essentials right—the sexual abuse, the sadistic touches, and so on. The things he got wrong didn't bother the police much, except for one man, my friend Jude Morgan, one of the investigators on the Slasher case. He was disturbed by some discrepancies, not only in Amber's killing but in the murder of Angel Price, only he couldn't get his colleagues to pay much attention to him. It probably wouldn't have helped."

"You're crazy," the lawyer said, out of the depth of the shadows. "You don't know what you're saying. You can't prove these fantastic accusations."

I leaned in toward him. "Yes, I can," I said, trying very hard now to keep my voice from shaking. "I've never believed in the death penalty, Flanders, but I hope they give it to you, you miserable piece of shit. Amber's only mistake, I'm sure, was to make it clear to you that she knew what you were doing. She probably said something to you about it, enough to make you feel you had to get rid of her. She must have known about the Melinda Kennedy caper and must have understood the real reason you arranged the whole deal. She had a lot of integrity and almost no sense of humor. She would have warned you, Lucius, but first she probably confronted you, Flanders, and she died for it. I wish she'd told me about it. We had a big fight the last night I saw her or she might have. Maybe I could have saved her, I don't know. Maybe not. Goddamn you,

Flanders, goddamn you to hell! You had your hired thug slaughter her like an animal, just so you could go on squandering Lucius's money and investing in your cockeyed get-rich-quick schemes. Fuck you and everyone like you! If I had any balls, I'd kill you myself."

Bedlington reached out a hand to touch me. "Easy, Shifty, take it easy," he said, in a low, trembling voice. "Can you prove what you're saying?"

"A lot of it, yes. Don't forget, we have Rougier. He's not going to want to go up for murder one just to protect you, Flanders, is he? No, he'll make a deal and sell you out."

"What about this other girl, Shifty? How does she come into the picture?" Bedlington asked.

"She'd worked in Italy and she knew Melinda from that period," I explained. "She also knew the truth about her and she was cunning. She figured out what Melinda was up to and she blackmailed her. Angel was basically just another Sunset groupie, a Hollywood party girl. A little smarter than most, but a victim, another loser. Like a lot of her kind, she drifted into drugs and paid sex. She and Melinda had been in that scene together abroad, I imagine, so she saw a chance to involve her old friend again over here. And she wanted to climb into Melinda's connection to you. She smelled money in it. She'd slept around with a lot of guys, including Ted Freeman, the man who runs Stage Two, Melinda's workshop. She got Freeman involved and for a while it was useful for Melinda. It gave her a cover, a way to get out of the house without making you suspicious, Lucius. She never went to any classes, of course. As for Angel, she got heavily involved, first with Lonny Richards, then with Jack Leone. She whored for him to feed her drug habit and got Melinda into that scene as well. Maybe not the drugs, but the prostitution part, yes. Leone and Richards were also putting over nice little betting coups at Santa Anita and then they also saw Melinda as a way to make that scam even more profitable for them. You had a racing stable, Lucius, and you were in love with Melinda. They got her to persuade you to use Richards on your horses and to get Charlie to claim some cheap animals they could fool around with. At first, Melinda went along with everything. They cut her in on the action to keep her quiet and they could also control her by threatening to unmask her. The culminating event was the phony Pick-Nine ticket, which Richards blew when he got into a fight with Lang in the jockeys' room and broke his hand. Charlie put up Carlos Medina, who gave the filly a perfect ride and won the race, thus screwing up the whole elaborate scheme. By that time, however, Melinda had had enough of both Angel and Jack Leone. So she came to you with her problem, didn't she, Flanders? And you activated Rougier again as the Westside Slasher to eliminate Angel."

"Melinda did that?" Bedlington asked. "She knew about this?"

"Oh, yes. Yes, she knew. She told me about Angel's death, about having heard it on late-night TV," I said. "Angel's body wasn't found until much later and didn't make the news until early the next morning. It wasn't even in the early editions of the papers."

Bedlington stared at Flanders, as if he had trouble seeing him, and I could understand why; the lawyer did indeed appear to be transparent, a shadow figure through which you could see beyond to the quiet, hidden life of the garden at his back and the rain falling through the leaves. "Why then did you object to my wanting to marry this girl?" Bedlington asked. "Why, if you were in it together?"

"Because he was afraid of losing control of your money, Lucius," I explained. "Melinda had served her purpose and he wanted her out of the picture, but he couldn't get rid of her. He couldn't have her eliminated, too, at least not now, and she knew it. They got together on different terms, strictly financial ones, with you as the perfect victim, being drained of money at both ends. You see, Flanders had to face the possibility that, if you lost Melinda, you'd go through with your suicide plans and he'd lose control of your assets. What does your will provide?"

"It leaves my entire estate to several museums and libraries," Bedlington answered. "Except for my G and S collection. That was to go to you, Derek." The old man heaved himself up out of his chair. "Please drive me home, Shifty."

"Yes, I guess we're through here," I said. "Might as well leave before the police arrive."

Bedlington put a hand on my shoulder as we walked slowly out. At the door, the old man turned one last time and looked back at his old friend. " 'Oh, thoughtless crew!' " he intoned. " 'Ye know not what ye do! Attend to me and shed a tear or two . . .' " He paused, waiting for the lawyer to resume the game, but nothing happened, not a word was spoken. The transparency of Derek Flanders remained silent, his face forever blurred in the shadows that had overwhelmed him. I took Bedlington's arm, which felt old and feeble in my grasp, and led him out into the street.

My car was about halfway up the block. As Bedlington and I moved slowly toward it through the rain, I heard the muffled sound of a single shot from inside the house. Bedlington, lost in his own thoughts, had evidently failed to hear it. I kept on moving until we got to the car, then I opened the passenger door and helped the old man into the seat. I got in on my side, started the engine, and pulled away from the curb. In my rearview mirror, as we drove away, I saw the front door of the building open and little Miss Finch came running out, screaming and waving her hands in the air. At least, I think she was screaming; her mouth was open and her face was distraught. Bedlington saw and heard nothing. I kept on going, turning the corner quickly into Orange Grove and away from the scene that I knew would haunt me now the rest of my life.

"What was that last quote, Lucius?" I asked, as we headed home.

"*Yeomen,* from the end of the opera, Jack Point's final lament for his lost love and the end of his life," he said. " 'For I have a song to sing, O! It is sung to the moon by a love-lorn loon, who fled from the mocking throng, O! It's the song of a merryman, moping mum, whose soul was sad, and whose glance was glum, who sipped no sup, and who craved no crumb, as he sighed for the love of a ladye!' "

"Very sad," I said. "Appropriate, as always."

Bedlington said nothing else until we turned into his driveway a few minutes later and headed up toward the house. "When will they come to arrest him?" he suddenly asked.

"I don't know, Lucius," I answered. "I imagine the police are on their way there now."

"Can you really prove everything you alleged back there?"

"I don't know. Some of it, I guess. Enough."

"And this man who attacked you, who killed these young women, what about him? Are you certain he'll testify?"

"I don't know," I said. "He's still in a coma. He was in the water too long and he may never come out of it."

Bedlington turned to look at me in amazement. "Then . . . then you had nothing . . . nothing . . ."

" 'I'm a dealer in magic and spells,' " I said.

Bedlington threw his head back and laughed, a high, cracked sound, more than a little hysterical. " 'In blessings and curses and ever-filled purses,' " he sang, wildly off-key, " 'in prophecies, witches, and knells!' "

Eighteen

WINNERS

"You know, Gino, I can't stand it no more," the familiar raspy voice said. "I can't stand living with that in the house no more. It's nag, nag, nag the whole fuckin' time. I can't stand it no more."

"I know what you're saying," his friend answered. "I know exactly how you feel."

"I mean, it ain't right," the voice continued. "I go to work, I bring home the money, only I got to get to the track two, maybe three times a week to keep my sanity, you know what I'm saying? I mean, what's so bad about that, Gino, I ask you? Is that a crime, to bet on horses?"

"Of course not," Gino said. "Of course it ain't a crime or we'd all be in the slammer, right?"

"So you know what I'm gonna do, Gino?"

"What's that, Dom? What are you gonna do?"

"I'm gonna divorce this broad, that's what I'm gonna do," Dom said. "I can't stand it no more."

"You gonna divorce her?"

"Yeah, I'm gonna get a divorce."

"After thirty-two years you been married, you gonna get a divorce?"

"Yeah, that's right. I decided I can't take this shit no more. I'm gonna get a divorce."

"What are you, crazy? Ain't you heard about community property? What are you, nuts?"

"It's worth it, just so I don't have to listen to her no more, Gino. You know what I'm telling you?"

"Yeah, I know, but look at it this way, Dom," Gino said. "You divorce this broad after thirty-two years, you know what happens?"

"I get some peace of mind, that's what happens."

"No, that ain't it. Peace of mind, my ass. Listen to what I'm saying."

"So what are you saying?"

"I'm saying that, after thirty-two years of marriage, you are gonna throw away your life, that's what I'm saying," Gino said. "First of all, you gonna get all your children pissed off at you, that's for openers."

"Fuck 'em. Who needs 'em?"

"And then this broad you been with for thirty-two fuckin' years is gonna get herself a lawyer and she's gonna have your ass. Half of everything you got plus fuckin' alimony for the rest of your fuckin' life, that's what's gonna happen to you, you dummy. You better listen to what I'm telling you, Dom, it's for your own good. You hear me?"

There was a long silence, then Dom said, "Yeah, maybe you're right. Jesus fuckin' Christ, what am I gonna do, Gino?"

"Hit her in the mouth one time," Gino advised him. "I mean, next time she starts that shit about how come you're always at the fuckin' track, belt her one, shut her the fuck up, that's what I'd do."

There was another long pause and then Dom said, in a small, plaintive voice like that of a young boy who is generally misunderstood by the world, "You know, Gino, all them stories you read about and you hear about all these fuckin' women getting their asses stomped by some guys they live with, you know what that's all about, Gino?"

"What, Dom, what is it all about?"

"They don't *listen*," Dom said. "They don't fuckin' *listen*."

"Yeah, that's right, they don't," Gino agreed. "They ain't like us, Dom, they're from some other fuckin' planet, you know what I'm saying? They're different from us. You're right, they don't fuckin' listen. It's a fuckin' tragedy."

I sat up on the grass and stretched. It had finally stopped raining after three days and the sun felt warm and comforting on my shoulders. Above me the back of the grandstand rose like a green wall and in the distance a mariachi band was playing, all brass and guitars and yelps of joy and passion. It was still about an hour to post time. I looked at Dom and Gino. The two fat men, friends once more after their earlier falling out over Dom's wife, were sitting in their usual spot, on a green bench with their backs to me and facing the main entrance gate through which the crowd for this early-April day at the races had begun to pour. I fell back on the grass again, my head resting on my folded *Form,* and stared up at the sky. Then I raised my left hand and flexed it slowly in the sun. The scar looked long and wickedly pink, much worse than the almost invisible but potentially far more serious wound in my side. Still, my hand, after these past two weeks of therapy and practice, was in fairly good shape. I'd be ready for the Pair O' Dice Inn in Reno next week and that suited me just fine. I was ready to go back to work at last, not only because it had been too long since I'd toiled at my craft, but also because I now had to get away. The winter season had been poisoned for me by what had happened and I needed to clear my head and cleanse my soul. In short, I needed magic.

In the uproar over the collapse of the Worthing Trust, Derek Flanders's suicide had passed largely unnoticed, simply as another small incident in the unfolding drama of investors losing their life's savings at the hands of the professional money men. Langley Worthing had cropped up on national talk shows. He had admitted no wrongdoing and spent most of his public time castigating the Communists in the government, who were deliberately bent on ruining him personally while bringing about the collapse of capitalism and the surrender of America to the Bolshevik conspiracy. He was a piece of goods, all right, as Charlie Pickard had put it to me that morning at Clockers' Corner. "It don't make no difference," Charlie had said. "The taxpayers of America will bail him out like they always do. Something's got to keep the system going, right?"

Right, Charlie. I thought about Lucius, with his house about to go up for sale and his best paintings at an auction house in New York. And I thought about Derek Flanders, lying behind his desk with a bullet hole through the roof of his mouth and his brains seeping through the back of his head. *I don't think he'll be missed, I'm sure he'll not be missed.* W. S. Gilbert had an appropriate phrase for every situation.

I wondered if Rougier would ever regain consciousness. Probably not, Morgan had told me, but it wouldn't matter, because he would only survive as a vegetable. It's hard to get a turnip to testify in court, Morgan had pointed out. Ted Freeman had been arrested, but his knowledge of events had turned out to be rudimentary; he knew about Melinda and her involvement with Flanders, of course, but nothing about the Blade and the copycat Slasher killings. He had blubbered and confessed everything he knew and promised to cooperate and he was out on bail, awaiting prosecution on a number of charges that Morgan felt would be hard to prove. "Everyone's dead or gone, Shifty," he explained to me. "All we have is circumstantial evidence and what he confessed to and that isn't much, my man."

Melinda Kennedy had fled, of course, and she was still being sought everywhere. "We'll probably find her eventually," Morgan had assured me. "She's too pretty to disappear forever. But I don't think we'll be able to nail her on any kind of a murder rap, Shifty. It's all what the courts call conjecture."

"Is that what they call it, Jude?"

He smiled. "Good fancy word," he said. "I'd call it that, too, wouldn't you?"

Conjecture. Conjecture killed the cat. I stood up and stretched, picked up my *Form*, folded it, and jammed it into my back pocket, along with my program. It was my own personal getaway day for the Santa Anita season and I'd picked a good one. Mad Margaret was running in the sixth and had been training so well Charlie had decided to stretch her out to a mile and a sixteenth instead of sprinting her again. "I think she'll rate," he said, "and she's got plenty of speed to get position on the turns. Let's find out what we've got, Shifty." Why not? And she'd pay a decent price, too, going long for the first time against more seasoned animals and after only one previous race. I was looking forward to a good getaway score.

As I started to leave, a small, elderly Japanese man in a black business suit, with a heavy camera dangling around his neck like a bell, smilingly approached Dom and Gino on their bench. "Excuse, please," he said. "You know wheah is Tough Crub?"

"Tough Crub?" Dom asked. "What's that?"

"Turf Club," Gino explained. "He means Turf Club. Japs ain't good with r's."

"Oh," Dom said, "Turf Club."

"Yes, Tough Crub," the little Japanese man said, bowing and smiling.

"Hey," Dom said, "you found Pearl Harbor, you can find the Turf Club."

I sat with Jay and Arnie and Angles for the first five races, making small wagers and breaking even, then I went down to the paddock for the sixth. Lucius J. Bedlington was standing on the grass, waiting for his horse and trainer to appear. He was dressed for spring, in black loafers, white slacks, a navy blue yachting blazer with gold buttons and a dark red kerchief. He carried a silver-headed cane and looked, nonchalantly poised in the middle of the walking ring, like a figure out of a nineteen-thirties Hollywood epic about the rich at play. "Ah, the magician," he said, smiling. " 'Ring forth, ye bells, with clarion sound—forget your knells, for joys abound.' "

"The Sorcerer?"

He beamed with pleasure. "You're getting quite good at this," he said.

"A lucky guess, Lucius. How'd you get here?"

"Drove, dear boy."

"Why didn't you call me?"

"No need to bother you, on the eve of your departure for the inhospitable wilds of Nevada," he said.

"You should have taken a taxi. If they stop you, you'll be arrested."

"I need variety in my life these days, Shifty, my lad," he said. "I'm easily bored. My best paintings are in New York and the house is empty."

"The Whistler, too?"

"No, dear boy. The old man and I are inseparable. We sit and commune by the hour."

"How's Scopes?"

"Alive. How should he be? When we go, we'll go together. He seems more cheerful since Melinda left. Turns out he never liked her."

"The man has taste."

"Oh, yes, he's a great butler, dear boy. The last of his kind."

"Like you."

"Yes, like me. Quite right. Very observant of you, my lad."

Mad Margaret looked terrific in the paddock. Her chestnut coat gleamed with health and she seemed to shine in the bright sunlight. There were half a dozen other decent horses in the race, but she looked outstanding to me, another class of athlete entirely. "How much is she going to win by, Charlie?" I asked, after the trainer had given Tim Lang a leg up and we watched her move out in the parade toward the racing surface.

"Anything can happen in a horse race," the trainer said. "Maggie's a good filly, but there's ten thousand ways to lose."

"And that applies to life, as well," Bedlington observed. "We'll make a philosopher of you yet, Charles."

Bedlington and I separated at the Turf Club entrance. "If she wins," he said, "go to the winner's circle, Shifty. Get your picture taken with her."

"What about you?" I asked.

He shook his head. "I never go to the winner's circle, dear boy," he said. "Public rejoicing is for the young." He raised a hand in benediction. " 'Farewell, magician—magician, farewell!' *Patience,* slightly adapted." He turned and walked jauntily away from us.

"He ain't looking good," Charlie observed, as we watched him go.

"No, Charlie," I said. "His heart is broken."

"Oh, is that all? Come on, let's watch the filly run."

It was a joke. Mad Margaret went off at seven to two, as the third choice in the race. She broke alertly, went a little wide around the first turn from the six-hole, mainly because she was so full of run that Lang couldn't hold her, then she settled down in third along the backside, moving easily, well within herself. Lang asked her at the three-eighths pole and she exploded. In a matter of seconds, she had opened up five, then came flying down the stretch with her ears pricked and her jockey just sitting there, along for the ride. She won by ten, a second off the track record for the distance.

"Holy shit!" Angles exclaimed. "She's a monster!"

"I would agree that this animal has a future," Arnie said. "What would you say, Jay?"

"I wish I'd bet more on her," Jay answered. "Shifty?"

"I did," I said, rising to head down toward the winner's circle. "I made the biggest bet of my life—a thousand on the nose."

"I should have figured the angle better," Beltrami complained. "She was the only one in here with legit speed."

"Should have, would have, could have," Arnie declared. "It's mankind's saddest song."

"Fuck you, Wolfenden," Angles said.

Not even Angles Beltrami, however, could blot out the spring.

The day before I left for Reno, Lonny Richards's body was found slumped over the steering wheel of his blue Corvette, parked down the street from his house in Sierra Madre. Someone had put a .25-caliber bullet into his brain at close range through his right temple. Jay called me up to tell me about it. I can't say that either of us was distressed. We had taken our lumps from Richards in the past, especially in connection with a good horse named Gran Velero, owned by a woman I had been in love with during a summer at the races in Del Mar a few years ago. "You know, you can't go through life stiffing everybody," Jay observed, "and not eventually be called to account for it. I wonder who did it to him? I suspect Leone, don't you?"

"Or the people he and Jack took with their phony Pick-Nine ticket."

"Anyway, who cares?" Jay said. "Dead jockeys don't cheat."

I enjoyed my time at the Pair O' Dice Inn in Reno. It was a new hotel on the outskirts of the booming little city, away from the more frenzied action downtown, and it was largely patronized by older couples on budget vacations. They proved to be appreciative audiences, but the gratuities were meager and I stopped working the dining rooms after my third day. I didn't make anything like the fifteen hundred a week Hal had predicted for me, but I benefited from my leisure time by renting a car and taking long drives into the countryside, out to Pyramid Lake in the desert and up into the forested slopes on the Nevada side of Tahoe. I went to Virginia City for a day and had a terrific time touring the old mining capital, the heart of the Comstock Lode, where the great California gold-and-silver fortunes had been made. I enjoyed being by myself, partly because I've always been something of a loner and partly because I needed time away from the track. I'd made quite a lot of money these past couple of months, but too many unpleasant things had happened and my time had been soured by them. In Nevada, I breathed fresh air and refreshed my soul by working hard at what I did best and what I loved most.

When I came back to L.A., I didn't immediately rush out to the races, but spent the first couple of days digging out from under my mail and generally putting my life in order. It wasn't until my second night back, when I dropped in for a bite to eat at Dudley's, that I heard about Bedlington. Arnie stopped by my table, with a pool cue in his hand. "I saw you come in, Shifty," he said. "Welcome back."

"Hello, Arnie. Hustling again?"

He smiled ruefully. "Well, Shifty, I need faster horses. They've been running slow on me ever since I saw you last. When did you get back?"

"Couple of days ago."

"Going racing tomorrow?"

"Maybe. I haven't seen the entries."

"That turf horse of Bedlington's is running again. Say, what about him?"

"Dummkopf? He'll run well."

"No, Bedlington."

"What about him?"

"You haven't heard?"

"What's happened?"

So Arnie sat down in my booth and told me. From what he said and from what Charlie Pickard added, when I finally got him on the phone later that night, waking him up out of a sound sleep, Lucius J. Bedlington had finally decided to honor his commitment to Pericles Thanassis. He had loaded himself, a basket of food and drink, and poor old Scopes into the Alfa and had driven up the coast of Malibu to have a picnic in the hills. Then, in midafternoon, he had come careening down Malibu Canyon at eighty miles an hour, missed a crucial turn, and plunged spectacularly to his death into a boulder-strewn ravine. He and Scopes were killed instantly. "I guess he got tired of sitting all alone in that old house, staring at the one painting he had left," the trainer said. "I hear he gave it to some museum in London."

"So you don't think it was an accident, Charlie?"

"No. Do you?"

"No."

"I'm only sorry for Scopes. I wonder if he knew?"

"He knew, Charlie. Lucius would have told him. He said they'd go together."

"Bedlington left a note. Wait, I'll get it. I wrote it down."

He left the phone for a couple of minutes, then came back. "Here it is. It was on the chair, facing the painting. 'Be happy all, leave me to my despair,'" he read aloud. "'I go—it matters not with whom—or where!' Must be one of them operas. Say, I'm glad you called. I didn't know where to get hold of you. You coming out to see your horse?"

"Dummkopf?"

"No, Maggie. He left the other ones to me, Shifty. I'm gonna sell most of 'em. But you got the filly."

"What?"

Charlie laughed. "Yeah, he revised his will, they tell me. He left you the filly."

"Are you talking about Mad Margaret?"

"Don't you want her? It's gonna take a while to probate the will and all, but she's yours, Shifty," Charlie said. "And you know she can run. I don't know how good she is yet, but we'll find out, won't we? . . . Shifty? . . . Shifty? . . . You there?"

I was there, all right, but for once in my life I was speechless.